MW00913008

RUN FOR ME TOO

Neva Gould

AuthorHouse™
1663 Liberty Drive
Bloomington, IN 47403
www.authorhouse.com
Phone: 1-800-839-8640

First published by AuthorHouse 8/19/2009

ISBN: 978-1-4389-9750-6 (e)
ISBN: 978-1-4389-9748-3 (sc)
ISBN: 978-1-4389-9749-0 (hc)

Library of Congress Control Number: 2009905924

Printed in the United States of America
Bloomington, Indiana

This book is printed on acid-free paper.

For my children, Ingrid, Karen, and Jim;
my grandchildren, Joshua and Michael;
and the people of my town of origin who perished in Croatia
during the pro-Nazi regime.

CHAPTER 1

The lights on Zrinska Street barely illuminated footprints stamped into the snow. Their author, Saul Kestner, walked along slowly, black bag in hand. His heart was light with fulfillment, though the rest of him was weary, and his head swam from lack of sleep. "I can no longer stay up with impunity the way I could when I was an intern," he told himself.

Not every day was his work and vigil so well rewarded. At last he had delivered Mrs. Lelich, despite her several miscarriages and the ominous murmurs of her rheumatic heart, of the baby she so desperately wanted. In most obstetric cases nature and the woman did the work, but with Milena Lelich he did not dare leave her bedside for a moment. And now he had a warm feeling inside, an inner satisfaction, as if he himself had bestowed life. An aroma of roasted chestnuts reached Saul from Vlado's kiosk, already shut. Too bad he was late, for he was fond of the chestnuts, Vlado, and Vlado's jokes.

Not many people were out on a dark, cold evening like this one, in December of 1940. It was snowing again, and the wind played with the loose surface layer, picked it up from one spot, twirled it around, and deposited it in another, quickly obliterating Saul's footprints. Thin streaks of light filtered through gingham-curtained windows and faintly reinforced the dim widely spaced streetlights.

In his mind Saul could see the flurry and scurry inside the houses, behind the thick walls. This was the time of day when the more prosperous men of the town read their newspapers, distracted by the odors of onions and garlic, fried meats and stewed vegetables their wives or cooks were preparing in the kitchen.

He knew it all so well. The little town of Slavonski Grad, which everyone simply called Grad, was located in the heart of Croatia, and since World War I had become part of Yugoslavia, was as much part of him as the blood that ran through his veins. It was not so for his parents; they had moved south from Hungary to this area, while it was still under Austro-Hungarian rule. But he and Robert were born here, this is where they belonged, and he felt a wave of pride sweep over him.

With delight Saul took in a deep breath, savoring the crisp clean winter freshness, and he realized that for once he was going to be on time for dinner! The twins would still be up. Darinka's soup would still be piping hot, the way he liked his soup. Perhaps he could even have a cat nap… or maybe catch the evening news; he had not had a chance to tune in for a couple of days.

Ah, yes, the radio, that devilish instrument that linked him to the world at large, which had become his compulsion lately. Like an alcoholic, he could not stay away from it, yet he loathed it, loathed the connection that was bringing in the tentacles from the outside world into his little paradise. The dark empty street now became suffused by gloom, and the deep shadows between the lampposts cast ominous shadows. What had started as an exhilarating walk now was oppressive. It was the same nagging ill-defined perturbation that had been intermittently haunting him for months. This was the quiet before the storm.

Saul turned over the possibilities. War might come… and if it did, they would have to flee to Bosnia or Serbia, which would remain in the free part, just as during World War I. The German army would be contained along the Balkan front, its progress arrested by the impenetrable mountain ranges. Or perhaps there would be no war. After all, Yugoslavia was not in Hitler's path, either on his way to the East or his way to the West.

He tried to cheer himself with his last thought, but the oppression clung to him and did not depart until he was well inside the gate of his own home. Barely audible ripples of "Per Elisa" emanating from Clara's piano seeped through invisible crevices and embraced him on the doorstep, dispelling all vestiges of gloom.

Darinka, the old cook, opened the door with a "Good evening, Dr. Kestner," and fluttered around to help him with his doctor's bag and overcoat. Clara's delicate arpeggios enveloped him more distinctly. "Well, what's new at home?" he inquired.

"Nothing much…. Farmer Babich brought eggs and a sack of flour. He sends you regards."

"It's been years since I treated his boy. He still stops by whenever he comes to town."

"Yes, he told me all about it."

"Oh, it was a small matter."

"No, sir, that's not what he said. He told me you drove up in the worst of blizzards."

Saul laughed, his left eye narrowing slightly, and Darinka could see a tiny twinkle, which she and many town folks found endearing. "Life is funny, Darinka. Sometimes I break my back and all I get are complaints. And sometimes, especially in the villages, the peasant folks are eternally grateful for my smallest efforts."

The music suddenly broke off. A moment later the living room door swung open, and Clara, smiling, came toward him.

"Hello, dear," she said and, raising herself on tiptoes, planted a kiss on his cheek. Then she tugged on his arm and led him into the dining room, where a white tablecloth gleamed, the places already set. "This will be a treat. You even have a few minutes to rest before dinner."

"Not so fast," he said, pulling her toward him, and bending down to kiss her on her lips. She rewarded him with a big smile, which momentarily erased the faint traces of matronliness that had recently made their appearance.

For an instant Clara looked just as she had when he asked her to marry him, with her light brown hair over one brow, her velvety brown eyes smiling from under.

"I thought you'd never ask," she had replied, clutching a bouquet of roses, which had been sent to her after her performance. Then she flung the roses, which nearly landed on the floor and abandoned herself totally to his embrace.

He had been very fond of Clara when he first met her, but it was her sister Tamara who had bewitched him and who had been the love of his life. When Tamara died and left him with an infant son – back in Zagreb after his training – everyone in his and Tamara's family had coaxed him, according to custom, to marry the sister. And eventually he made up his mind to confront Clara, feeling certain that she would turn him down, and that she would never give up the prospect of a career as a concert pianist to become the wife of a small town physician.

"Not only do I get you to love, but I even get a baby without the pains of labor," she told him, flashing a meter-long smile. He often didn't know what words to expect from Clara, what words would tumble from her mouth. He had offered to start his medical practice in Zagreb, rather than in Grad as he had planned, if she wished to continue at the conservatory. She shook her head emphatically and gave him another kiss. But that was a long time ago, in another life, and Clara had brought into his daily existence a quiet, steady love that warmed and comforted him, a contrast to the tumultuous flames of Tamara, that sometimes threatened to consume him. She had grown by his side from a somewhat brash young girl when he had first met her, to a most caring and loving wife and mother, and a remarkably logical and levelheaded observer of the life around them.

"Did Mrs. Lelich deliver?" Clara's words brought Saul back to the present.

"She did, and without much trouble. The baby is a bit small, but vigorous. I'm sure they'll both be fine."

A ruckus erupted nearby, something like the charge of the cavalry, and the twins, Ljerka and Rajko, made a noisy entry unbecoming of their nearly ten years. Screeching "Papi, Papi," they threw their arms around Saul's neck, each child tugging him in the opposite direction, as he bent down to their size.

"Did Mrs. Lelich get a baby?" Ljerka asked.

"Yes, she did. A beautiful little girl, but not quite as beautiful as you are."

The twins giggled and ran off.

"Now you lie down," Clara said, pointing to the sofa, "while I peek into Darinka's pots and pans. You look awfully tired."

"Where is Peter?" he inquired about their sixteen-year-old.

"He went to see Silvia. He should have been back by now!"

Left alone, Saul contemplated the sofa. It was lucky that he could catch little naps under most circumstances, and that was what gave him the strength to endure the rigorous demands of a rural medical practice. But before he had settled himself comfortably, he heard

Clara's excited voice in the hallway, and a moment later she entered with Peter, their oldest – actually his and Tamara's boy.

"Oh my God," exclaimed Saul when he saw Peter enter, his face smeared with blood, and the right eye nearly shut.

Steering the boy to the sofa, he inspected his face. With a little pressure the bleeding, which came from Peter's slightly prominent nose, stopped. Darinka, who had entered with a tureen of soup, went back as quickly as her small heavy frame would allow, and returned with a carefully wrapped shard of ice from the ice box, which she carefully applied to Peter's eye.

"Peter, I've never known you to pick a street fight," Clara said sharply, but not without some surprise.

"I didn't, Mami! They attacked me."

"Who? What happened?" Saul asked impatiently.

"I was late coming back, and I didn't want you two to worry, so I took the short-cut along the park."

"And so?"

"Well, as I was coming around the bend, an ice-ball hit me in the back of my head. Someone yelled 'Kike,' and four boys sprang out of nowhere and pinned me to the ground. They shouted 'Son of a bitch dirty Jew,' and took turns punching my face and stomach. Stjepan's younger brother called me a 'Bastard Jew Christ killer'."

"To think that you delivered that boy," Clara said with rancor, addressing herself to Saul.

"The bully Vukovich," Peter continued, "who was their leader, suddenly ordered the boys to let me go. But as I tried to get away, he stuck his foot out, which I didn't notice, and I fell headlong into the snow. Then they laughed and attacked me again, cheering that idiot's cleverness. They tugged so hard on my scarf I thought they were going to choke me, but instead they tied my arms with it and rolled me down the hill. At the bottom I managed to free my arms and get away."

As Saul listened, the blood left his face, washing away doubt, surprise, and anxiety. Then it rushed back in a whirl, till he felt his temples bursting, and he was swept along by a fury that made his fist come crashing down on the dining room table, rattling the porcelain and tumbling a glass.

"Clara," he shouted, waving his arms, "I'll break their necks!" He paused briefly. "I'm through! I'm done with this lousy place!"

How could this be? His own son beaten up in their town! His roots ran deep in this corner of the world, but he would sever them. He would not allow weeds to choke off the fruit of his existence. He started pacing up and down the dining room floor. Turning to Clara again, he said, "We will leave as soon as I can arrange it. We'll go to Canada. I want to get out of here!"

Clara looked quizzically at her husband, as if trying to decide whether this threat of departure was genuine or merely the flash anger in which he sometimes indulged.

Peter found his voice again. "Father, why do we have to be Jewish?"

Saul felt a knife thrust into him. Why? Why indeed? He was at a loss. How could he explain such matters to his children, when his own convictions were muddled? Judaism had been a burden to him on a number of occasions, and he himself had often wished not to bear the stigma. It had been a detriment to him in the Austro-Hungarian army, and it had complicated his progress in medical school. And why?

As he sometimes put it, Saul considered himself "a Jew by habit," the habit by which others viewed him, simply because his parents happened to be Jewish. At one time he had seriously thought about conversion. His friend, jolly old friar Boniface, after whose health he had looked for some years, had told him many times, with a mischievous wink of his jaundiced eye: "Just a little Holy Water over your head, and you will be one of us. You don't even look Jewish."

But it had not been as simple as all that. In his heart Saul had wanted to get out of Judaism; but that meant not only shedding one religion, but trading it for another. It was this exchange that he was not convinced about. He knew he would offend his mother; not that she was particularly religious, but could he look her in the eye after admitting that it was expediency and cowardice, and not conviction, that had prompted his conversion? His father's dogma and sectarianism he could clash with, but his mother's adherence to tradition he did not wish to slight. And so he let the friar's offer rest.

Somehow, even after his parents' death, Saul failed to undertake the metamorphosis. Perhaps he was wrong not to have acted. He would have spared Peter the beating.

"Why, Papa?" asked Peter again.

Saul faltered. He did not have a plausible answer. Unexpectedly, Clara came to his rescue with characteristic brevity and razor-edge logic. "A Jew is a Jew before the Nazis, even if he is now Catholic."

The salt in Clara's words had scarcely had a chance to sting the wound in Saul's flesh, when the door opened and the two younger children burst in.

"When are we going to eat?" moaned Rajko. "I'm hungry."

"What happened to him?" exclaimed Ljerka, pointing to Peter.

Finding his tongue at last, Saul whispered, as he gently caressed Peter's head, "Let's talk more about that later. And about Canada."

A drill-like sound intruded itself on everyone. It was the shrill noise of the office buzzer, so unmistakably different from the regular chime, telling Saul that the outside world needed him again.

"It is the wife of the journalist," Clara said, after answering the call. "He'll need you before long."

"The journalist? The journalist you said?" He repeated more as a mental exercise than a question, and the second time he sighed involuntarily. No, not him! Not him again! He could do so little for that poor newspaper vendor, and such he was, though everyone in town had promoted him to the rank of a journalist.

And besides, he did not wish to leave home after the events of the evening. Looking into Clara's eyes, into those soft, deep, brown pools of mystery that had soothed his soul after Tamara died, unwanted words of frustration spilled over, words which he immediately wished to disown. "Why ever did you marry a small town physician? You could have gone on to bigger and better things!"

"Nonsense," she said playfully. "I would never have made it, and you were my way out. You saved me from a showdown."

"That's not what they thought at the conservatory. You play Chopin like an angel."

Clara's face became serious. "I do love the piano, but it does not kiss me or hug me or love me back. So please go now, and come back as soon as you can."

With a knot somewhere inside him, he kissed Clara's lips, and in the distorted perspective of proximity, her soft brown eyes melted into a pool deep within which he saw the journalist, with his body withering away, and his eyes like tarnished silver. He shuddered.

"Won't you eat with us, Papi?" Ljerka piped up coquettishly, and momentarily took Saul away from his morbid patient. With her round little face she was the image of his mother and particularly precious to him. Though far more timid and serious than Rajko, in her brother's presence she sometimes became infected with his frolics.

Saul took her hand into his – it was a charming hand, he thought, no longer a little child's but not yet fully grown – and pressed it to his lips.

"No, darling," he said, "I'm not hungry."

Then he mussed Rajko's hair and wondered for the nth time what made the boy's large grey eyes look deceptively sad, for the moment the boy smiled, which was very often, his face became a picture of joy and mischief.

Saul kissed the twins good night, for those two lovable monkeys were certain to be asleep by the time he returned. As he took leave of Clara and Peter, Darinka entered with the reheated dinner.

Several moments later, Saul found himself walking down the same street along which he had returned home. It had stopped snowing, making it one of those wonderfully clear moonlit winter nights, the air absolutely still and pure, that one gets only after a snowfall. The crisp air was soothing his raw nerves and infusing him with the strength he needed to face his patient. He wished Peter were along with him. He enjoyed immensely the company of his older son, whom he had sometimes taken along on house calls or health inspections. No matter how hard he tried to be objective, he could not suppress an enormous pride in Peter. The boy was turning out to be everything a father's heart could ask for; and one day he would be a physician like himself. He and Peter understood each other so well, and he always knew where he stood with him. Not so with Rajko. His younger son was an enigma to him. Rajko vibrated at a different frequency than the rest of the family, and as Clara had put it once, "was a delightful stranger in their midst." Saul often amused himself with the thought that Peter was like himself, intense and brooding, and Rajko was as he would have liked to be, cheerful and easygoing. Peter was his image; Rajko was his dream.

The events of the evening pressed again on his consciousness. If only he could take Peter's bruises unto himself. But enough of such foolish thoughts! They had to leave! Tomorrow he would see about the visas.

As he approached the quarters of the newspaper vendor, his steps became slower and shorter. He would give the journalist something to numb the pain, but besides that, he could do so little for the man. Then he braced himself, bit his lower lip, and knocked on the door.

CHAPTER 2

Peter awoke with an ill-defined ache – a vague yearning he could not pinpoint. With an effort he got out of bed, and his eyes, which normally would quickly slide across the smooth surface of the mirror hanging on the opposite wall, were arrested by his own reflection. He contemplated the spectrum of purples, greens and yellows encircling his right eye. Then, moving to the window, he looked out frowning.

Across the street was the courthouse, with its complicated architecture of turrets and cupolas. The other buildings were more plain but sturdy, two storied, covered by red tile roofs. He looked in the direction of the town center, but all that he could see were the red tile roofs, and to one side, the small snow-covered hill, shaped like an inverted saucer, which had been set-aside as a park many years ago by the town elders. It was along the park edge that he had been attacked. In his mind's eye, he could see the town's central plaza, ringed by modest Baroque buildings, and the more humble cozy houses, radiating centrifugally along half a dozen outward stretching streets. What had been a pleasant town had suddenly become an odious place, with mean little dwellings strung in irregular rows. What only last week he had seen through his window in the neighbor's courtyard as sun rays gracing the branches of a snow powdered dormant lilac now looked like spotlights on a miserable shrub. How different everything had become! He knew that it was he, and not the town nor the bush, that had changed.

His glance wandered onto the balcony outside his parents' bedroom. Tiny holes in the snow indicated where his mother – Clara was the only mother he knew – had strewn breadcrumbs, and several sparrows were busy finishing off the morsels. With a rapid flutter of its wings, one of the birds dove towards another, jabbing its competitor with its beak, and chasing the other ruffled and screeching away.

Peter shivered. He wished he could reach out to the little fleeing grey creature and tell it how well he understood. He could still feel his own trembling, when those boys had attacked him, and how his heart had hammered, as if he had been a little field rabbit pounced upon by hunting dogs. He could even now taste the blood, which had trickled from his nose and made its way between his lips, with its nauseating sweetness.

The discomfort with which he awoke was still with him, as he groped with an inner bleakness. But a force was luring him from the confines of this miasma, and he yearned for restoration of beauty in life in general, and for Silvia's lovely face in particular.

And lovely indeed was Silvia's delicate face, with those green eyes, like two green jewels, peering out at the world, and framed by a halo of black curls.

Peter gulped. It was only a few weeks since Silvia Weinberg had come to Grad, yet so much had happened within that short stretch. When she had turned on him those bewitching eyes of hers, his knees went liquid, and his heart seemed to flip over in his chest, then race ahead. He could hardly believe that this was the ungainly obnoxious kid from Zagreb whose family had spent the summer a few years ago at the same Dalmatian resort as his own family.

Once more the mirror caught his attention, and as if it were magical, he was drawn to it, approaching it with questions. "Would Silvia mind seeing him like this? Had she missed him as much as he had missed her?" Craning his neck and turning it from side to side, as far as his eyes would allow, he took inventory of the ravages of battle. Silvia's visit to her grandmother was soon coming to an end, and she would be returning to Zagreb. That was far worse than his bruised exterior.

It was bad enough that Silvia would be leaving, but the thought that she might return to some former boyfriend was utterly unbearable. Silvia had lit a fire inside him, fanned by her flirtatiousness, which was consuming him. This was not the quiet steady warmth of love he had been familiar with, which he bore his family, teachers, or friends, but the tormenting flames of some purgatory he had not known before.

Looking deeper into the mirror, he tried to assess the plusses and demerits of his features beneath the discoloration. Though some people claimed he looked like his father, save for his mother's large hazel eyes and for a slightly prominent nose, he could not see the resemblance. He simply did not have his father's good looks, and above all lacked his father's elegant bearing which exuded conviction and confidence.

But still, Silvia did seem to favor him. And if her love was uncertain and elusive, he had enough for the two of them.

"Peter." He heard his name called, and a moment later his father entered the room. If I could only be like him, Peter thought, he always is so sure of himself. A faint odor of Lysol told him that his father had already been at work. Though his dad's manner was as easy as usual, the little flicker, or whatever it was, that made his father's blue eyes often seem as if they were smiling, was not there. Peter knew his father was worried.

"Are you going out?"

"I think so," Peter answered vaguely, though he had already decided in his mind to see Silvia.

"It will do you some good to finally get out. Besides, I need you to take some medicine to your professor. Two more days, and then he can stop." He handed Peter a small packet with a note, adding, "and he needs someone to cheer him up."

Peter walked briskly down R Street, turned the corner into J Street, and continued halfway down the block to Number 17. Then he skipped up a flight, two stairs at a time, leaving a trail of snow, which promptly turned into little puddles, and finally disappeared behind a door bearing the sign "Professor Emil Petkovich."

Professor Petkovich was a conspicuous member of the real gymnasium in Grad, where he had for many years taught European history. He was an outspoken and somewhat eccentric man, always in pursuit of truth, no matter how devastating that truth might be. Because he had no patience with stupidity, he had acquired a small but ardent group of enemies. The "Old Fox," as some of his inferior colleagues called him, had an adoring group of young followers among his students. He knew how to captivate their imagination, nurture their thirsty minds, and make even a boring lesson interesting.

The professor was always on the lookout for bright students, and took a special interest in them. Often he would have his "pets," as they were referred to, over to his bachelor flat, and on many occasions marathon debates ensued about the past, present and future. The Hundred Years' War and Napoleonic battles were fought over again. The large comfortable living room served as the battleground for many wars and conflicting "isms."

Despite advancing years and a considerable degree of sophistication in several fields, Professor Petkovich retained a certain idealism and simple-mindedness in his political views, and forever dreamed of a United Europe.

The professor now sat in a rocking chair close to a little blue tile stove, his small bent frame wrapped in a wool blanket. He was convalescing from pneumonia, which had nearly cost him his life, and which had taken away all the extra padding around the shoulders, the neck, and under the chin. As he looked at Peter, deep furrows appeared between his brows.

"I was so sorry to hear what happened to you," he said. "We have a few rotten apples around, but you realize, don't you, that they do not represent the general sentiment."

Peter nodded. The room was unbearably stuffy, and he had trouble concentrating. He sat at the table, not quite knowing what to say, and alternately rubbed one ear, then the other, and every so often his nose, which still felt like an icicle. The last few months had brought Peter less often to the professor's doorsteps. In particular, he avoided the professor's home when Francek was there, because the boy had come under the influence of a new right-wing Catholic party, heavily tinged with anti-Semitism.

And recently there was Silvia. Ah, Silvia! The thought of her made his mind wander and momentarily leap out of the stuffy room.

"It is not the discord within our country that I fear, but the crushing pincers from Germany," the professor said in a barely audible voice, as if speaking to himself. Then addressing himself more clearly to his young friend, "Peter, I am very worried about what is to come. I feel Yugoslavia is next on the firing line. If we try to resist, we will be crushed under foot."

The professor's words brought Peter back into the room. He had never seen the professor look so old and sallow, and the physical debilitation seemed to have ushered in an unusual degree of pessimism. This is not the way he used to talk. Where had all those uplifting thoughts and lofty ideas gone? Peter recalled his father mentioning once that patients recovering from pneumonia might became depressed.

The comment had hit a raw nerve in Peter, as a dentist might have with a drill, and he raised his voice by several decibels. "I hope you are wrong, Professor, I certainly hope so!"

"Hm, I hope I am, but.... You know, this illness has removed a film in front of my eyes. Things just don't look good to me now. Look here! There is war next door in Greece. Hungary and Romania have aligned themselves with the Axis. So much of Europe has already been devoured. And France, the protector of the 'Little Entente,' our greatest hope...oh, my heart aches, how it crumbled! Do you seriously think that Yugoslavia can offer resistance to Hitler? Ha, a brave thought!"

"There was no spirit in France," shouted Peter, barely able to remain seated in his chair, forgetting all the rancor of the last several days. "My uncle Robert went to Paris a couple of years ago. He says the French hate the English almost as much as they hate the Germans. But ask the people in this country. They'll fight the Germans. Of course, this area will have to be sacrificed, my father says, as in the last war, and the front lines will have to be moved to the mountain ranges of Bosnia. The tanks will do the Germans no good there."

"It won't come to that. We will be given an ultimatum to join the Axis, like Romania. What else do you suppose we'll do but accept the terms? You know, for you and your family that would be best. The present regime would remain in power, and they would not allow serious harm to come to the Jews."

"The Serbians will fight rather than permit their King to become a puppet." Peter returned to the previous topic, his cheeks now aflame like his frostbitten ears.

"We would only have England on our side, and look at Britain, how it is bleeding. It still stands only by virtue of its natural moat. And not for long. The Germans will probably land there in the spring."

"What about the Russians? They are afraid of too strong a Fuhrer."

"Russia certainly will not attack first. Nor will Germany attack Russia as long as there is an England left…unless Hitler believes himself above his own theories. Incidentally, did you ever read *Mein Kampf*?"

"Yes. And if the Germans are to walk in here, it would be best for my family to pack up and leave quickly."

"Is your father really applying for visas?"

"He is. But I'm not sure he really wants to go. By the way, did you get to meet Julius?"

"No."

"He was staying with us for a while, until he could enter Palestine. He is from Hamburg. Three kids in his family. The father, I understand, has been in and out of concentration camps for the last three years." Peter rambled on, then hesitated for a moment, changing the subject somewhat, probing his mentor's mind. "His older brother, he told me, is working in a munitions factory." Without dropping his voice at the end of the sentence, he paused to read the clues in the professor's face, but there were none. His temples now throbbing, he continued, "Imagine, his brother is making bombs that might kill you or me, or some English soldiers fighting to defeat our enemy! He should refuse to work!"

"What alternative does he have? He would be shot like a dog right then and there. Perhaps some day, Peter, you'll know how difficult it may be to walk a straight line. What else did Julius say?"

"He didn't say. He seemed to fear his own shadow." Then Peter added pensively, "There is something wrong with him, Professor. There is something wrong with all of them, those German refugees. I feel it, but cannot put my finger on it."

They returned to the question of Yugoslav neutrality versus involvement, opposition versus compromise, the prospect of containing a German invasion, and what might be the fate of the local Jews. Hitler had made life unpleasant for German Jews, they agreed, and many had left already for near or distant shores. But was that all, was that enough, to leave Germany for the Germans? Did he just want their wealth and to be rid of them? What indeed would happen to the Jews of Grad if Yugoslavia were to come under German occupation?

And so the conversation went on and on into the afternoon, the sanctity of the local lunch hour totally forgotten by both Peter and the professor.

After the stuffiness of the professor's living room, Peter drew in greedily a few deep breaths of fresh air. He had become so wrapped up in the conversation, he had forgotten about the existence of such a thing as time. In fact, he had even briefly forgotten about Silvia, which he could hardly believe, for lately she had been in his thoughts from the moment he awoke to the moment he fell asleep. Her face floated up to him invitingly, and his step quickened. He just simply had to see her. It was late, but not too late for them to take a short stroll by the river before it got dark. The air was crisp, but with the proper attire, a walk would be invigorating. He had to see Silvia, and see her alone, without her relatives hovering over them. He bent down, scooped up snow with his gloves to make a snowball, and then dribbled it down the street till it fell apart. Seeing no one in the street, he slid and skipped virtually all the way to the Weinbergs'.

Much to Peter's surprise, Silvia, the grandmother, and other members of the extended Weinberg family received him warmly as a hero of his recent anti Semitic confrontation, and not as its victim. The grandmother was baking goodies for Hanukkah, and the whole house was filled with the most delicious aroma of baked buttered and yeast-leavened dough. She brought Peter slices of mouth watering walnut and poppy-seed rolls, for which he was most grateful, as by now he was absolutely famished. And as a crowning glory to a hero, the grandmother allowed Peter and Silvia to take a walk un-chaperoned, provided they returned before it was pitch dark, and in winter that meant early.

"Be good," she told them, as she went back to the kitchen to concoct with the cook more oven-baked delicacies.

That day Silvia was in a somber mood, which was rare for her temperament. The walk took Peter and Silvia along one of the paved streets, away from the center. They paused on the steel bridge, which traversed the river's bulging waist just beyond a small dam, as it meandered near one edge of Grad. Holding hands, Peter allowed himself to dream while they watched the water tumbling down, the cold not sufficient to freeze the running stream. He had even forgotten about his recent humiliation and his discolored right eye. Silvia did not seem to share with him the magic of the afternoon walk. She was irritated and compulsively returned to the fulcrum of her irritation.

"Some nerve, those people! The Goldsteins. You know, the refugee couple I told you about from Austria; the ones who are staying with the Weisses. They have supper at Uncle Max's, and have – or use to have – lunch with us. Well, they didn't like our meal and made a big fuss. Grandmother thought that what was good enough for us on the day the cook was off ought to be good enough for them. And do you know what Mrs. Goldstein did? It was dreadful! She laughed and laughed in Grandma's face, and said, 'Hitler will get you too.' It was like some sort of a curse." Silvia shuddered, and then added, "Peter, I don't understand. We have really been nice to them, and yet they hate us."

"It seems they envy us that we still have what they have lost."

This explanation did not satisfy Silvia. She got angrier and angrier the longer she dwelt on the subject. "Those people have no pride, anyway! They come around like beggars in Zagreb, droves of them; every day new ones ring the doorbell, with sad-sack stories. Why don't they go to work?"

Peter winced. He did not expect such words from her. She ought to know that foreigners could not work without special permits, and most of them could never get them. With a sigh, he added, remembering the professor's words, "I only hope we won't have to do the same some day."

"Not I! I'd never do that! I'd never crawl before people, begging them to throw me a few crumbs. I'd rather be d…."

"Don't say it, don't!" Peter felt an oppression engulfing him again, a feeling that time was running out, that his world was ebbing away. The anguish gave him the impetus to do what he otherwise might not have dared yet; as if in a trance, he embraced Silvia, and found himself planting awkward kisses on her ruby lips.

"I love you! I'll always love you," he stammered, tightening his embrace, and kissing her again. For one instant he felt her tremble. It was a momentary quiver, something like the fright of a captured animal.

She was so close to him now, that he imagined their skins melting, and their bodies and souls uniting. "Do you love me?"

"Yes," she whispered, after a moment of hesitation, and kissed him back.

Peter was seized by delirium, and all the recent meanness and ugliness in the world fell away.

"I could never love anyone else. Maybe," he paused. "Maybe when we get older we'll get married."

But a moment later, the gulf between them opened up again, though he held on to her for dear life, and with a searing sensation he saw visas within the gap, and marching armies, strange lands, and the darkness of the unknown.

"Silvia, oh Silvia!" his voice cracked, as the streetlights went on.

CHAPTER 3

"Doctor, doctor, come quickly," Abraham Kohan's daughter shrieked hysterically.

As Saul was roused by the screams, he had a strange sensation that he was mired on the floor of an immense ocean, rapidly resurfacing after only ten minutes of sleep.... His head was still swimming somewhere in the depths; in fact, he was still asleep, three-quarters asleep, but a certain segment of him heard, "Where is the doctor?"

Saul groaned. He was so tired, his head would not stop swirling, and he was falling back to the bottom of the sea. He had been constantly on the go the last two days and the night between. At the wee hours he had attended the delivery of the miller's wife, his vigil having been divided between her and an asthmatic child whose attack was uncommonly resistant to the usual treatment.

At the crack of dawn, when the doctor's work seemed finished, a frantic young villager came to fetch him, and off he was driven in the horse-drawn wagon. The rocking motion of the carriage and the crunching noise of the half frozen snow under the wheels lulled him to sleep and fortunately gave him a short reprieve. When he returned, he found a long line of patients waiting for him at the office. Then there was one house call after another, one sick patient after another. When he finally returned home late that afternoon, he literally collapsed on the sofa.

"Quickly, quickly... father... doctor... come," echoed in the hallway.

The last wave of screams lifted Saul from the bottom of the ocean and off the couch.

"Come, doctor, quickly," yelled the hysterical woman, as she burst into the room, wearing only a negligee over a nightgown, and a flimsy pair of boots, to which the snow still clung, her tinted red hair flying in all directions.

Old Abe Kohan, Saul thought, did not have much luck with his children. The daughter was an old spinster and a recluse, sleeping till noon every day, and the son was of subnormal mentality, very amiable and friendly, but totally incapable of conducting the family business. The old man had always been a shrewd and industrious merchant, but since the death of his wife, he had abandoned himself to a growing bitterness toward his children and an inordinate craving for money. What had been a frugal disposition in earlier years, when he was poor, turned into miserliness in old age.

Saul got up, ran his left hand through his hair, and with the right reached for his coat. Then he picked up his black bag and followed Abe's daughter into the January dusk.

En route, Saul questioned the distraught woman, but she was incoherent, and he could only gather that the problem concerned her father and their younger store clerk, Vaso Pamich.

As they walked through the gate, Saul was startled to see the crumpled figure of the old man lying in the snow. The small lean frame seemed even tinier than usual. Saul knelt down and at close range saw old Abe lying in a pool of blood. "A bleeding ulcer, perhaps," he thought, and reached for the hand inside the sleeve. It was cold, the pulse gone.

The daughter switched on the doorway light, a solitary dim bulb. Saul bent down again, and his breath froze. There was old Abe with a slash across his neck, froth and blood clinging to the wound.

Saul was overcome by a feeling of nausea. Beads of sweat cropped up on his forehead. In the inevitable pursuit of his profession, he had thought that he had come to terms with death, no matter in what guise it came. His gut seemed to twist, as it had done in the trenches of World War I. Perhaps it was the lack of sleep that made him ill. He breathed in slowly and deeply to calm himself as sweat continued to pour down his face.

The murder of Abraham Kohan, the "stingy old Jew," as people referred to him, electrified the little town of Grad. Vaso Pamich, the junior store clerk, readily confessed to the deed and was arrested.

Saul had not had time to even grab a cup of coffee for breakfast. But now at 10:00 o'clock there was a small welcome respite, and he stopped at the deli for a snack, which he enjoyed doing on the rare occasions when time permitted.

"Poor Vaso," someone said at the next table. "He has a wife and two children to feed. Hard to get by on a junior clerk's salary. Have you seen his kids go barefoot? Probably the old Jew wouldn't give him a raise."

"He shouldn't have gambled at cards," someone replied.

"He has been desperate to pay off his debts. Poor Vaso! And now his family will suffer, and all on account of that stingy Jew."

When Saul returned home, Clara was there in the foyer to greet him. She had a sixth sense for knowing when he needed her most.

"We are leaving," he declared, finally free to release his pent-up exasperation. "Vaso's cause has been taken up by some pro-Nazi groups, and he has suddenly become the victim. Of course, the courts will convict him, but there are people who are saying that 'after all, it was only a Jew who had been killed.'"

"Come and sit down. Darinka will bring you some coffee."

"I should have pushed the visa business more vigorously!"

"But you have been working so hard, you've hardly had time to breathe."

It was true, he had gotten bogged down by an outbreak of severe respiratory infections.

"And it is not that easy to get entry visas for Canada or the U. S. without friends or relatives over there to vouch for us." Clara's logic argued against his self-flagellation.

"Perhaps Australia would be easier. Anywhere, just out!"

When Peter was beaten up, it was his pride that had spoken out, but now it was time to leave, he felt it in his bones. Yet he really did not want to leave, nor did Clara. He loved this little corner of the world where he had grown up, and it was frightening to start all over in some remote country. But times had changed, and he ought to change too, he told himself.

"You know, Clara, this year a man was murdered because he was mean and Jewish, and next year he will be murdered simply because he is Jewish."

"If you really think that we should leave, then we'll leave."

A few days after Abe Kohan was interred, Saul found some free time to stop at the town hall and renew his efforts to obtain emigration papers, but encountered a new obstacle. He was told that he and the children could get a visa for the U.S., but Clara's visa would be delayed, because her place of birth, following the break-up of Austria-Hungary, was now in a different country with a different quota.

"We are not going until we can all go together," Saul declared.

He was also informed that all that he would be able to legally take out of Yugoslavia was fifty dollars, and with that he would hardly be able to start a medical practice anywhere. Big businessmen found ways to transfer their funds to Swiss bank accounts, but he, a country physician, was at a disadvantage.

Under the burden of expanding demands of his medical practice, Saul felt his strength sagging, and out of fatigue arose hesitation and postponement, and out of postponement, a hope that the political situation might stabilize, so that after all they need not leave. And while most of his time and energy were consumed by the urgency of the moment, his world spun headlong towards war.

CHAPTER 4

Saul and Peter were already at breakfast when Clara tuned in Radio Belgrade, which she did religiously to hear the 7:00 A.M. newscast. Rajko and Ljerka were still asleep next door.

"Are we going to Zagreb for Easter?" asked Peter, hoping to see Silvia, but neither Saul nor Clara seemed to hear his question.

As spring had approached, Saul was feverishly following every newspaper report and radio communiqué, each minute counting. A few days before, the Premier and Prince Regent Paul had been summoned to Vienna to negotiate with Germany for free passage of German troops through Yugoslavia to assist the Italian campaign in Greece. Saul realized that the time for Yugoslav neutrality was vanishing and that signing a pact with Germany was tantamount to becoming an Axis satellite, the consequences of which filled him with great unease, creating a queasy feeling in the pit of his stomach. Refusal probably meant invasion by Germany. As Professor Petkovich had predicted, the Premier and Prince Regent, whatever their true feeling may have been, accepted Germany's demands, and a pact was signed and sealed in Vienna on March 25, 1941.

Peculiarly enough, that morning only the national anthem came across the air. A few minutes later the agitated voice of the announcer came on: "King Peter, though not quite of age, has taken over the reins of the government, on this 27th day of March. A coup was successfully carried out by General Simovic and his followers, ousting Premier Cvetkovic and Prince Paul, and voiding the pact with Germany. The General has been given the mandate to organize a new cabinet. An attack can be expected from Germany at any time. Please stand by...."

"Ta – tata – ta," the anthem again.

Saul's hand jerked, and he spilled coffee on the tablecloth. Yugoslavia was on the brink of war!

"What now?" Clara gasped. Saul felt her and Peter's eyes on him, as if he were an oracle.

"We'll have to wait and see," he managed to squeeze out. There were a few chances in a million that war might still be averted. And a few in a hundred that Clara's visa might come through in the next few days.

After finishing his café au lait and fresh baked rye bread with homemade plum jam, Saul had intended to go downstairs to the office and catch up on paperwork, but instead he lingered on in the dining room, conscious of every breath he drew, and of the throbbing in his temples. He felt an impulse – perhaps some atavistic response to imminent danger – to look in on the twins. Rajko, who had apparently been awakened by the radio announcer, was jumping on his bed, very excited.

"Papa, somebody ought to teach those Germans a lesson," he shouted, and proceeded to take that task upon himself. General Rajko cupped his hands around his mouth, produced a trumpet-like noise, and commanded his imaginary troops to attack.

"Oh, shush! One can't even sleep in peace around here any more," Ljerka protested with a big yawn.

"Peace, who's talking about peace, when a war is about to start," Rajko announced proudly to his sister. "Yoopee! Fire!"

"Papi, Papi, I'm scared of wars." Ljerka burst into tears. Saul sat down on her bed, trying to comfort her. But what could he truthfully say to make her feel safe? That the war will not come, or that wars are not scary? All that he could do was just hug her and kiss her, and dry her tears. That strategy seemed to work, and after a few snivels, she jumped out of bed.

"Papa, I love you."

When Saul returned later that afternoon from his sick calls, the radio still blared the national anthem, the commentator periodically explained the official position of sovereignty and the continued neutrality of the new government, and Berlin had not made any moves, diplomatic or otherwise.

"Papa," Rajko pranced up to him like a little colt, as Saul passed through the gate into the courtyard. "This is great. No school today.

Pow, wow," and he threw an invisible grenade, which destroyed a whole platoon of Germans.

Rajko was obviously thrilled with the idea of Yugoslavia beating up the Germans. Nor was he the only one. Saul had seen a number of adults walking about as if intoxicated, overcome by a frenzy to wage war on Germany. It all seemed so unreal, but he was certain that he had read about something similar in a Russian novel.

The threat of danger did not occur to Rajko. He was a happy-go-lucky boy with a notion that nothing bad would ever happen to him. In early childhood he had caused Saul to worry about trying to climb a seat near one of the tile stoves, which his small limbs could not negotiate, and he repeatedly fell down.

"Does he not learn from mistakes?" Saul had asked Clara. And in his own mind he had wondered whether this represented a deficiency of intellect, or was an indication of future shallowness. Certainly Peter had not acted that way.

Peter had been very different. More sensitive and introspective, Peter had come to him with all kinds of questions: "Papa, why am I 'I', and not someone else?" And later, "Why do I see everything through the eyes of Peter Kestner, and not someone else?" And the inevitable extrapolation, "What happened two hundred years ago, and through whose eyes did the world exist then?"

Such thoughts did not seem to occur to Rajko as he got older, though Saul became assured that there was no intellectual deficit, but thoughts of this type seemed to slide off Rajko, like rain off a tin roof.

Ljerka dashed up to Saul in the hallway. "Papi, is it true that there is going to be a war?"

"I don't know, sweetie."

"How can people live with a war going on?"

"Let us hope there won't be any."

"Papi, do you remember the war expo we saw last year? That was awful!" And she burst into tears.

Of course he remembered the frightening gas masks and horrible Lewisite skin burns shown at the Zagreb exposition, after which the children had nightmares. It had been wrong for Robert and Bettina to take the children when they were visiting over vacation.

Saul embraced Ljerka, but again there was nothing he could say that would sooth her, short of reassuring her that there would be no war, and that he could not promise her. Her whole terrified body shook in his arms as he kissed her and whispered in her ear, “We’ll just have to wait and see, princess.”

CHAPTER 5

Peter looked around his room, trying to absorb all the details, to indelibly commit them to memory, for that was all that would be left to him. His father was notified that their visas had been approved, and they would be leaving in a few days. He walked to the window and looked out. It was already Palm Sunday, the 6th of April, and still uncommonly chilly. The three trees his father had planted, one for each of the children, stretched their bare arms towards a pale sun, hesitating to spread their foliage. His glance slid over a few low tile roofs, towards the tallest hill skirting Grad, on top of which he could barely make out the three crosses, conferring to it the name of Calvary. He remembered sledding there once with Silvia. Oh, Silvia. His heart ached. He might never see her again! He looked in the direction of her grandmother's house, which he could not see over the intervening taller roofs.

From the distance suddenly rose a wailing sound, which everyone in Grad recognized as the siren from the one and only factory, which infallibly announced the end of its workday from Monday to Saturday. But on a Sunday around noon, it sent Peter running downstairs. He found his mother clasping and unclasping her hands, his father pacing up and down the floor of the living room, and the radio on, loud and clear.

"The Luftwaffe has attacked Belgrade, without an official declaration of war," the announcer informed, "coinciding precisely with the sirens of an early morning air raid drill. People going to mass were machine gunned at close range, caught unaware by the perfect timing of the attack. As you all know, our capital had been declared an 'open city,' and there is no anti-aircraft, allowing the pilots to fly low safely in order to strafe, and drop bombs with great and deadly precision. There are numerous casualties, but as yet there are no estimates available. Attempts at diplomatic contacts have failed to clarify the situation, and by this act of aggression we appear to be at war."

Peter felt his heart stand still for a moment and then race ahead to catch up with itself.

"Clara – ah." A groan came from his father. "War has finally broken out, and we are still here in Grad! And it's all my fault! We should have left a year ago. No, two years ago. But I stalled, and now it is too late! The borders are sealed, and there is no way out."

"You are not to blame."

"Like a fool, I had hoped the war would not come. What had I thought? That it would go everywhere else but here? That it would simply evaporate into thin air?"

"It is impossible to justify the hope and logic of yesterday in the light of events of today."

A couple of explosions and tremors interrupted the conversation, and Peter saw his father spring rapidly from self-recrimination into purposeful action. As they later found out, two disoriented Yugoslav pilots had flown their airplanes over Grad and between them discharged four bombs, killing one servant girl and injuring a dog.

Saul promptly arranged to send his family out of town, to the safety of a nearby village, though he could not go himself on account of a few very ill patients. The physician in whose care Saul usually left his office during brief vacations had been called up by the general mobilization two weeks earlier, and now Saul had to carry the other man's load as well.

Peter tossed back and forth on a pile of straw long after the candle had gone out, unable to fall asleep. He now shared a peasant cellar with Rajko, Ljerka, and several young adults. His mother was accommodated upstairs, dormitory style, sharing the floor of the main room, a combination living room, dining room and kitchen, with several older Jewish couples who had fled Grad.

Peter strained his ears. Everyone seemed to be asleep, except Ljerka, who cried almost imperceptibly, giving herself away with faint sniffles. Not Rajko, he snored heartily. "Funny kid," Peter thought, "he really likes to sleep on the floor better than in his own bed. He is the only one who is enjoying himself."

There was something odd and unreal about the cellar. Peter was aware of everything that was happening, though it did not seem to be a part of his life. In fact, the last three days had felt at if he were a spectator watching himself on a stage. No, that was not his life, he was still in Grad, a student at the real gymnasium, expected to graduate with honors next year and go to the university. And this week, as they did every year, his family would go to Zagreb for Easter vacation, to visit Aunt Bettina and Uncle Robert. And then he would see Silvia. His throat tightened, and he had to swallow hard. In his mind Silvia was standing next to him. He threw his arms around her, and he smelled lily of the valley in her hair.

"Are you asleep, darling?" Peter heard George ask his wife, and the words instantly dispelled his dream and brought him back to the peasant cellar.

Marta and George, like so many young Jewish people from Grad, had stretched their wings as soon as they were able and had flown away to Zagreb, which they considered culturally like a bit of Vienna. George had completed his studies there in jurisprudence, and had opened a law office. Because of the holidays and the political situation, they had returned to Grad, to stay with their parents.

"Yes I am," mocked Marta.

"Everybody's asleep."

"So?"

"So, I love you, and I need you, my little one. Will you be my wife tonight?"

"But George, suppose…."

"Can't you hear the snoring?"

"How can you think about such things these days?"

"Being so close to you day and night, with the entire world topsy-turvy, that's the only thing I can think about. The only thing I am sure of is our love. Please don't fight me."

Peter hardly dared to breath, lest he be discovered awake.

"You're hurting me, dearest."

"Relax."

"Enough, darling, please. Suppose the kids…."

"I love you, and I need you."

"I love you too."

Peter was overcome by a feeling of revulsion for the pair, and thorough dissatisfaction with himself. He had been an intruder in someone else's life. He could have stopped his ears, but for some inexplicable reason, had failed to do so.

Ljerka's corner was now entirely quiet, and Peter wondered whether she too had heard the amorous gasps of the couple, Ljerka who still believed in the stork. Peter had once overheard Rajko tell her some "funny stories" he had heard about "making" babies, but she dismissed them very quickly as absurd and totally illogical.

"You know, Rajko," she had replied to her twin, "if it were as simple as all that, then everybody could have a baby. Mrs. Franich wants a baby, but she hasn't got one because God didn't send her one."

Sleep came easily and sweetly to the lovers, but for Peter it seemed like ages before it came to his rescue, and allowed him a reprieve.

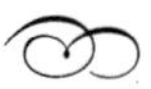

In the morning Peter could not wait to get away from the farmhouse. His mother was fretting about Ljerka having the prodrome of some illness. One look at his sister told Peter that she was suffering from growing pains, and that she was no longer the innocent little girl of the day before. And so life was closing in on Ljerka, and making her come face to face with the gentle and the harsh, the sublime and the ridiculous, the cruel and the bittersweet, no matter how their parents tried to shield her.

At the gate Peter ran into the orphan boy, a scrawny eight-year-old with the face of an owl who had been taken on at the farm as a servant. Gossip had it that he was the illegitimate child of the farmer's oldest son, stemming from the fact that he was treated kindly. The farmer had said that when it came to work, the boy was as good as any grown man.

The boy carried an armful of sticks. He stepped quickly out of Peter's way and stared at Peter with large vacant eyes, without returning the greeting.

Outside the village Peter found a little stream that caught his fancy. As he listened to the soft ripple of its flowing waters, it seemed to soothe him, and to slowly, slowly wash away some of the pain within him, just as it did in time wear away its own bed of earth and rock. He could now think of Silvia, dream about embracing her, without the enormous pain that usually accompanied his yearning. He remained there, as if hypnotized by the swishing sound, until the sun and his stomach told him that it must be noon.

Inside the farmhouse the atmosphere was unbearable. The women from Grad were quarreling over the minutest trifles. Now that they seemed to be all in the same boat, they had to assert their non-existent superiority over one another. So much steam was generated, that George, who tried to act as peace-maker, was dripping with perspiration, gallantly bearing a fingernail scratch across his cheek, inflicted accidentally by one of the women while he was separating her from her best friend during a face-slapping and hair-pulling episode.

"I know what's bothering you," Rajko winked knowingly at Ljerka. "You're in love with Captain Odin," referring to their parents' friend, the handsome young cavalry officer.

"I have had enough of this," Clara declared. "Without telephones and electricity, all we do is argue and fight, and no one knows what's going on. I haven't heard from my husband since we left Grad. In times of war it is best for families to stay together."

Before anyone found words to reply, the farmer entered the room, having just returned from Grad.

"The German motorized units are swarming in from all sides and closing in rapidly." His long mustache quivered with every word. "Our army is disorganized… there is no ammunition, no command! Here and there men with rifles and bayonets have tried to stop the tanks. And our curse, our separatists, are assisting the enemy. I heard that a significant number of Croatian soldiers have already deserted their posts to welcome the Germans."

"You have been kind to us, Ilija," Clara spoke up, "But I think the time has come for us to go home."

"If you like, Ma'am, we'll hitch up the horses, but family and friends of our doctor are always welcome to stay."

"Hey, Ljerka," Peter heard Rajko say, "We'll have another one of those great hay rides."

A procession of three horse-drawn peasant wagons left the village in a hurry that afternoon, heading for Grad. It had rained earlier, just enough to quench the thirst of the dirt road, so that the two carriages ahead, driven by Ilija's sons, did not raise dust. In the first carriage sat the orphan boy. Peter had seen him help hitch the horses, and he was rewarded by being allowed to come along. With his owlish eyes and without a word, the boy had blinked at Rajko, and presented him with a painted Easter egg, as they were leaving the village. It was Friday, Good Friday, two days before Easter.

Peter was nearly lulled to sleep by the rhythmic beating of the hoofs, and the occasional interspersed whistling sound, as the farmer whipped the air above the mares. He was about to dose off again, when a loud noise jolted him, and the mares reared. Ilija had managed to stop the horses and jumped off as if he were still eighteen. The first carriage was tilting badly by the bed of a small creek, and its horses were neighing wildly. Presently the farmer came running back.

"What happened?" Clara asked.

"Ma'am, the wooden bridge was mined."

"Is anyone hurt?"

"The boy's got his leg near ripped off, and the horses are in a bad way." Then he cursed and spat. "We're close to Grad, Ma'am. Maybe your husband can help the lad."

"Tie the stump tightly and keep the boy warm," Peter heard himself say, as if someone else were talking through him, remembering his father's comments. "We should rush him to the hospital directly."

George and Ilija carried the moaning child, while Ilija's sons led the second and third team of horses across the shallow stream, and everyone else followed in a wide arc around the remnants of the bridge, leaving behind a broken wagon and two dying horses.

"Oh, Mother of God," Ilija grumbled, "whose sins is that poor bastard paying for."

CHAPTER 6

With amazing swiftness Saul saw Germany defeat Yugoslavia, and on Easter Sunday, April 13, one week after the invasion started, a puppet "Independent State of Croatia" was created. Gone were the brief days of intoxication and foolhardy saber rattling. After a restless night, Saul was up early. The streets were deserted, and an uneasy quiet prevailed, interrupted only by a rare firecracker set off by some pro-Nazi sympathizers, celebrating the birth of the new nation. Most homes remained shuttered up, and neither patients nor summoning relatives came to call.

In the evening, someone needed Saul, and a policeman came to fetch him. With his black bag as usual, he set out, accompanied by the officer, who led the way to the police station. A badly beaten victim after an interrogation, Saul thought. Only after being shown into a large room with the entire male Jewish population of Grad present, did Saul realized the gravity of his own situation.

"So that's what it has come to, and so quickly," he told himself, beads of perspiration cropping up on his forehead. "What a fool I was not to have gotten out two years ago!" He slapped down his useless bag and collapsed into a chair. But an inner voice, or perhaps it was Clara's voice, reminded him that it would have been more like tearing himself away. His life had been so intertwined in the fabric of this inconspicuous corner of the world, that unless he were expelled, he could not depart.

In a flash, Saul recalled the early twenties, and all the optimism that had accompanied those years. Those were the days when he was young, and energetic, and full of dreams and hopes. After he recovered from the loss of his beloved Tamara, he was caught up in the wave of nationalistic fervor, arising out of the ashes of the Austro-Hungarian Empire. He and his brother Robert promptly received Yugoslav citizenship, while the leaders of the newly formed country pledged to give equal opportunities, rights, and justice to the previously stateless Jews. And so it was with exhilaration that

Saul returned to Grad, the town he loved so well, after an absence of a decade, with the war and his studies behind him, ready to start a new life with Clara. He had always had a sense of belonging there, of being an integral part of it, of its green valley, of its people, its fortunes and foibles, of its fertile soil, and its very grains of sand. Even the Romans, in their own time, had called it the "Golden Valley – Valis Aurea."

And now that whole world had crumbled! He had seen the change coming, had cried out against it in wounded pride rather than genuine conviction, and in the end his ties had muddied his judgment. So here he was now, in jail, thrown together with sixty some men, with most of whom he had very little in common, except for Judaism, and that in his own mind was just a rubber stamp. He looked around at his fellow prisoners with a certain amount of annoyance, and swore that if he ever had another chance, he would get rid of this unwanted burden, this religious stigma.

The new chief of police then addressed his captive audience, rolling each word in his mouth with pomp and relish.

"Gentlemen, you will be released in the morning unharmed, provided you cooperate with us and hand over all guns, moneys and valuables you own. Nothing more will be asked of you in the future, I can assure you. Our new government will not tolerate that Jews be rich, when so many Croats are poor. Jewish wealth will be returned to our people to whom it belongs, and from now on only poor Jews will be tolerated." Waving his arms imperiously, he continued. "Anyone withholding the items requested, or trying to hide them, or hiding even a small part, will be executed in the morning. Under our new martial law, every infringement, every offense, no matter how small, will be punished by execution. I will leave you now to think things over."

The men stared at the receding doughy bulk of the chief of police, at each other, at the white walls of the detention room, the chuckling rifle-toting guards, their faces reflecting a mixture of confusion, terror, and disbelief.

Zvonko Adler, a former gymnasium classmate of Saul's, spoke first. "In Hungary, considerable autonomy is given to the local government, and though there are many restrictions and injustices, life somehow still goes on. It is best to deal with the local authorities and keep the Germans out."

"Luxury is not a necessary ingredient of life," added Steiner, "We can live modestly without diamonds, or furs, or a lot of money, if we have to. Jews have periodically been plundered by mobs, their possessions expropriated by inspectors, or were threatened by inquisitors, judges, and police. When black clouds gather, we have to be clever and lie low, till a warmer climate returns, and then we can flourish again and regain our wealth and our status."

"And what choice do we have?" said a religious old man. "Obviously it would be foolish to lose one's life over a ring or a bracelet, and leave behind a fatherless family. No, it would be more than foolish, it would be vain and sinful and Philistine to value gold and possessions above the life that God has given us."

So they mulled things over, debated and debated, and after a time some of the terror thawed, while their optimism was fanned by the chief of police, who gave them, over and over again, his solemn word of no further abuse.

"Perhaps the initial excesses like this round-up will subside," Adler ventured a guess, "and a reasonable balance will be reached. Whenever there are radical changes, in whichever direction, the Jews seem to receive the blows."

That was true. Saul remembered only too well that at the end of World War I, when Austria-Hungary collapsed, there was a local outburst of anti-Germanism, and before the Serbian government could establish order, outlaw groups sprang up in Croatia, attacking and plundering long-time German settlers. In the ensuing chaos, many Jews whose names may have been German sounding were burnt to the ground, as was the house and general store of his own parents, and they found themselves destitute overnight. It was his older brother Robert who helped him finance his medical studies, and when Saul went into practice, he had to build, as the saying was, "out of the ashes."

Before dawn, the chief of police started interviewing his prisoners, one by one, in a cunning scheme, in which he extracted lists of everyone's possessions, while threatening them with the firing squad if these did not match completely with all the valuables the wives were instructed to bring. The wives were told about the itemized lists, but not their contents, and were instructed to hand over everything of value, if they ever again wanted to see their husbands. Thus the chief of police rekindled the terror in the hearts of the men, lest they omit some little trinket, and into the hearts of the women, lest they condemn their spouses by hiding a ring or a pin.

At last, after that endless night, Saul's turn came.

"Sit down, sit down, doctor." The chief of police waved him to a chair. Saul thought he could detect a shade of deference. "Dr. Kestner, you have the respect and friendship of our citizens. We know that the post of county physician pays little, and that your private practice during the depression could not have made you rich. It is not people like you that we are after."

Well, Saul thought, maybe Zvonko was right. The police overreacted, and they are already loosening the grip. But he did not like his interviewer's squint; he preferred to look a man straight in the eye.

"Have you anything to declare?"

Saul hesitated. It was common knowledge that he owned a rifle, having distinguished himself at the local range two years ago, more by default of other contenders than by his own merit. And so he acknowledged his firearm, but made no mention of a small sum and a few pieces of Clara's jewelry, which had secretly been buried for him a few days before in the garden of a Christian friend. He would need those if he ever dreamed of getting away.

"You can go now, doctor. I understand the journalist is having another one of his attacks."

Momentarily Saul found himself outside the police station, blinking as the sunrays flooded his face, after a night of darkness. The Jewish women of Grad were lined up on the pavement with their money and valuables, ready for the exchange.

The sun infused the curving street with a bright glow, as if it were a festive day, though the air remained chilly as Saul walked home with Clara, her hand gripping tightly his arm. There was so much to tell her, but his tongue seemed to stick to the roof of his mouth, and they walked in silence. As they turned the corner, Saul saw a large yellow placard on the gate of their home. Even from some distance he could read the words in German and Croatian, "This is a Jewish house," followed by the six-cornered Star of David.

"This is to warn people, as if lepers live here," Clara added bitterly.

Peter appeared in the doorway and rushed up to them. "Are you okay, Papa?" Peter's sharply chiseled features were underscored by lack of sleep. The two embraced, and Saul imagined for an instant that he felt their hearts beat in synchrony.

Inside the living room the twins were busily discussing the new poster.

"I don't know why they make such a fuss about Jews," said Ljerka.

"Yeah," Rajko agreed. "Why can't they pick on someone else?"

Then they noticed their father and ran to give him a hug.

Saul felt physically and spiritually exhausted and lay down on the sofa, but try as he might, he could not fall asleep. His mind was like an over-wound spring, spinning about a central fulcrum, and asking, "What's to come next?" He replayed the various possibilities back and forth in his mind, but his logic prevented him from coming up with an answer. "Maybe there is no logic. This is sheer madness." That would be the sort of thing Clara would say. Noticing the morning paper, which had arrived from Zagreb, on the table, he picked it up in search of some clues. Suddenly his eyes caught a small article. "What's that?" he exclaimed, and jumped up. "The colorful professor, Emil Petkovich, of the provincial town of Grad, was found dead in his apartment yesterday. The cause of death was a heart ailment."

Saul felt the floor sway under him. "So Emil did it, after all!" He had heard Petkovich say it, no, swear to it, that if the Germans won, he would not participate in the aftermath. Saul had taken his friend's veiled threats as verbal flair for the dramatic. And who would know better than himself that the man's heart was sound. Yes, sound and in the right place!

"Oh, what a world it has become, when a sane man resorts to suicide," Saul told Clara. It was not madness, he knew, nor any personal matter, that had prompted Petkovich to such rash action, but an unwillingness to bend to a rule which was abhorrent to him, and of which he wanted no part. "Yes, when a sane man resorts to such action, and an insane one rules the world."

The article continued with statistics and minutia of the Professor's interesting, though eccentric past for the morbid curiosity of the avid obituary fan.

The doorbell rang, and Saul opened the door by reflex, his mind still dwelling on his deceased friend and patient. To his surprise, he found himself staring into the face of the same policeman who had fetched him the night before. Unable to control the bite of sarcasm, he snapped, "Need a doctor again, eh?"

"No, sir," came the reply, "we want your son."

Saul felt his gut twist inside him. Peter! Why Peter? Couldn't he go instead? He wanted to say something, but he could not find the words, and he stood there tongue-tied on the threshold.

"He is to report tomorrow morning at 8:00 at town hall." And before Saul could summon a word, the man spun around on the heels of his boots and was gone.

And why not Peter now? Nothing seemed sacred to that chief of police. The promise he had given Saul and the others was still wet on his lips. Saul knew he had appraised the man correctly, but he felt no satisfaction in that knowledge.

And what did they want with Peter anyway? Saul felt one more convulsive twist inside him. Ahead of him was another endless night, even worse than the one before.

It was not till the following evening that Saul could breath a sigh of relief. The Jewish youngsters were humiliated, but not otherwise harmed. They had to go wash windows and clean the lavatories in various public buildings. This was for the benefit of the citizens of Grad, so they could see the sons and daughters of the well-to-do Jews become their servants for a week. But that was not so bad. In Zagreb, for instance, all the eighteen and nineteen-year-old boys were sent out of town for hard labor and came to be knows as Group D. They were to be held as hostages for a huge ransom in money, gold, and jewelry, which was left up to the entire Jewish community to collect.

It could be worse, Saul told himself, but how could he be certain that tomorrow would not indeed be worse.

A few days after Easter, Saul saw the first German occupation troops march into Grad, concomitant with the creation of the pro-Nazi state of Independent Croatia in the geographic mid-portion of the defeated and disintegrating Yugoslavia. The troops were from Saxony, and were quartered with local Aryan families. Surprisingly few complaints ensued from the general population, who conceded how clean and orderly the troops were. Stores which had closed the week before reopened, and business was suddenly booming, as the German soldiers and officers had far more spending money than their Yugoslav counterparts ever dreamed of having. The politically uncommitted citizens breathed a sigh of relief as the town resumed a relatively calm and orderly pace.

A photographer lived in back of the Kestner house, and many a uniformed German now passed through the common courtyard where the children were playing, in order to develop rolls upon rolls of film to send home, documenting their conquests. Ljerka and Rajko owned a ping-pong table, a gift from Uncle Robert that had been the envy and attraction of the neighborhood children and provided backyard entertainment now, while the schools remained closed. Soldiers and officers stopped to watch the game, and some asked politely to have a turn. A baby-faced corporal, who introduced himself as Werner, came back several times and brought chocolate for the children.

After two weeks, the first occupation troops left abruptly and were replaced by Bavarian units. Saul was notified that the courtyard was to become a platoon field kitchen, with the woodshed providing a partial roof; the laundry room, attached to a separate small building in the rear of the courtyard that at one time had housed a carpenter shop, would supply the necessary water and double as a larder. Another low building, angling around the courtyard and now abandoned by a workers' union meeting place, was requisitioned for an officers' mess hall.

Soldiers and officers now poured into the yard en masse. They seemed like a different breed of beings. Perhaps this was not mere chance, Saul thought, but carefully calculated strategy. There were no more polite requests for a ping-pong game, but the paddles were snatched away, the children pushed aside. These soldiers behaved as one would expect a "master race" to behave, their heads swollen with pride, noses turned up, and their boots ready to kick below. In a week the town became bare, the shops completely emptied, as if locusts had descended.

When Saul returned before noon one day after making a few house calls – he still saw patients, though now he was obliged to wear a yellow band with the star of David – he found Rajko on top of the garage roof. The German field cook always placed an enormous kettle with food under the adjacent overhanging roof. A rain gutter spout ended just above the kettle, and Rajko, his pockets bulging with pebbles he had collected, was rolling them down one by one into the stew, a mixture of glee and angelic innocence illuminating his impish face.

"Ah, that boy," sighed Saul. "Is it courage or lack of judgment?" But whichever it was, he was glad that it was he and not some Bavarian, who put an end to it.

While a German Lieutenant cursed and spat out some gravel from the stew, which had almost cost him a broken tooth, Saul had sat down for lunch with his brood. But no sooner had he had two spoonfuls of Darinka's caraway soup than the wife of Milovan Stankovich came for him.

The Stankovich family, one of the oldest and wealthiest in the area, was, so to speak, local aristocracy, and Milovan, the latest scion, had served in the Yugoslav foreign service. Knowing that Milo was one of several liberals arrested a few days before, Saul abandoned his meal, and black bag in hand, departed immediately.

The Stankovich home, usually bubbling with activities, was like a tomb, and Saul found his patient in a darkened room, lying face down. As Saul approached the bed, Stankovich rotated slowly, but as he tried to prop himself up, an involuntary groan parted his lips before he fell back.

"Easy Milo, easy," cautioned Saul, "Don't stand on ceremony with me!"

"They were all our people, those curs! Not one of them was German."

Saul inspected the gashes on Stankovich's back. They were oozing, but there was no evidence of infection.

I'll tell you how I got those…the chief of police – that swine – he has three brutes…and they gave me a going over. They stripped me and tied me down to the floor. One of them jumped all over my back with spiked shoes." Milo was out of breath, and had to rest before he could continue. "I was lucky, but with Zorina…they really had it in for him…they used a table as a jump off. They broke in his chest and made minced meat of him."

"They managed to cut up your back and crack a couple of ribs, Milo, but thank God, they have not done you serious damage. I want your wife to put sulfa powder over your back for a week."

"Saul, they are not human," Milo's voice sounded muffled, as if it came from somewhere beyond. "They are animals, and they'll kill us all." And he fell silent, bathed in perspiration, his mouth twisted in pain.

"You'll be fine, my friend. Rest now." He handed his patient a codeine tablet, gave him some water, and carefully strapped his chest. "I'll look in on you later," he promised as he departed.

The gloom of Stankovich's flat enveloped Saul and followed him into the street. Indeed, those were distressing days, with mockery made of justice, liberty, law and order, all the things that he had come to expect in a civil society. On the one hand innocent people were abused and tortured, and on the other the jails were opened, the old condemned thieves and murderers were given amnesty and released all over Croatia – nay, were embraced and taken into the governmental fold. These became overnight the most loyal followers of the new regime, its ardent proponents, enforcers of law and executioners of justice. Vaso Pamich, who was in the local jail for having slit old Abe Kohan's throat, was released on Easter Sunday, the day the Germans had entered Zagreb and declared Croatia independent. He donned a black shirt and promptly became a party official in Grad.

Deep in thought, Saul cut diagonally across the square in front of the main church and its tower, the most visible man-made structures in Grad, coated with a pale yellow stucco, and housing the bell by which the local citizens could tell the flow of time in fifteen-minute intervals. A bronze statue of the legendary local hero wielding his sword against the Ottoman oppressors stood on a pedestal in the middle of the square. A few linden trees surrounded the hero, and grass and weeds covered much of the ground around the pedestal.

As Saul turned the corner, he saw a German truck parked in the street. New field kitchen supplies, he decided. Darinka, their old cook, opened the door for him, her usually red and puffy eyes even redder and puffier than usual, and before greetings passed between them, she burst into tears. Saul then noticed her old shabby suitcase and several bundles piled up by the doorway. A new ordinance had just been issued that Jews could no longer have Christian employees, domestic or otherwise, because Jews, by virtue of their inferiority, could not give orders to Aryans, who were superior to them.

"God bless you, Doctor," she said as she reached out for his hand and kissed it. "I will pray for you and your family." She picked up her belongings and waddled through the door, which an amazed Saul held open for her, and then proceeded out the gate, fifteen years after she had first entered it.

The next moment Saul was nearly knocked down in the hallway by three German soldiers carrying armchairs. Clara stood in the middle of their guest drawing room, now empty, staring at the naked parquet.

"Our good furniture has been requisitioned for a German officers' club," she explained.

"Furniture can always be replaced," Saul countered, but he knew well that that was not true for one confiscated item – Clara's piano, which she loved dearly, and which was a particularly fine one.

"The requisitioning officer liked my piano. He said it was too good for the club, and he is sending it to his wife to Munich." Then she shrugged her shoulders, and added,

"One less room to clean, now that we have lost Darinka. As long as the family stays intact!"

"That's my girl!" He planted a kiss on her lips; Clara was always a trooper, he could count on that.

It was worse for the Steinbergs. Once the hoodlums and criminals in Grad were released from jail, they had to establish themselves commensurate with their newly acquired stations in life, and this could be readily accomplished by obtaining a police permit to requisition any mobile belongings from any Jewish family as they pleased. One such rehabilitated thief turned collaborator desired a painting from the Steinberg apartment. Josef Steinberg, who was an art lover, treasured that particular painting, though it was of no great value, and objected to its confiscation. The collaborator simply arranged for deportation orders, and Steinberg was whisked off twenty-four hours later to the recently created concentration camp in Jasenovac, the first and only deportee from the area.

Such were the early days facing Saul and the Jews of Grad under the Independent State of Croatia, the newly minted satellite country in the Nazi constellation. Saul spent many hours worrying, and reckoning, but at the end of all those cogitations, there was an ever-present question mark; the future lay hidden behind a thick fog, impenetrable to the probing searchlights of his mind. The general situation seemed to be getting worse. The persecution of Jews took place in every city, town, or village, though there was considerable variation on the basic theme.

After his radio was taken away, Saul felt himself completely cut off from his source of information from the world beyond. Radio London had extended the only ray of hope in those bleak days. He knew that the BBC broadcasts were embellished, because the news was not favorable, but the propaganda envisioning the eventual future was such a source of spiritual sustenance and boost to the morale, that he and Clara, like many other people, risked their lives to listen, and some claimed that they simply could not go on without them. Thus Radio London had come to be known under another name, that of a newly discovered vitamin – Vitamin J – the J standing for Jewish.

CHAPTER 7

Radich, a Catholic friend of Saul's brother Robert, arrived from Zagreb on some business in Grad and called on Clara and Saul. From his inner pocket he extracted a letter from Silvia for Peter, and he promised to stop by the next day and pick up Peter's reply. Jews were discouraged from using the postal service except in emergencies, and even then it was uncertain whether delivery would be honored. After the preliminary exchange of greetings and regards, Radich said somberly, "I have bad news. Of course, the newspapers have hushed up everything."

"What is it?"

"It's about the boys of Group D."

A dysphonic sound of surprise and dismay broke from Clara's throat. "You mean they did not raise the money?"

"No, not that! The required amount and more was raised, but the boys were not released."

"And what now? They want more?"

Radich shook his head. "One day it was announced that Group D would be transferred to another job."

"So?"

"So the boys were led off by armed guards. They were marched for three days and three nights into the hills, with hardly any food or water."

"And then?"

"On the fourth day, weak and exhausted, the boys were marched up a slope at bayonet point." Radich hesitated, his eyes darting from Clara to Saul, and back again to Clara. "To the edge of a precipice, and shot, their bodies landing in the crevices below."

Saul gulped. He saw Clara stare at their visitor, her eyes reflecting a momentary lack of comprehension. Then the corners of her pretty mouth twisted, contorting her face, before she covered it with her hands.

"Was Silvia's brother Marcel in the group?" Saul inquired.

"Yes."

"It could have been Peter if he were a year older, and we lived there," Clara gasped, and dashed out of the room, no doubt to throw her arms around the boy, and to hold on to him while she could.

Saul shut his eyes. Before him appeared stark, nearly vertical cliffs flanking a small plateau, which some boys were trying to climb. He saw shining guns and blades closing in, as he had seen on the battlefields of World War I, and a bottomless abyss ahead; he even heard shots and screams. A flock of birds, which had nested on the crags, scurried frantically away, and added their shrieks to those of the humans. Oh, if they only could have been birds! But then there would have been no need to flee.

Even with his eyes open, the vision lingered, and he could see the flock of birds up in the sky, circling around and around, grudgingly eying their cliffs, silent witnesses to a terrible day. And far below was a valley in which vultures circled – The Valley of Death.

"Now I know what the 'D' really stands for," he told Radich.

In the silence and privacy of his room, Peter reread Silvia's letter once more.

"Dear Peter,

Mr. Radich has kindly offered to be my carrier pigeon and deliver this letter. So much has happened since we saw each other last. You probably know that my brother Marcel was taken away with all the Jewish eighteen and nineteen-year-old gymnasium boys, and we don't know his whereabouts. Initially we received brief messages from him, as did the other parents, but lately we have not had any news, and the authorities will not give us any information. I miss him very much. Mama and Papa are very sad and nervous, and sometimes I feel that they don't care for me and Albert half as much as they do for Marcel. Now they are talking about sending us away to relatives in Hungary. I don't want to go, even though some of my cousins in Hungary go swimming and picnicking, while I am bored here in Zagreb, all cooped up in our apartment.

I often think of my last visit to Grad, but it feels so long ago and so far away, that I sometimes wonder whether that was really me. I remember our walks across the bridge, with the stars twinkling above, and the water churning below. I cherish those memories, but forgive me, Peter, they no longer feel a part of me. What I am trying to say is that I like you, that I will always remember you, but if you meet another girl you like, don't hesitate on my account.

Your friend (I hope still),
Silvia

P.S. I feel better that I've gotten this off my chest."

Peter paced up and down his room. The first reading was the most painful, but with each rereading, the blows seemed to get softer. Didn't she say that she would never forget him? That she cherished their time together? Was it her way of disengaging herself from him, or did she wish to set him free in this age of terrible uncertainty? He sat down and wrote.

"Dear Silvia,

Mr. Radich has been very kind to be our letter carrier. I am so sorry about Marcel. I know how much you admire him, and how much you all must miss him. I am told that the Croatian authorities are going to relax restrictions, now that they have secured their position, and perhaps Marcel will be able to contact you. Perhaps going to Hungary would not be so bad. The situation there is much better than here, but wherever you go, I am envious that I cannot go too, and that we cannot see each other.

You say that you will always remember me. I have you always in my thoughts. I just wish I could whisper those words in your ear and dispel any doubts you may have. I have none! I love you, and I know I always will. I know that time and your current sadness are numbing your feelings. Please have courage and faith.

Promise me that you will keep an open mind, and when this is all over, we shall meet again.

Love You,
Peter

P.S. The stars still twinkle above the bridge, and the water is still churning in the river, but neither is the same without you."

After the news of Group D seeped into the marrow of his bones, Saul felt himself drawn into a vacuous depression. Wherever he turned, he met Clara's anxious glances, Ljerka's perplexed eyes, or Peter's suffering countenance. Only Rajko, bless his heart, remained capable of laughter. Saul wondered how much bleakness he himself would be able to stand and desperately felt the need to grab at something – anything – that would pull him out of the muck into which he had sunk. The urgency and immediacy of a medical crisis could still distract him temporarily and plunge him into someone else's problem, but with resolution, his own dejection returned.

When Saul returned late one day, he found Clara in tears.

"Why do you stay out so late? You know there is a six o'clock curfew for us," she chided. Of course he knew! He had been notified at least a dozen times officially, and there were big placards posted in the public square forbidding Jews to be on the street after six, but somehow when he was involved with a patient, he lost track of the time and was not accustomed to watch the clock.

As Clara hung up Saul's jacket, a big yellow metal button with the six-cornered star pinned to the lapel caught a tangential ray of sun seeping through the window. Just as their houses were marked, so the Jews were required to mark themselves with a yellow band, patch, or button, whenever stepping outside.

"The penalty for any infraction is the firing squad," she went on.

But Clara's fretting did not bother him just then, and he tried to wipe away her frown with a kiss.

"I think we'll be all right," he said finally, kissing her once more. "I met Milich, the county clerk. He really knows the lowdown. You know, he has a chance to see all the new directives from Zagreb, and he reassures me that everything is stabilizing, and that this will all blow over soon. Individual excesses, like the slaughter of Group D, will not be repeated. We just have to have a little patience." Saul felt buoyed by this latest news, even if it was not entirely convincing. He needed something to grasp, to latch on to for dear life and lift him out of the paralyzing gloom, which had enveloped him, even if it were only for a few days.

"What about the ditch digging?" Clara inquired. "They need your talents there, maybe?" Saul's name had just been added to that detail.

"They cannot very readily omit me from a complete list. I won't really have to dig, but I'll have to show up for a few days, and then I'll be able to go back to the practice."

Nothing could squelch Saul's sudden optimism, not even Clara's Cassandra tongue. With abandon he gave himself up to an inner germination of hope and renewed vitality, which throbbed inside him and began to unlock the shackles of his former depression.

"Anyway, let's have supper," Clara whined. "I am sorry the vegetables aren't very nice. You know I am not allowed before eleven to the market, and by that time most of the farmers are half way back to their villages."

"We won't starve."

"I know we won't, but it is aggravating. In fact, it is the proverbial straw breaking my back. Oh, Saul, I can't take much more of this!" And she burst again into tears.

Saul squeezed his wife's hand and reminded her that the swing of the pendulum of persecution was about to be reversed, and that it would seek a new and more moderate level.

"They say the children will not be allowed back to school when they reopen in the fall," she moaned, as she mopped her face. The current year had abruptly come to an end before Easter.

'Here they come now," he warned. "Pull yourself together."

"I don't know why that soldier insisted on calling me Sarah," Ljerka said puzzled, as she and Rajko came in. "There is a drunken German soldier downstairs. I told him my name was Ljerka, but he kept calling me Sarah."

It did not occur to Ljerka that she was being identified with her biblical ancestor. In fact, none of the Kestner children were very familiar with their religion. The two or three major holidays, which had been observed when grandfather was still alive, had recently gone by unnoticed. Ljerka was the only Jewish child in her class, and with all the stories the maids and the cook had told her over the years, she seemed to know more about Christianity than Judaism.

"Why are people persecuting the Jews?" she had asked at dinner last week. But that history was repeating itself, and that there had been many persecutions...and executions...between herself and the real Sarah, she was totally unaware.

Saul sympathized with his daughter's bewilderment. All of her friends were gentile, and it had never occurred to her that she was in any way different. He too had not felt himself different from his next-door neighbor, the shop keeper diagonally across the street, or the baker at the end of the block, and now something was being forced down her and his throats, whether they liked it or not.

Lifting her chin with his index finger, Saul said, "Whether you are Ljerka or Sarah, you are my little girl." He bent down and kissed her on the nose.

After dinner Saul remembered that he had been so busy the whole day that he had just shoved his mail into his black bag and had later forgotten to read it. There was nothing that had seemed important to his cursory glance, but now that he looked again, there it was, the letter, which he had been expecting. It bore the seal of the Ministry of Health, and even with his eyes closed and the letter unopened, he could see the curt typed words relieving him of his duties as county physician, but for sake of appearance, it was he who had to send in his resignation. His replacement would be that alcoholic quack who had been a disgrace to the medical profession and an embarrassment to Saul and the other three physicians who practiced in the area.

As Saul sat in his chair, the dozen years of his work telescoped into a series of images. He saw clearly the long lines of children he had vaccinated in various villages scattered through the valley at the end of long, tiresome, muddy roads into which the wheels of the carriage transporting him had cut deep furrows. He could see their frightened faces and hear their cries, especially the little babes with rosy cheeks and unbelievably snotty noses, the kind you would never see in town. He had amused himself with the notion that the peasant women in his county did not believe in handkerchiefs.

A procession of children passed him by, the ones he had delivered – why practically half of the town below the teens, or more. Innumerable nights of vigil flashed by, with deathly ill patients and their families, the scarlet fever cases who had to be placed on a strict diet and their urines checked frequently, and the diphtheria cases, who had to be given anti-serum and had to be watched like a hawk for respiratory obstruction, and could still die weeks after they seemed well. The cases of tetanus should have been hospitalized, but the local hospital took in mostly surgical cases, and it was a miracle that so many had survived – a tribute to wifely or motherly devotion and numerous house calls on his part. And even rabies he had to deal with, but for those poor victims there was nothing he could do but isolate them and watch them die. And then, of course, there were asthmatics, cardiacs, and diabetics.

It had taken a great deal of hard work, but there had been rewards, too, and intellectual excitement. He had witnessed certain medical mysteries unravel and new modes of therapy develop since he had completed his studies. Now he could treat diabetics with insulin, and patients with pernicious anemia with the new vitamin B-12 preparations. With the advent of certain dyes and drugs, especially sulfa, he was now able to restore to health a number of people with severe infections, who, he was certain, would otherwise have succumbed.

Saul's wandering thoughts returned to the present. In a way the dismissal was a relief, because his official position had made him more and more uneasy. There were more and more frequent death reports to be submitted in the county office, in which a collaborator's pistol had gone off by accident and had killed a prominent anti-Fascist, or as happened the other day, a Freemason was found run over on the railway tracks, with evidence of preexisting trauma.

Now all those things, good and bad, were coming to an end. He was still allowed to continue with his private practice; there were simply not enough physicians around.

Despite the dismissal, and despite the new ditch-digging list, Saul remained in good spirits. He had worried so much lately, that for the moment he could worry no more.

As Saul's resignation was about to take effect, Vaso Pamich came to see him, wearing his black shirt decorated with insignias, very polite and flattering. He had taken his cap off and was pawing it awkwardly, shifting his weight from one foot to the other.

"We will not lay a finger on you and your family," he finally began. "Doc, you'll see! You'll be taken off the ditch detail. We'll fix it. And you can keep your county job; just leave it to us! You are a fine doctor and an honorable citizen. The folks around here love you, rich and poor. You have taken care of their sick and have broken bread with them."

Everyone knew how unsatisfactory Saul's replacement was going to be, and people still remembered how that man had mishandled a typhoid epidemic when he was the town health officer. In the end, Saul was called upon to bring the small outbreak under control, which had earned him a gold medal from the Red Cross.

"Yes sir, you are a fine doctor and an honorable citizen," Vaso repeated. "I can't say the same for the others," referring to the rest of the Jewish population, "but you are an exception." Saul shuddered. Coming from the mouth of this man, there was something venomous in the word "exception," and for the first time in his life, Saul felt himself less apart from those "others" that Pamich was referring to, than ever before.

"We are offering you our protection by making you an honorary Aryan," Vaso continued, as the emissary of the local collaborationists. They could not have picked a worse representative, the murderer of old Abe Kohan. "What do you say to that?"

Saul was at a loss. The only two truly poor Jewish families in town had already been declared "honorary Aryans," since they did not get rich on the backs of the Croatian population, and instead of a yellow button, they had to wear a white one, which marked them just as well. The tailor Levin, who barely eked a living for his family, bragged how now he was safe and better off than his well to do cousin, but nobody really knew what the next moment might bring. Saul felt that at any official's whim such designated status could be revoked. The thieves who were running the government could not be trusted. On the other hand, to turn down such a "generous" offer as complete immunity might be construed as plain impertinence and could provoke retaliatory action.

Vaso noticed Saul's hesitation and added, "O. K., Doc, think it over. Let me know in a couple of days."

Saul vacillated. The offer was not to be discarded too lightly. Vague rumors of murderous deaths in concentration camps were beginning to circulate around. He had not brought his children into this world so that they should be hunted down and killed like stray dogs. And after all, he would not be collaborating with the enemy; he would merely be exchanging protection for medical services. There was nothing he could do for the other eighty or so Jewish families; the time for concerted action was gone, and now it was each man unto himself as best he could, and he would do well to look out for himself.

Saul was not allowed to ponder for long, for duty was calling again. Five men had suddenly and mysteriously died in a near-by small village, and he was summoned to investigate.

Once Saul had performed the appropriate examinations, it was clear to him that the five deaths were no mystery, and that each victim had several bullet wounds in various sites. That was all he was asked to address himself to. As to how the men came by their metal trimmings was a matter for the police. What he did gather unofficially from other villagers was that all five were Serbs, and that a rowdy group of Ustashe came by and used them as target practice. After the shooting, their houses were burned down and the women and children driven away.

When Saul returned to Grad, a young man in Fascist uniform was waiting for him.

"Hi, Doc," he greeted beaming. "How did you like those five Serbs? The one with the bullets through his neck is mine! Neat job, eh?" he gloated, displaying proudly his death weapons and caressing the pistol barrels; then he sauntered off on another errand.

Saul could hardly believe his own ears. Obviously this was not a man simply carrying out orders, but a murderer given license to kill. With governmental blessing, uninhibited by threat of punishment, he felt absolved of any sin, and devoted himself with lust and inventiveness to his task.

All that night Saul stayed up, pacing back and forth, sipping coffee, and considering the offer of immunity. He confided his anguish to Clara, his fear that without special protection she and the children might fall prey to the sport of such a man.

"All my life I have fought to preserve life, to relieve pain, and now I have to make compromises with men whose principles are diametrically opposed to mine."

"What principles? They have no principles."

Next morning Saul sent in his resignation. As for any repercussions, Vaso was promoted to a higher rank in the local pro-Nazi establishment, and the offer of immunity simply died on the vine.

With his days crowded by events, a few days seemed to Saul like weeks, and weeks like months, but in fact it was only several days later that the town was bustling again with news. The events that stirred the town had taken place in the middle of the preceding night, when the good people of Grad were off the streets and safely tucked under their blankets. Not only was there a six o'clock curfew imposed on the Jews, but there was a nine o'clock curfew for the rest of the population, except for the police, the Ustashe, and the German occupation troops. A carload of SS men arrived in the middle of the night, and under cover of darkness, broke into the Jewish temple. Windows were smashed and benches overturned. Prayer books were heaved out in front and set on fire, and the Torah torn and dirtied. Lastly, a brass calf was planted in the center of the synagogue. This mission accomplished, the troopers proceeded to raid the Jewish cemetery.

At daybreak, curious passersby stopped at the gate of the temple, and some gathered enough courage to walk in. This was the first time any of them had stepped inside – they believed it was sacrilegious to entered the house of worship of another faith – and the frosted glass windows had kept out the eyes of the idle curious. Word spread now rapidly about the golden calf, and there was general consternation among many citizens of Grad, even among those who had Jewish friends or counted themselves as anti-German, that for years such paganism had existed in their midst. Saul wondered how many of these good people would eventually be disabused of this notion.

Several imps had sneaked into the Jewish cemetery at dawn, which was the origin of a number of fantastic tales that began circulating about coffers of gold and unbelievable riches buried with the dead, as would have been befitting only a powerful Pharaoh.

On the way home from a house call, Saul passed by the temple. Smoke was rising from half-burnt heaps, with a few cinders still glowing beneath seared pages and crumpled white shrouds of ash. There they lay, the remnants of the prayer books with the strange letters that he had found so hard to decipher as a little boy. These had never meant anything to him, except a boring hour at Sunday school.

As Saul approached, he felt that people cast probing, perhaps even remonstrating glances in his direction. He averted their gaze, and as he observed the blue-grey curlicues issuing upwards from a smoldering pile, he felt self-conscious, if not frankly embarrassed.

Walking away from the crowd, Saul felt their eyes still piercing his back. Suddenly an episode that he had all but forgotten came to his mind. It had taken place some years before, and he had not remembered it in the intervening years, until this precise moment, when it sprang forth from some remote recess of memory. Yes, he remembered clearly the events of that scorching summer Sunday, when he had gone to the river for a swim. His teenage cousin Andrej, whose family had since moved to Zagreb, and Andrej's friend came along with him.

It so happened that it had rained heavily the preceding week, and the river was swollen and quick beyond its usual limits. Shortly after they arrived, at the spot where previous generations of town elders had chosen to swim, and their more recent descendents had built little wooden changing booths, a little schoolboy was swept away by the current into the deeper portion of the river and disappeared from sight. The shrieks from bystanders alerted everyone, and Andrej and his friend, both excellent swimmers, plunged into the river and pulled out an unconscious pallid boy from the murky turbulent waters. Saul positioned the limp child so water could flow out freely and initiated artificial respiration. He worked quickly and steadily, and in fairly short order, the boy came to, a bit dazed at first; it was not long before he ran off home.

The hot spell continued all that week, and the following Sunday the sun was even more searing, the unpaved side streets even more dusty. Saul and Andrej headed again for the riverbank. As they were walking along leisurely and chatting, they were hit by a barrage of stones, and a squeaky voice yelled, "Kikes!" Saul turned around to see who it was that was stoning them, and there he was, the little schoolboy who had nearly drowned in the river the week before.

So involved had Saul become between the silent judgmental crowd at the temple and his reminiscences of a past summer, that for the first time in his life he had walked past his own gate and had to retrace a few steps. The brief period of optimism fueled by Milich's comments had dissipated, and he was trying very hard to keep an even keel.

Inside the courtyard he found Rajko with several neighborhood youngsters. The German field kitchen had recently been moved to some unknown destination, along with the occupying Bavarian troops, and the yard had returned to relative normality.

Rajko was in the middle of a heated argument with one boy who had installed himself in the swing hanging off a tree branch and refused to relinquish it. Saul heard Rajko asking for a turn, and then howling "It is mine," after a more polite request had failed to unseat the usurper.

The boy, unaware of Saul's presence, laughed lazily. "Tomorrow it will be mine. You own nothing! Anything I want that's yours, I can have. All I have to do is ask 'them,' and 'they' will give it to me. Ha, ha, ha!" He laughed boldly.

Saul felt his temples bursting. He had had enough humbling for a day. He would teach that snotty kid a thing or two. Before Saul had a chance to commit his crime of passion, his target had slid off the swing and slipped out the gate. This gave Saul sufficient time to reflect on how foolish his rashness might have been. The boy could report Saul to his youth group leader, and then who knows what might happen. Meddlesome creatures, those youth group leaders, and powerful too, making even parents afraid of their own children.

"Come on, Papa," Rajko tugged at Saul's sleeve. "Let's go inside. Swings are too babyish anyway." Rajko's large eyes seemed even larger to Saul, as if magnified by a film of water.

CHAPTER 8

Clara hurried down the corridor to answer the office buzzer. She opened the window and looked down into the courtyard.

"Is the Doctor in?" inquired a middle-aged woman with a shopping basket over her arm. Clara, after a few moments, recognized her as the junior assistant in the pharmacy.

"No. He had to go to one of the villages early this morning. Shall I tell him that you called?"

"No, I just wanted to know whether he was in today," and she walked away.

This was the second person calling on Saul who just asked for him, but didn't wish to leave a message. People were acting strangely these days and becoming secretive. Clara returned to the bedroom to complete her toilet. She looked in the mirror straight ahead, then into the side-mirror on the left wing of her dresser checking out the left half of her face, then examining her right profile in the right wing. "Not bad, not bad at all," she told the woman in the mirror. Two large brown eyes looked back at her. They were her best feature for sure. A few grey hairs peppered the chestnut brown, and a curl hung over her right eye. That curl was chic when she was eighteen or twenty-four, but now it should go – only Saul seemed to still like it. The nose was regular, with a slightly rounded tip, not perfect but acceptable, and fortunately not too long, like the noses of several members of her family. The lips were full, but not thick like Aunt Stefi's. Kissable, she had told Saul; yes, they were definitely meant for kisses.

Clara looked again in the mirror. She decided that the face was actually attractive. She was too severe with herself. Several people at the conservatory considered her quite pretty. But nothing like her gorgeous older sister Tamara. An unintended sigh escaped her lips. Was he still so much in love with Tamara and thinking of her often? The thought caused her considerable pain. She, Clara, was much better for him than that gorgeous self-absorbed willful sister of hers! Did he realize that? And why did he hardly ever mention Tamara? Did he want to keep her memory all to himself? He shared his thoughts with Clara about so many things, but Tamara seemed to exist in some other sphere, in some hidden territory that only he was allowed to visit. Or did he avoid talking about Tamara in order not to hurt her? Did that mean that he was still very much in love with Tamara? Another sigh escaped her lips. Then she sank into an old reverie. She remembered the first time she had met Saul, when Tamara brought him home to meet the family. "Wow," she told herself, looking over the handsome young doctor with those marvelous grey-blue eyes and wavy sandy hair, "I wish I'd seen him first!" But it wouldn't have helped. Tamara would have lured him away. She always seemed to win the prize. Clara was no match for her.

At one point Saul had turned to Clara, and with a twinkle in his left eye asked, "What do you think about having me as a brother-in-law?"

"Are there any more like you in your house? Any younger brother for me, for instance? Something close to a replica."

Saul laughed. Clara's mother seemed embarrassed. "Don't be so forward," Tamara scolded. Clara felt like snapping back, but this was a special occasion, and she bit her tongue. Forward, bah! What about such short notice for a wedding! The custom was to have a long engagement. It was probably Tamara's idea to get married right away, and she would surely get her way. She always did.

Clara looked again at the handsome doctor as they were having dinner. She was already totally and hopelessly infatuated. Oh, well, Tamara was never required to study anything or do anything. The parents assumed that she would marry and marry well. But she, Clara, was expected to study French and play the piano; perhaps the family thought that would help her support herself, if necessary.

No one realized when Clara was little that she had considerable musical ability. She herself considered the piano a challenge to be pursued defiantly and obdurately. Tamara had the looks; she had the piano! That eventually got Clara into the Zagreb Conservatory where several faculty members predicted a bright future. That was a laugh, she thought! It was fortunate her parents belonged to a new "liberated" society that no longer forced unwanted husbands on its daughters. The only tradition they had observed was to encourage widowed Saul, when that time came, to marry Clara, his deceased wife's younger sister. It was only after Clara married Saul and gave up the piano as a career, that she really came to love the piano, and in her playing, what was lost in consistency of technique for lack of sufficient practice was replaced by a new warmth. It had gained a soul, she would say.

Clara walked into the children's room to check on the twins and was surprised to find all three on the floor playing a new type of rummy a neighbor had taught Rajko recently.

"Mami, Peter is playing with us," announced Ljerka enthusiastically, while the boys were too absorbed in the game to even acknowledge their mother's presence.

The buzzer went off again. Clara wished Saul were back already. It made her uneasy these days when he was gone so long. A man in the courtyard asked for Saul.

"He is not in," Clara replied, "but he should be along soon, and you can wait for him in the waiting room. It is open."

"No, no, I don't need to see him. I just wanted to know if he was around this morning," and then the man went away. People were becoming more strange than ever, Clara told herself, shrugging her shoulders. She returned to her previous ruminations. Saul did love her, she was certain of that. He told her so. And she could tell by the way he embraced her, by the way he kissed her, by the myriad small ways in which he showed his concern for her. There would be moments, however, when he would look very sad, and Clara's old searing pain and torment would return. She could never get him to open up at such times to sooth her reopened wound.

A screeching noise from the outside told Clara that a wagon with recently shod wheels had turned into the courtyard. She hurried to the window and caught sight of Saul jumping off the wagon, quite agile and innately elegant, but showing that his work and the years were taking their toll. There was a lot more gray than sand in his hair. He stopped for a moment to talk to the driver, shook hands with him, and spun around to enter the house. Clara breathed a sigh of relief, and all that weight that had born down on her shoulders only a few moments ago simply melted away.

"Hello, darling," he said, plopping down his black bag. A moment later she was safely in his embrace and their lips were sealed in a delicious kiss. He loved her! How could she ever have had those cowardly doubts?

"I sure missed you," he said. The buzzer rang and interrupted the domestic scene. Rukavina, a court clerk, stood in the courtyard outside Saul's office. "Oh, Doctor, I just wanted to see you."

"Duty calls," Saul sounded almost apologetic to Clara. He planted a quick kiss on Clara's cheek and went down. Clara remained by the window, and as she looked down saw Rukavina embrace Saul and hug him and kiss him. At some length, the two exchanged words that did not reach Clara at the upstairs window. Then Rukavina left.

When Saul came back upstairs he explained. A man of Saul's age and height with graying hair, wearing a leather jacket of the type Saul owned and frequently wore, was found dead on the railroad tracks. His face was swollen and distorted from beatings, and rumor spread that the dead man was Saul because of the incriminating jacket.

"I wonder if it is Vojnovich? He is the only one around here who owns a leather jacket like mine. He is a Freemason. A quiet sort of person, never known to be in trouble before. They probably planted him on the tracks after killing him."

"How awful," said Clara, and after a moment added, "So that is why so many people stopped by today and asked for you, and they all said they didn't really need to see you." Then a shiver went through her. "Oh, my God, it could have been you."

"Where are the children? It is too quiet here," asked Saul.

"They discovered a card game that even Peter is willing to play."

"Come, my dear, before either the children or another patient pulls us apart," Clara heard Saul whisper in her ear. His arms wrapped around her body and their lips met again. She clung to him, unwilling to let go of his embrace and of the moment of bliss he had planted on her lips. Ah, she loved him so much! Over the years her love for him had grown, which she would not have thought possible. Yet deep inside she felt that another tree of love had grown, even larger and mightier. She was reluctant to admit – she would not have thought it possible – that she loved the children even more than she loved Saul.

CHAPTER 9

Saul found Clara in the dining room engrossed in preparations, "just in case," she explained to him. Because there were new rumors that any day the entire Jewish population of Grad would be sent to various concentration camps, everyone was getting ready. The Croatian Jewish communities had heard about the camps of the 1930s from fleeing German Jews, some of whom had been released. Saul and Clara compared them to rigorous prison sentences that one could manage to survive.

"We just have to bide our time," Clara continued. "No one in his right mind doubts that Nazism will collapse; it is all a temporary matter."

Saul was aware that predictions about the duration of the war ranged anywhere from three months to a year, though realists like himself felt that it would last at least two years, and that was a long time to survive in a camp, especially for the children – especially the children…especially the children; the words repeated themselves like a hammering in his head.

"The U.S. and Russia, everyone says, will soon enter the war, and then there will be a landing in France in the fall – or perhaps only next spring – and after that it will all be over in no time," Clara continued, echoing the sentiment of the persecuted. "All we need to do is to hold out a bit – survive – for just a little." That was it! That was the paramount word, "survive" till the conflict was over. "That's what everyone says," Clara added.

So Clara, like everyone else in Grad bearing the stigma of Judaism, packed a few necessaries into backpacks, one per person, as that was all that would be allowed. She carefully stuffed them with warm underwear, tins of sardines, bars of chocolate and so on, giving priority to high caloric items in the smallest possible volume. Then she dumped everything out, and with trembling hands repacked them again, trying to stretch the confines of the space. When she had finished, she called the children to explain to them what was where and why. "We may be separated and sent to different camps," her voice faltered. "Then each one of you will have to look out for yourself."

The twins stared blankly, and Saul's eyes caught momentarily the blue of Ljerka's before she covered her face, the tears streaming down. "Mami, Papi, I don't want to be alone! What can I do all by myself?"

Yes indeed, how could she last for a few years, his little girl! He was dejected again, certain that it would be a long war.

One by one, Clara removed the articles and set them down on display, like a magician pulling a remarkable stream of items from the backpacks. Vaguely Saul noticed a little pot for each pack, as Clara explained that it was for boiling water – there were rumors there was typhoid in the camps – but the remaining display of items seemed to be blotted out of Saul's mind. Beyond the little pot, he saw sand, oceans of sand, not like the beautiful Adriatic beaches where they had vacationed, but the sands of a desert, and beyond the dunes, another lifeless desert, in which Clara's droning voice sounded like the distant buzzing of a fly.

When the twins left the room, Clara could no longer keep her composure. She literally slid into her chair and wept.

"Don't cry, Mami," Peter said, and after a silence added, "You're the best mother in the world," as he bent down to give her a hug.

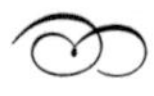

Every Jewish family in Grad was now waiting for that final knock at the door. Every day people were saying goodbye to friends for the last time. But nobody came. Were the deportation plans not yet ready, the time not fully ripe, or was it all a lie and it was not going to happen at all?

In the meantime, wild rumors about concentration camps were becoming more frequent, insistent, and ominous. After an exhausting day, Saul tossed in his bed, turning over dark thoughts, a crumpled letter from Robert in his hand. He noticed that Clara was still awake.

"Somebody in Zagreb was released from the men's concentration camp, from Jasenovac I mean," he whispered. "He is an expert in mining, and the Ministry of Interior had him released. Robert has sent me a letter via another Catholic friend. The man claims that nobody has a chance. They hardly get any food and have to lug big boulders. If they cannot do the work, they are whipped to unconsciousness or shot. Clothing is so scant that in the winter he is sure they will all freeze to death. He thinks that nobody can last more than a year, unless he is shot sooner. The camp is so well guarded that it is very difficult to escape, but no one is even trying it, because for every successful escape, he says, a hundred inmates are shot."

"Oh, Saul!"

"Women and children, it seems, are no better off. There are stories that in the women's camp on that hellish Adriatic island, they are taken out in small boats, stones are tied to them, and then they are pushed overboard."

"What are we to do?"

"So far, the deportations have been from the cities. There is hope that they will leave the rural areas alone."

"And if they don't?"

"Then it's all up. One or two of us might make it, but to hope that the whole family would survive…that's impossible. The odds are against us, especially against the children."

"We won't go, Saul. I'll not have my children go through that. I didn't bring them into this world to suffer such ordeals!"

"And what will you do?"

Clara opened the drawer of her night table, searched briefly, and then pulled out a bottle marked with a skull and cross-bones. "Let's try to make it, Saul. Let's not give up too easily. But if they come, they won't get us! Let's not give them that satisfaction. There's enough here for all five."

Saul could hardly believe how resolute Clara was on this point, when only a few weeks before wilted vegetables had upset her. But he had long ago come to recognize the resilience and resourcefulness of human nature in general, and of his wife in particular. Over the years he had come to know another Clara beneath the initial frosting of lace, and music, and roses. He winced a little, as the image of Tamara made its sudden appearance. No, Tamara would never have had the guts that Clara had. He had been unfair to Clara to keep the old fire burning.

"Clara, I've been thinking the same thing. I've been turning this over for some time. How ironic, that I, who always considered life to be precious, should be considering suicide!"

"Is it a deal then?"

"It's a deal."

In the adjacent rooms, Peter, Rajko, and Ljerka were deeply asleep, and did not in their wildest nightmares imagine the dark future that was being contemplated for them next door. Saul felt an urge to look in on them, as he had often done when they were small, or when he returned very late from house calls and had missed sharing dinnertime with them.

Peter was sleeping with his face to the wall, and all that Saul could make out was the outline of his dark curly head of hair. Lately the boy had drawn even closer to his parents, his beloved professor dead, and he had been dropped by several old friends who were no longer comfortable to be in the company of a Jew. He hardly ever mentioned Silvia, but it was very obvious to Saul and Clara that Peter was suffering in silence on her account.

In the next room, a band of light from the hall fell across Rajko's bed, and in the semi-darkness the boy looked so small and still that it was difficult to imagine that this was the same Rajko who attacked the enemy in the flank from the garage roof.

In the third room was Ljerka, recently moved out of the room she had shared with her twin, a replica, Saul imagined, of what his mother must have looked like as a youngster, her head framed by a ruffle on the pillow, like a water lily resting on a leaf in a pond. She had reached the awkward age, with the face of a little woman and the body of a child.

For a moment, Saul was oblivious to his circumstances in the contemplation of his sleeping children, but in a split second the background knowledge slid back into focus, and he felt a wave sweeping him up. The walls spun around, and he had to grab Ljerka's bedpost to steady himself. "My God, must these children perish?" He smashed his fist against the wall. Ljerka stirred and moaned in her sleep, as if echoing the pain in her father's heart.

Saul was still awake at 2:00 a. m. when he heard someone banging on the main gate. In the old days it was not unusual for him to be called in the middle of the night, whenever a medical emergency arose or labor ensued, but with the curfew, people had to foresee medical necessity or wait till the morning.

Clara jumped out of bed like a gazelle and peered around the edge of the curtain. "I didn't think we'd be needing the contents of that bottle so soon." Her voice cracked, and her right hand trembled ever so slightly.

Under the dim streetlight, Saul discerned a man in civilian clothes along with two armed policemen.

"It's no use ignoring the knocking. If they want, they can break down the gate. I'll go and see."

When Saul opened the gate, he recognized the civilian, an Ustasha collaborator. The man glared at Saul, swept past him, and entered the apartment, followed by the two policemen with lowered rifles and mounted bayonets. Saul gulped. Clara was right, the moment of reckoning seemed at hand. The collaborator charged into the living room, nearly colliding with Clara. He then barked out orders to his underlings to search the premises. It was only after the three men walked through the bedrooms – fortunately the children slept soundly – that the Ustasha informed Saul that the search was for "hidden communists on this twenty-third day of June," and that on the day prior, Hitler had launched an invasion of Russia. Communists had to be routed from all the Jewish and anti-fascist hideouts.

The search failed to uncover any "Reds" under the beds or in closets, and the intruders departed.

"So Hitler has invaded Russia!" Saul told Clara after the intruders left. "This is good news. He is lagging ten days behind the date chosen by Napoleon, and Hitler too will find frost and ashes wherever he looks for winter shelter."

His mind was somewhat eased because a respectable counterweight had been added to the forces dominating Europe; England was no longer alone in its struggle to tip the scale in the right direction. Saul finally fell asleep. He dreamt of apple and cherry orchards in a distant and strange land he had never seen before. The next moment, he was still a child, stuffing himself with aromatic grapes in a vineyard on the slopes surrounding Grad.

CHAPTER 10

Late that summer Grad was flooded with a contingent of people from the northern part of Slovenia, which had been annexed by Germany. The first thing that Saul saw of these people was their hands, as an afternoon errand had taken him past the railroad station. He had first run into Zvonko Adler on Main Street, outside the Adler General Store. The Adlers had been for three generations the most prosperous merchants in Grad, and their store was the closest to a mini-department store that Grad could offer.

Zvonko, the latest scion of the Adler family, stood on the sidewalk, broom in hand, sweeping vigorously. Saul had hardly seen him since that night at the police station.

"Greetings," Saul said, genuinely pleased to see his former schoolmate. "How are you?"

Adler shrugged his shoulders. "How should I be, when after working hard to expand the business, all that I am allowed to do is sweep the floors, while Markovich, my lowest clerk is now the manager? As you know, he turns the income over to the authorities – that is what's left after he fills his own pockets. Mariana and I have hardly anything left to live on.

"And do you think, Saul," he whispered, raising the broom emphatically, "that I could perform this marvelous function of mine after closing time? Oh no, I have to do it in the middle of the day, so that the lowest bum in the place can see the Jew-boss put in the proper place."

Saul winced. Every Jew in town seemed to have a different story, and yet they were all the same. The Ustashe wove threads of humiliation into the net they were spreading over their victims. "We certainly have to swallow our pride," he muttered without conviction, for lack of something better to say.

"Don't misunderstand me, Saul. There is nothing wrong with a bit of manual labor. My grandfather, when he first opened the store, did everything. He scrubbed and cleaned and polished and thanked the

Lord that he was his own master. But this," he pointed to the broom, "is calculated to humiliate me. These bastards really know how to hit where it hurts. How I would love to walk up to Markovich – that scoundrel – and spit in his face! But I won't Saul, if not for my own sake, then for Mariana and Anika and David…and if sweeping the floors, or cleaning dung, or whatever, will save my wife and kids, then I'll just go right on doing it. I just need to vent from time to time."

They exchanged a few more furtive words, and then Saul took leave. He walked on automatically, along the curving street, past the bakery, still thinking about the conversation, hardly paying attention to his surroundings, which were so familiar he felt he could find his way even if he were blind.

At the station, Saul's eyes gathered up the image of a train, though his mind had not immediately become aware of it. There it stood on the tracks, a long string of sealed cattle cars attached to a locomotive, which was spewing puffs of white steam. Several raindrops fell, and Saul abruptly stopped, his limbs pinned to the ground, as if by a sudden paralysis. From the cattle cars, between the slats, sprouted human arms, large and small, to catch a few drops of rainwater.

Saul gasped. He finally saw. But what he saw was surely a hallucination. Then his mind began twisting fact and fancy, and he no longer saw the cattle cars, but enormous wooden crates on wheels – or perhaps giant-sized coffins – hitched to the steaming locomotive. And there were no people inside, only writhing arms and cupped hands in search of a few drops of water. Rationally Saul knew that behind these there were parched lips and beating hearts and desperate souls. He turned his face away, but his heart had already leaped out of his chest and jumped aboard the train, and there it hugged and kissed the faceless Slovenes and stayed with them, begging them not to suffer so much.

The following day Grad was overrun by new faces – saddened, tired, frightened, and above all, perplexed faces. After spending the night in the army barracks, the Slovenians were, so to speak, let loose on the town to scrounge for food. Saul saw an old Slovene couple in his office seeking a prescription. They told him that they were from Maribor, in the northern part of Slovenia, near the border with Austria. The Reich had embarked on a program of expansion of its territory, they explained, and had redrawn the borders. This involved Germanizing a portion of Slovenia, with complete removal of the original Slovenian population and their resettlement in Serbia, while the evacuated Slovene territory was to be settled by pure-blooded Germans. The couple was given short notice to leave their home in Maribor. They were allowed one backpack and one small suitcase per person; the rest had to be abandoned. At the station the suitcases were loaded into a freight car, and the couple, with the rest of the transport, were shoved into and sealed inside the cattle cars. Before the train departed, however, the freight car, which was the last in line, was apparently unhitched, and all that the Slovenes were left with was what was on their backs and in the backpacks.

When the Slovenes reached Grad, they had been en route for several days. None knew their destination – the German commandant had withheld that information – and none knew by what route they had come thus far. Some claimed that they had gone around in circles, disoriented and half-starved, left here and there on abandoned side rails, till they were certain they had been forgotten and would perish. Why these people were eventually brought to Grad seemed a mystery to Saul, as it was a small out-of-the way town, with round-about train connections to the main thoroughfares, certainly not on the path to Serbia.

Soon the day arrived when the Slovenes were to return to their sealed "stables" and be on their way. They said good-bye to the town's people and returned in the evening to the barracks, to hear whereto the morrow would bring them. And that was the last that Saul or the citizens of Grad saw of them.

The next day Grad was full of stories of how the Slovenes were assembled in the army barracks, how the doors were bolted, and how they were machine-gunned at close range. The barrack grounds were off limits to the civilian population, but no rules or regulations or threats could entirely eliminate the daredevilry of some of the town hooligans, who had spent much of their lives on the streets, and they brought back ghastly accounts of a massacre, and heaps of dead bodies. But these were the same youngsters who had spun some fantastic tales before, leading to several false rumors, and this time they were not believed.

CHAPTER 11

In October Saul was notified that he, along with all the other Jewish families, had to move out of his home into a dilapidated section of Grad that was to become the ghetto. Orders like these came from the government in Zagreb, setting the general policy, but the details were to be worked out by the local authorities, police, or prominent party members, the Ustashe. Three days notice was given to complete the moving in Grad, most of which was done on foot or in wheelbarrows, as there were nowhere near the number of movers in the little town as there were households to be moved. Whatever could not be moved within the specified time was to be confiscated.

Saul was one of the few to get a vacant apartment, which happened to have at the far end a separate entryway with a small room that could serve as his office. Most people could find only tiny flats, and many had to double or triple up, or even sublet cellars. Once the moves were completed, a strange spirit of quiet optimism descended on Grad and its "ghettoites." Everyone said that the Jewish problem of Grad had finally been solved, that all the Jews now lived in miserable quarters, that they were nearly penniless, that they had been sufficiently humbled in the eyes of even the lowest of local citizens, and hence could no longer be a source of envy, which many theorized, was the root of anti-Semitism. They would now be allowed to remain in this impoverished state, as they no longer represented a financial threat or competition to anyone, and had satisfied the appetites of the greedy. Having lost everything they had, nothing more could or would be taken from them. Talk of deportation ceased, for the ghetto seemed to have offered an alternative way of "concentrating" the Jews. One only had to have patience now, and wait till the war was over.

From Zagreb there still seeped word of sporadic deportations of men, but somehow the pattern in Zagreb had been altogether different. The urban Jews had been more affluent, influential, and meddlesome than their rural counterparts, and most of them had been in conflict with the Croatian nationalist movement. For that obvious reason, the capital had adopted much harsher policies than the towns and rural areas did.

Whatever Saul's feelings were about Judaism, his lot was now thrown in with the rest, and while he was still allowed to practice his profession and see private patients, the numbers had considerably dwindled. When the schools reopened after a six months closure, Peter and the twins were not allowed to attend, and Saul was glad to press Peter into service as office help. When all this madness would be over, he would send Peter to Vienna to study medicine, as he had done himself.

Ljerka indulged in daydreaming, when she did not fret about school. For Rajko no school was just fine. He was very busy making plans to join the guerillas, but he had no idea where to find them. He had heard about them striking here and striking there, but they always seemed to disappear into thin air, and no one he knew had ever seen them.

It was sometime in the middle of December that Milich, the county clerk, sent word to Saul to come and see him about a very urgent matter. Some weeks prior, Milich had casually mentioned to Saul that the medical situation in certain areas, in particular Bosnia and Hercegovina, was catastrophic, and that the families of Jewish physicians who volunteered to go there were exempted from deportation. Saul had considered the suggestion, but had doubts about promises made by the current regime, as he had had doubts about the title of Honorary Aryan. Because the government would have a list of the handful of physicians, their exact relocation, nothing could prevent the authorities from instantly rounding up their prey at a later date. And so far he was proven right, as the two families who were declared Honorary Aryans in Grad were equally expelled from their dwellings and were now in the ghetto.

"The only attraction of Bosnia," Saul confided to Clara, "is that it is where most of the resistance is located, in the steep remote mountain ranges. That could be a possible escape for you and me and Peter, but not for Rajko and Ljerka. I doubt the twins could survive the rigorous mountain winters or long marches, not to mention the dangers of battle."

Saul went to see Milich, more out of courtesy than conviction. Milich was one of those old-timers, colorless, inconspicuous, reliable, who was not replaced by the new administration, precisely because he was inconspicuous, and because there were not sufficient local pro-Nazis to fill all of the little slots. It was a known fact that the members of the police department and the town council were Nazi sympathizers from A to Z, but the county office, which was mostly administrative and apolitical, was left to the old guard.

"Dr. Kestner," Milich spoke up when they were alone. "During the depression you treated my wife when I couldn't pay. I never forgot that. Now it is my turn to do something for you." Milich leaned forward, his horn-rimmed spectacles bouncing on his nose, and he dropped his voice to a barely audible whisper. "I have reliable information that all the Jews of Grad and the surrounding county will be deported before the end of the year. I don't know the exact date, but there is little time left. Please go away and don't come back. Save yourself and your family. I told you before that I would give you yellow passports to Zagreb to get an assignment in Bosnia. Well, here they are." The travel permits had already been prepared. "Go to Zagreb on that pretext and volunteer for Bosnia, or disappear, but don't come back. Better leave tonight or tomorrow, and good luck to you."

Before Saul could collect his thoughts, he found himself outside in the chilly street with five duly processed traveling permits in his pocket. "By golly, this is our chance," he thought. His heart seemed to beat so hard and loud, it echoed in his ears like a drum. "Our chance to escape," he continued the inner dialogue. "But I'll have to be very careful...careful and lucky is more like it." Escape was a dangerous thing, like walking a tight rope without a net. One false move, and there was no second try.

After recovering his equilibrium, Saul reflected on what Milich had told him. He thought about the other Grad Jews and the impending disaster, and felt torn between an impulse to warn the others, and a desire to look away, hide, and be gone. When he ran into Hoffman, the impoverished carpenter who had been one of the honorary

Aryans, Saul could not resist his healer instinct. In a subtle way he tried to explain the situation to Hoffman, and asked him to quietly pass along the word to the others, but Saul could not get anything across. Hoffman had developed all the signs of a harmless maniac since Saul had seen him last.

Saul then stopped by Zvonko Adler and told him that "according to a very reliable source," the Jewish population would soon be deported. This was the time for everyone to escape, and he urged him to do so, but Zvonko laughed and shrugged his shoulders. "To tell you the truth, Saul, we've had so many false alarms about deportation, that I doubt this one too. They have just moved us recently, so it doesn't make sense to move us out again."

With so many rumors and "highly reliable" accounts that proved utterly inaccurate, it was no small wonder that people did not know whom or what to believe, and what to disregard. No amount of persuasion seemed to work now, and Saul felt hollow with impotence and frustration.

"Oh the hell with them," Saul told himself as he left, his sense of guilt somewhat mollified. But deep down inside he knew he was kidding himself. In reality, Adler and the others were trapped, because to get away they needed traveling permits. Such permits were required to go from one town to the next, and were issued on white paper to Christians, and on yellow paper to Jews. Though in theory Jews were allowed to travel, yellow papers were almost never issued. Unconsciously Saul reached into his pocket to make sure the permits were really there.

The next day Clara hurriedly packed two suitcases. That would have to do for all of them till the end of the war. She let neighbors believe that they were going to Zagreb so Saul could obtain a transfer for Bosnia from the Ministry of Health, and that they would shortly return for the remainder of their shrunken ghetto belongings.

Saul chose an evening local train, requiring a transfer to the main line, avoiding the more visible bus connection. Rumors had it that it was safer to travel by night, when the wolves slept in comfortable beds. That rumor seemed to hold true, as the Kestners encountered a minimum of fuss on the night train with their yellow passes. The twins were promptly rocked to sleep by the rhythmic motion of the train and the hypnotic tapping of the wheels against the rails, while Peter and the adults sat silently in the compartment.

On arrival in Zagreb, Saul took everyone directly to his brother's apartment. He rang the doorbell, but there was no answer. He tried to remain calm, but alarming thoughts whizzed through his head. "They have taken Robert and Bettina away…and I didn't even know about it!" He pressed the bell again, but still no answer. Saul leaned against the wall, beads of perspiration cropping up on his forehead. In a flash he recalled the side street in Grad where he had grown up, where Robert had taught him to ride the bike. It was Robert who had answered Saul's myriad questions, rather than their ever-so-dignified and inaccessible father, who did not want to be bothered by stupid and childish questions. And it was Robert, who, after World War I, had become the family's bread-winner and helped finance Saul's studies.

Why don't they answer?" Rajko piped up. Then the door flung open, and Robert stood in the doorway. The brothers embraced and kissed.

"What a surprise! Come in, come in," Robert exclaimed. "I wouldn't have opened the door, had I not heard a child's voice. You never know who might be ringing. Bettina, come here, come quickly," he called to his wife, who had hung back, obviously frightened by the doorbell. "And bring milk and bread and butter for the children. I am glad I was able to buy some on the black market. And make more ersatz coffee for the adults."

They all sat down around the large dining table, the Venetian blinds shut, and the lighting rather dim, evoking an eerie atmosphere in the room cluttered by large old fashioned pieces of furniture. After retaining a youngish appearance for many years, the passage of seasons had finally caught up with Robert, and Saul was surprised to see how much his brother had aged in the short interval since he had seen him last. Robert's thin graying hair was now snow-white, and the lines in his face had lost their crispness, so that he looked old and puffy.

"So what brings you all to Zagreb?" Robert inquired.

"Grad is to be deported. I've been tipped off. I could go to Bosnia, but I don't want to."

"You have two possible havens," Robert said, "Italy and Hungary. Shari, Bettina's cousin, has gone back to Budapest, to her parents, and so far things are not too bad there. But who knows for how long? I don't trust the Hungarians."

"Italy? I've heard something about Italy."

"In April when the war broke out, a few Jewish families from Zagreb ended up in Dalmatia, in the part occupied by the Italians. They had not sought out the Italians, but had naively believed, like many of us, that Germany would be unable to defeat us completely, and had fled to the coastal region, which they expected to remain free. They have sent back favorable reports, and since then a number of others have escaped to Italian occupied territories. What will happen in the end, no one knows."

A faint snoring sound came from Rajko, who had satisfied his hunger, and now was curled up in one of the large armchairs. Ljerka sat in Clara's lap and poked her fingers through the holes in the crocheted border of the tablecloth, while Clara exchanged words with Bettina, as she was trying at the same time to follow the men's conversation.

"You know my former business partner, Blumenfeld. He and Mira managed to get away to Abbazia, and they have sent word that they are well, and that the rest of the family should come and visit. Censors being what they are, they can't be more explicit. Recently the police tried to arrest Ivo, Bettina's nephew, but fortunately he was not at home, so he and Luci managed to quickly get away to Split, which is now occupied by Italy. The situation in Split is not as favorable, and it has become more and more difficult to be smuggled into Split."

Peter could no longer contain himself. "What about the Weinbergs? Are they still here?" He had hoped that Silvia had remained with her parents, and that somehow he could see her.

"They are. They are sending Silvia after Christmas to her Hungarian grandparents near Novi Sad; that's under Hungary now. And Marcel, as you know, was taken with Group D."

Peter turned his face to the wall, not to show his glee, but to keep his joy, his secret, all to himself.

"With money one can still buy a passage here," Robert continued, "but it keeps getting more and more difficult."

"I would think that in the long run," Saul interjected, "Mussolini would have much more autonomy and freedom from German interference than the Hungarians would."

"I myself favor Italy. Of course, everyone's dream is to somehow reach Switzerland, but nobody that I have heard of has managed to buy his way quite that far. What you need first of all are traveling permits to a border town. Near southern Slovenia is best. Yellow permits are not issued for border destinations, but false white papers can be purchased for a price. I know where one can buy them. The real obstacle is how to get across the river Kupa to the Italian side."

"What about you and Bettina? Are you going to stay here like sitting ducks? Come with us."

"To be honest, Saul, I've been toying with the idea for some time. My patience is reaching its limit. Till now I have been shielded because of my lumber expertise, but you never know what will be tomorrow. As you saw this morning, we were afraid to open the door for you. But Bettina hesitates to make the trip because of her arthritis and heart condition."

"Dr. Rosen exaggerates your cardiac status, believe me," Saul addressed himself to his sister-in-law. He had examined her a number of times himself, but her hypochondriac tendencies seemed to prevail. Then in a voice so stern he surprised himself, words came tumbling out of his mouth: "Bettina, you must come. You should not stand in my brother's way!"

"I have not been altogether idle in this matter," Robert went on, "Bettina is my witness. I have prepared a plan, but have kept it in abeyance – just in case."

Robert then explained how he and his colleague, Joseph Weinberg, Silvia's father, had charted an escape route from bits and pieces of information received from sympathetic foresters and land surveyors with whom they had had business dealings in the past. The plan revolved around an abandoned little wooden bridge in a mountainous area, which spanned the river where it was still young and narrow, and which supposedly was not patrolled, because it had been totally overlooked by both the Croatian and Italian authorities after redrawing of the boundaries.

Rajko was awake by now, and tried to persuade Ljerka to play hide and seek. Peter paced around the apartment, hands thrust in his pockets, his mind hovering somewhere in the clouds.

The following day, without further ado, Robert obtained white traveling permits for all of them.

"The day after tomorrow we'll be in Italy," he declared cheerfully. "I just needed a little pull from you," he told Saul, "to overcome my inertia and finally leave."

"You are such an optimist," Bettina countered. "What if that bridge isn't there?"

"I have every reason to believe it is. I'm telling you, Joseph and I obtained very detailed descriptions. Italian occupied territory is on the other side. For a part of the way we'll have a guide, and afterwards we should not have any trouble locating it."

"And what if we find it, cross it, get over to Italy, and then the Italians hand us back to the Germans or the Ustashe?" Bettina continued with her pessimism.

"That's a chance we must take," Saul interceded. "No, it's not even a chance! We have no alternative."

"What about the Weinbergs? Are they coming?" Clara asked. "Robert, didn't you say that you and Joseph mapped this route together?"

"They are reluctant on account of Marcel. They are sending Silvia and Albert next week to Hungary."

"To the grandparents?"

"To a farmer who will hide them, as arranged by the grandparents. In fact Saul and I were going to go over shortly, to try a little persuasion. And Peter should come with us."

On the way to the Weinbergs, the three Kestner men ran into Samuel Friedman, a former resident of Grad who had migrated to Zagreb a decade earlier; his only son had been taken with Group D and had perished together with Marcel Weinberg. Everyone except their parents knew about the tragedy that had befallen the boys. With unprecedented solidarity the Jews of Zagreb united to shield the boys' families, to surround them with a wall of silence, and to protect them from the truth. And so the parents went on hoping, despite occasional transgressions and inevitable indiscreet comments by unknowing bystanders. Soon rumors sprang up of fantastic rescues and miraculous escapes, which the parents much more readily accepted, no matter how improbable, than that their sons, their pride and joy, had been killed.

Avoiding his usual greeting of "How are you?" or "How is your family?" Robert stammered, "Well…well, long time no see!"

"I just got some wonderful news about Group D." Friedman could barely control his euphoria. "Some of the boys have been seen in Albania. It seems that all of them are there. I've written to the Red Cross in Switzerland."

"I'm happy for you," Robert managed to squeeze out, then seemed to choke on the words, as Friedman walked away exhilarated, without taking leave.

"Poor Sami," Saul commented as they moved on. "It was his only son, begotten at an advanced age."

"Only a father or a mother could put any faith into such vague reports as 'have been seen in Albania.' Have been seen by whom?" Robert added. "The last time I saw him he announced proudly to me that the boys were fighting in the woods with the underground. And his letters to the Swiss Red Cross, have probably all landed in the wastebasket at the central post office."

As they approached the next corner, Robert made Peter and Saul cross to the other side, because Fein was coming down the street. "Today is the day to run into everyone."

After pulling his hat further down over his brow, Robert explained that although he was one of them, the Jews of Zagreb despised Fein, and in the past when he had paraded around like a cockerel had feared him more than the devil. Not so now, but they still crossed the street to avoid him. One rarely saw him nowadays, and always with crutches or a cane.

"Fein had been one of the men appointed to the committee to collect and appraise the ransom for Group D," Robert explained. "It was he who received Lilli Weinberg's jewelry, when she gave all her valuables so that Marcel would be quickly released. Later Fein's wife was seen wearing Lilli's best ring. Some people excused Fein's stealing, saying that that much less would be shipped to Germany, and in any case, the required sum and more was collected, but the boys were never released.

"But his other activities could not be excused. Once gold ran in Fein's veins, his appetite became insatiable. He became an informer for the police, often blackmailing and extorting money from others. He imagined himself protected from persecution as an undercover agent, but the police soon had no use for him. To them he was just another Jew, only a bit more despicable than the rest. So one day they sent him home from the police station with two broken legs. Word has it that he was strapped into one chair and his feet onto another, and then some brutes sat down forcefully on the portion spanning the gap, till the bones cracked. I don't even know if you can break bones that way, but that's what people said." Robert shook his head. "I guess there are all kinds."

Saul glanced sideways at Fein. A strange mixture of pity and fear filled him: Pity, because there was something pathetic about the way the man literally crawled on his crutches; and fear, because Saul felt something inside him, something he hoped would never come out. Somewhere inside him, he suspected, there was a Fein. And he wondered how much it would take for him to become a traitor. And was he not already a coward and a traitor, not to a whole community, but to one person? Was he not a coward and a traitor when he came crawling to Clara, to beg her for her hand, when his heartstrings were still whispering "Tamara" in his ears?

Fortunately for Saul, they reached their destination, and he was saved from further plaguing thoughts triggered by Fein.

The adults sat at one end of the large comfortable living room in the Weinberg apartment drinking ersatz coffee.

"We're leaving tomorrow," Saul told Weinberg. "Come with us, Joseph! Our families have always been friendly, and now our children are bringing us closer. Let's try our luck together."

"You and I have planned this route together," Robert weighed in. "Don't back out now."

"I told you: I cannot leave while they have Marcel. They might kill him, if we escape. Or, he might need our help.... They may actually release the group for Christmas."

"Christmas, bah! They promised to release them several months ago, after the ransom was paid."

Weinberg seemed dejected, on the verge of tears. "You are a pest, Robert, I told you a million times, I won't leave!"

In the far corner of the living room Peter and Silvia stared at each other as they held hands, seemingly unnoticed and nearly forgotten by the adults.

"You are even more beautiful than I had remembered," Peter whispered.

Silvia blushed and looked away.

"How I have longed for this moment, to see you again...and perhaps to hug you!" His voice broke off. "But instead of a hello it is a good-bye." He swallowed hard, then resolutely added, "We'll meet again when the war is over. Never give up! That's the only way to get through. When it's all over, we'll be older, and maybe wiser, and if we still love each other.... I know I'll never stop."

"A few years is a long time," Silvia looked away to avoid Peter's eyes. "One can never tell what may happen. So much has already happened in the last few months, that a few years seem like an eternity.... I wonder if I'll still be around." Silvia paused for a minute, and with a tremulous voice added, "Peter, I don't want to die, I don't want to die yet! I'm too young to die!"

Peter drew her towards him and kissed her hastily, desperately, as if to drink in tenderness and passion for the years ahead, but her lips were like ice.

At the other end of the spacious room, the men were still arguing.

"If I were in Otto's shoes," Weinberg said feebly, "you can rest assured that I would go. He won't leave because of his house and his fancy rugs and furniture. About those things I care little, but I am in a completely different situation."

"Joseph, everyone fancies himself in a 'different' or 'special' situation, presuming that he would know exactly what to do if he were someone else," Saul added.

"What about Silvia and little Albert? Save what you may, while you can," Robert insisted.

Rather than break into tears again, Weinberg exploded. "Get out!" he hissed, jumping up from his chair and wiping off the perspiration from his forehead. "It is bad enough as it is, without everybody giving advice and meddling into what is none of their business."

Saul hesitated. Everyone's nerves were worn thin and had become frayed. They jumped at their friends instead of their enemies. Should he tell Weinberg about Group D, or shouldn't he? Perhaps the man should not be deprived of the last grain of hope, yet this hope was counterproductive and prevented him now from saving the rest.

Apparently Robert had the same idea, and he spoke as if reading Saul's mind. "Real friends have to speak up when they see their pals put a foot into a trap, whether the advice is asked for or not. You have an obligation to your wife and the other two children as well. Sending Silvia and little Albert off alone to Hungary is not a good plan. The way the Ustashe work, you won't be able to help Marcel anyway. Er... there are ugly rumors, er... about Group D. You are staking your wife and two children for something very uncertain, er...for someone who perhaps isn't..."

Weinberg jumped up, spewing insults in a high-pitched hysterical voice, and asked his guests to leave. With a flurry, he opened the entrance door, waved them out, and then slammed the door.

"There is nothing one can do," Saul remarked, "when a man stops his ears to the truth and shuts the door on it."

A minute later there was a scurry of footsteps on the stairway, as Weinberg caught up with them and hugged each one of them in quick succession.

"Good luck to all of you! Have a safe crossing. You understand that I can't go. Lilli, too, absolutely refuses."

Saul and Robert nodded their agreement in complete unison. Saul was about to say something, then held back his words. After all, was it certain that the mountain bridge really existed?

It was already dusk when Saul, Robert, and Peter found themselves in the street, like three beaten dogs. Not that it was that late, but the cold pallid December sun had just set.

"Let's hurry or we won't be back before curfew," Robert reminded. "Bettina will go out of her mind."

Saul put his arm around Peter. He guessed the boy was suffering, but there was nothing soothing he could say, and he remained silent. All three stared ahead to avoid each other's eyes. Further down the street Saul saw a commotion, and suddenly he noticed a barricade.

"This way!" he yelled, indicating an about-face to Robert, and giving Peter a yank. "Run!" He ran in the direction from which they had come, with Peter right on his heels, but at the far end, too, he could see the police setting up a blockade, and momentarily he stopped in his track.

"Papa," Peter exclaimed, and pulled his father into a narrow side street, which Saul had not noticed. They ran straight ahead, then turned sharply to the left, then to the right, and left again, along narrow virtually empty streets, which zigzagged upwards to the old city.

"Stop," Saul barely managed to expel the word from his painful throat and heaving chest. He felt dizzy and leaned against the adjacent building wall. "We're out of the trap, now. Further running might arouse suspicion."

Only then did Saul realize that Robert was not with them. Neither he nor Peter could remember seeing him after the barricades.

"Perhaps he took another route. He knows Zagreb better than we do and is heading home," Saul suggested. But inside he felt a pressure in his chest, as doubt cast a shadow across his heart.

"We're in the old city. There's no time to waste."

The clock struck half past six as Bettina opened the door for Saul and Peter. An eternity later it struck seven. There was no trace of Robert. Bettina wrung her hands and dashed every few minutes to the window.

"Perhaps he hopped on a trolley somewhere, and it got stuck again." Saul was grasping for plausible delays.

"He doesn't ride any more. Trolleys are a likely place to get picked up."

"Then perhaps he met someone he knows."

"He would hurry back. He knows I worry."

"Or he is still hiding somewhere."

With that suggestion silence fell. Food was brought in, but only the twins, who were uncommonly quiet this evening, ate heartily, and Peter chewed on a piece of crusty bread, when he was not chewing on his fingernails.

Half past seven. Saul became acutely aware of his own breathing, and he forced himself to draw the air in and out slowly, slowly, trying to calm himself. With all his might he tried to slow his respirations, slow his pulse, slow down time, but all these seemed to escape his grip, as his heart raced, not with definitive fear, but with diffuse apprehension and gloomy forebodings. And the vision of Tamara in her sickroom intruded into his consciousness. "Yes, I've been here before."

Even Bettina stopped looking out the window and was sitting still, in frozen perplexity.

Eight. Silence. There was nothing anyone could do but wait. There was no phone to make a call – telephones had been removed from all Jewish home some time ago. And who could be called when people were swallowed up by the night, and were never heard from or seen again? What magical number could be called to bring back one's loved ones on a dark cold December night in 1941?

Nine o'clock.

Ten strokes. Every doubt left Saul. He knew it all. Until now he had hoped that there was some bizarre circumstance delaying Robert. That perhaps he had been arrested for mistaken identity and released later, which happened once in a while. Bettina wore a knowing horrified look on her face, and Clara, after she tucked the children into bed, had tiptoed back into the room. Even Clara, who often found the right word to say at critical moments, was silent. Nobody stirred, like an arrested moving picture frame, stopping the flow of time, as if trying to capture forever the past moment in which all was well, before it is lost irretrievably to the present.

Saul clenched his teeth. A piece of his flesh had been torn out. He slowly got up, parted the curtains and looked out. All that he could see was a dark, deserted street lined by concrete pavement incompletely covered by patches of ice and snow. He stared into that cold and dark outside world, his face wet with tears.

In the hallway the lamp burned deep into the night, flickering frequently, due to power shortage, mimicking its predecessor, the candle, which in addition to being a source of light, was a memorial to the dead. Now even the electric bulbs appeared to quiver and tremble over the vast darkness, which they had come to illuminate.

In the morning Saul found Bettina still sitting in the living room, her eyes red and hollow, but dry. "It's urgent," Bettina said, "that you move out of here right away. The police may come." And after a pause, quiet and resigned, she added: "I guess that little bridge to freedom just wasn't meant for Robert."

"We'll have to find another bridge, or a boat, or even a tunnel," Saul replied. "Without Robert and his contacts we cannot risk that route. And you must come with us."

"No, not I," Bettina insisted, shaking her entire short and slight frame. "You must go, Saul, but I have to stay, even if Robert would want me to go. If nothing else, I can send him packages to the concentration camp. They allow packages, one small one per month, and that might just be the difference between life and death." She countered Saul's arguments with a dignified no, and added, "It will be all right for the women."

"Your packages may not be delivered, Bettina. And it is just as bad, if not worse in the women's camp on that devilish island. It is a veritable hell! Clara and I have heard that the limbs of women and children are tied, and others say that stones are tied to them, before they are pushed overboard; which it is, God only knows, for none have come back to tell."

"That camp is being discontinued. It is terrible enough for the women to lose their men."

"It is true, the camp on Rab is being discontinued, but not for the reason you say. The island is inconvenient and inefficient, so two new women's camps are being organized on the mainland. There are even rumors that the camps will be moved to Poland."

"What won't they think of next!" sighed Bettina. "How much more frightening is a camp on foreign soil and so far away, but I still cannot go with you."

"I understand you completely," Clara addressed her sister-in law, and then turning to Saul, added: "I would also not leave if they got you. We are in it together, you and I."

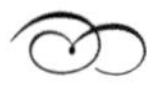

As adamant as Bettina was about staying, so was she about Saul and Clara leaving. She contacted some old and devoted Gentile friends of Robert's, who were willing to hide Saul and his family for a little while, till he worked out another escape route.

Saul now tried to contact people reputed to be in the black market, who were smuggling people across the border, but these proved to be elusive. His leads were either false, or the smugglers had stopped operating, as conditions had become more risky. The situation looked very bleak as the days went by. The only good news was that the United States had finally entered the war. But the end was still so far away, that it looked like a mirage, constantly teasing Saul to get over one more hurdle, but evading his grasp as he reached out, till he felt he would fall to the ground utterly exhausted.

One day, while trying to locate a contact, Saul found himself face to face with a Nazi sympathizer from Grad, whom he had actually not seen for some time. It was too late to turn the other way, or to hide his face in a shop window; the man had already seen him. Much to Saul's relief, the man tipped his hat, and the next moment he was gone. Perhaps the man had gotten tired of his new bedfellows, as some people did, who were initially seduced by Croatian nationalist and separatist propaganda, but had a sense of justice and became disillusioned with the excesses of the current fascist regime. Or perhaps the man was out of touch with events in Grad. Saul wore no yellow button, as it was more dangerous to be with it than without it, counting on the fact that nobody would know his face on the streets of Zagreb. In fact, Clara had flushed theirs down the toilet with gusto on the night train to Zagreb.

Time was flying by now. Saul would be expected back in Grad with his Bosnian assignment, and when the Jewish population was rounded up, his absence would be noticed. After that, Saul did not know what would happen. Would they be hunting for him right away? Obviously his tracks led to Zagreb. Or would they forget about him and go on to some more pressing problems, and the local government surely had a wide selection to choose from. Hopefully the chief of police did not wish to appear incompetent in letting someone slip through his fingers; it might look bad for him to call on the Zagreb police for help.

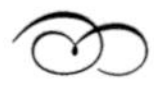

As reality is often stranger than fiction, two days after Christmas, the family quartering the Kestners was visited by a couple who had come to spend the year's end in Zagreb, and who owned a little restaurant at a remote and obscure railroad station somewhere in Croatia. It was precisely past that station that the Jews of Grad were taken on route to a distribution camp, and Saul and Clara thus learned that the deportation had taken place as planned.

"Late on Christmas Day," the innkeeper began, "after our villagers had lit their candles and sung 'Peace on Earth, Good Will to All Men,' a train arrived with the deportees from Grad, who had been gathered up on Christmas Eve. The guards brought small groups at a time into our restaurant and asked for hot tea."

Clara inquired about her friends, describing their appearances in great detail, but all that the innkeeper and his wife could remember was a blur of men's and women's faces, fused into one shivering mass of humanity clutching the warm teacups.

"With one exception," added the innkeeper's wife. "I cannot get out of my mind the face of a little girl – I'd say she was four or five – as she sat there whimpering when I brought her the tea. With her golden locks and blue eyes, she looked just like one of the little angels painted on our church altar."

"At least they were given something hot," someone commented.

"Nonsense! The whole thing was irrational," the innkeeper said. "Those people didn't need tea. A train inspector who ate at our place told us the next day that only a handful of people got off that train at the end of the line."

"What happened to the rest?"

"No one knows."

"They are d-de-demons," Clara stammered. "No doubt about it. Directives stated before the end of the year, isn't that true, Saul, and they had to pick Christmas Eve."

"For those who die it makes little difference whether it is Tuesday or Wednesday," words flowed from Saul's mouth as if someone else were speaking for him, as if a hypnotist had extracted them from his subconscious mind.

"There was something else extraordinary that happened," said the innkeeper. "In our village we have a peasant woman, a poor kind soul who dearly loves children, and took care of nieces, nephews, orphans, for weeks and months on end, to stifle the disappointment of a childless marriage. You can imagine how happy she was, when after many years she conceived and bore her husband a son. But her happiness was not long lasting, because the infant was not well and soon died. This was enough to drive the woman out of her mind, and after she recovered physically from her confinement, she started wandering around at all hours of the day and night, looking for her child. This became a problem when the curfew was imposed, but after a while, the patrols began to ignore her and the village dogs stopped barking.

"That night, on Christmas, when the transport from Grad came through the village, I saw her hanging around the station, but I didn't pay her any mind. Later, when all the people were taken back to the train, I thought I saw an arm reach out of a window and toss something out. The half-crazed peasant woman, who till then had hung back in the shadows, moved to the spot, picked something up, waved after the departing train, and soon disappeared into the night.

"The day after Christmas, there was a big commotion in our village. The peasant woman claimed that a miracle had happened, that her dead child had come back to life, and in her arms she held an infant boy no bigger that her dead one had been. Many speculations and theories swirled around the village, and one woman claimed that she had seen a comet in the heavens, but no one thought of a connection between the train and the mysterious child."

The adults fell silent, overwhelmed by the various accounts. No one had even noticed that Ljerka and Rajko had fallen asleep, curled up on the couch.

Now that the Jews of Grad had been deported, the pressure was even greater on Saul to find a hiding place quickly, till the madness was over, to perhaps find a place where they could hibernate like bears, till the winter passed.

The Kestners' hosts decided to go out of town to visit relatives till after the New Year and left their apartment key with Saul. It was safer for them that way, and altogether there would be fewer people coming and going. Several nosy neighbors were becoming a problem. According to regulations, every household had a certain accounted for and registered number of people living there, and no guests were allowed to stay overnight. If a house were searched, there would be trouble, even if the excess souls were Aryan, as they might be political fugitives or partisans. Travelers who checked into hotels or inns had to duly register with the police, so that control would be maintained over the entire population. Needless to say, Saul never registered.

Bettina sent word to meet a prospective guide in a coffee house, but the man did not show up. Joseph Weinberg sent him an address via a former employee, but all that Saul found in the back of the building at the end of a dilapidated hallway was a pawn shop that was the front for an illegal foreign currency exchange. He was desperate by the first week in January, the longest week in his life since the trenches, when he finally tracked down a certain Mr. Ruber, whose plan for crossing the border seemed plausible. It involved being smuggled across the river Kupa by members of a thriving black market ring. Final arrangements were made on the spot, and Saul had to hand over in advance the entire demanded sum, which was considerable. Saul had no choice; time was running out. Ruber must have sensed a hesitation on Saul's part, and explained that the money had to be split three ways, amongst himself, a peasant on this side of the river, and a group of Slovenian youths on the other side.

On the appointed morning of that same week, the Kestners were met by Mr. Ruber at the railroad station, where they were to board the train for Karlovac, the last stop in Croatia before entering Italian-occupied Slovenia. Ruber introduced his fiancée, Miss Blankety-Blank, to Saul, whom they were to follow at some distance. The exact details were not revealed. And that was the last that Saul saw of Ruber.

Though the train was fairly crowded, Saul found some seats for everyone. The Fiancée sat in another compartment, some distance away. She made especially sure to be nowhere near when the police came by to check identification papers. The policeman found no fault with the falsified credentials Robert had procured for Saul's family before his arrest, and the train pulled out of Zagreb without further ado.

Two middle-aged women, who apparently traveled that route frequently, shared the compartment with the Kestners.

"Do you know, sister," one of them said to the other, as she picked up a dropped stitch with her knitting needle "that Jews travel on this very line in all kinds of disguises in order to cross the border? You won't believe how many have been taken off the train."

"I know, I know, sister! One day a whole bunch was caught swimmin' across the river and shot. That day our muddy Kupa ran bright red."

"Why, just the other day a man was snatched by the border patrol and hanged off a lamppost near the railroad station in Karlovac."

The women told their tales without the slightest emotion, exchanging stories to pass the time, as they might have exchanged recipes in former days, trying to outdo each other, each new story more gruesome than the previous. Saul wondered what he had done to have locusts sent upon him. Clara's hand trembled as she dabbed the perspiration off her face with a handkerchief. As if entranced, Peter and Ljerka stared out the window at the snow-dusted countryside, while Rajko squirmed in his seat, glaring at the women. As Rajko was about to stick his tongue out or thumb his nose at the women, Saul poked him and sternly told him to keep still. Every so often Saul noticed the Fiancée going up and down the aisle to check whether they were still aboard.

In Karlovac, Saul had to show his papers again before leaving the station. Rajko, wide eyed, looked around at all the lampposts, but there was nothing out of the ordinary.

The Fiancée then led the Kestners, who according to instructions, followed her at a respectable distance – supposedly not to arose suspicion, but more likely, not to endanger her in case of trouble. She led her flock into an inn, sat down facing them several tables away, and gave her order to a waiter. It was way past the lunch hour, so Saul ordered a big meal, because he didn't know when, where, or whether dinner would be coming. And what else was one supposed to do in an inn but eat, so not to arose suspicion? Their guide seemed to have forgotten all about them, absorbed by her chicken stew and a newspaper.

Long after their dishes were removed, more and more soldiers, officers, and various uniformed officials seemed to pour in and out of the inn. But the Fiancée just sipped more coffee, and every so often peered over the edge of the newspaper. Saul began to wonder whether this was a trap.

At twilight the woman finally called for her bill, and Saul did likewise. She then led the Kestners through a tangle of streets, walking faster than she had done from the station, so that between the dusk, the children, the two suitcases, and the slippery half frozen ground, they nearly lost sight of her. Saul became convinced that she was trying to lose them, and that suddenly they would find themselves walking around in circles in an unfamiliar town, with the money and the guide gone. Then unexpectedly she turned into a small farmhouse, and before Saul's eyes accommodated to the poor lighting in what was a combination kitchen and living room, she was gone. It was strange; Saul had not so much as exchanged one word with her, nor did he quite catch her name when Ruber introduced her at the station.

The farmer turned out to be a hospitable chatty old man. He made the children sit on a bench set against the tile stove and had his wife bring them water.

"I am poor and sick," he apologetically said to explain his situation to Clara and Saul. "In my old age, I can no longer make an honest living off my land. My plot lies foul, too close to the new border. So now I try to make ends meet by smuggling. But with prices going up and up, I am not sure for how long my old woman and I can keep up. Let St. Anthony and St. Joseph, and all the other saints in heaven be my witnesses, that what I get from Mr. Ruber is barely enough to get by."

Saul found it quite believable that the three-way split Ruber talked about was uneven, and that the risk involved may have been inversely proportional to the financial compensation. Then the farmer talked about the government and the weather, at the mercy of which he sometimes found himself, and both of which were often truculent. Lastly he talked about his stomach ulcer and tortuous leg veins, which gave him much trouble, eager to obtain medical advice when he discovered that Saul was a physician.

"Now it is time for you to go," announced the farmer abruptly, as he peered out a window. "My wife will take you to our son-in-law, some three hours by foot. His house is near the edge of the river. Do not talk, as the voice carries at night, and there could be guards out on patrol."

The darkness outside was palpably thick, with the clouds blanketing the sky. The farmer's wife led the Kestners through fields, up and down low bluffs, and through brush. It was hard to follow her in the moonless night. The furrowed half-frozen soil formed irregular ridges, which at times were iced over and difficult to negotiate, and in other spots, the midday sun had softened the ground into a slippery paste. Everyone, except for the peasant woman, who seemed to glide in her pointy peasant shoes, was tripping and stumbling all the way. Peter fell once into a ditch, and frightened everyone with the noise he made, but fortunately there was no one else around to hear it.

At the son-in-law's Saul and Clara were told that they had to wait till the early morning hours to be rowed across the river, and that it was best for them to sleep for a while. Each was given a crust of bread and water, which they consumed by the dim light of an oil lamp - electricity had not arrived at this outpost - after which four of them were put up cross-wise in a double bed, while Clara settled herself in a rocking chair. Nobody except Rajko fell asleep.

Suddenly the door flung open and two gendarmes in uniform walked in, each with a rifle precariously slung across one shoulder. A chill passed over Saul as the cold outside air swept into the room and carried with it the pungent smell of bayonet grease, mingled with the fetid odor of cheap boot leather and perspiration-soaked uniforms, so characteristic of the Croatian low-ranking guards and recruits. He gave them an icy stare, and they reciprocated. Peter and Ljerka fidgeted nervously, and Clara looked as if she had not one pint of blood left in her body. After scrutinizing the Kestners for a while, as a farmer might livestock, or a merchant, barrels of exotic goods, one of them spoke up.

"What have you got here? Ahem, some guests again?"

"Yes," reassured the son-in-law. "Come have a glass of slivovic."

"Well, maybe just a little one. Just to warm up. It's getting raw out there again."

Clink! "To your health."

"Another one?"

"If you insist."

Crash! The glasses collided again. "To the Independent State of Croatia!"

To Saul's amazement, the officials departed "without seeing anything suspicious," and without taking him and his family along. The son-in-law then explained that all the border gendarmes had already gotten their palms greased, but would come around at inconvenient moments to show the necessity for continued payoffs. "What they are most interested in is the smuggling of cowhides, which is very profitable, and which goes on between midnight and dawn. You and your family have to wait till that is finished, so that we can use some boats for your crossing."

Just before the crack of dawn, as the son-in-law had said, everything was ready. The river Kupa was a few hundred yards beyond the house. The temperature had dropped, and there was a chill in the air. A thick fog engulfed the whole bank, so thick that one could barely see beyond the tip of one's nose, provided it was not very long.

The son-in-law and a young farmer rowed two boats swiftly across, with Clara, Rajko, and Ljerka in one, and Saul and Peter in the other. On the other side was Slovenian territory under Italian occupation. As the rowboats approached their destination, pallid rays of a rising January sun began piercing the fog, revealing a gentle embankment.

There were no Italian guards around. The leather smugglers, the son-in-law explained, had fired a few shots into the water on the preceding evening, and whenever they did that, the Italians, figuring that there was some trouble and wishing no part of it, would invariably disappear for at least twelve hours, to patrol some other, quieter portion of the river border. Three youths and three elderly people awaited the Kestners just beyond the riverbank. The boys were the Slovenian guides, the last relay in the Ruber setup. The others, a married couple and a single man, were refugees, originally from Austria, and whispered among themselves in German. That meant that they had been on their pilgrimage for several years already, that this was not their first crossing, and that they had eluded Hitler by escaping to Yugoslavia. Compared to them, Saul realized that he and his family were novices. And who knew how many more times they would have to do such things? Only there were fewer and fewer places left to go to, or borders to cross. After Italy, there seemed only Switzerland remaining, and who could tell whether that little country would be able to remain neutral.

The boats had left as soon as the Kestners were deposited on the shore. The Slovene guides motioned to everyone to move away quickly from the bank and keep silent. Daylight was filtering through, but irregular patches of fog still bedeviled the small group, trying to keep up with the procession. There seemed to be no road or path, only bare undulating frozen hillocks with rare frost-bitten shrubs. Saul prodded his brood to keep up, as he and Peter struggled with the suitcases and Ljerka whimpered that the air was cutting her cheeks. Rajko had to be silenced, as he counted aloud his steps in a game he had just invented.

After another half an hour, the little troop arrived at a tiny deserted inn, run by the family of one of the guides, a small isolated stone structure in the middle of nowhere, flanked by a few scrubby pine trees. Dark coarse homemade bread, chunks of smoked rather dry sausage, plum jam, and water were brought for everyone, and adults got hot bitter ersatz coffee. Sugar and milk were hard to come by and were not offered. The Kestners and the Austrians eagerly refueled, while the young Slovenes ducked mysteriously in and out of adjacent rooms. An uncomfortable hour of procrastination followed, though Saul could not extract a satisfactory explanation for the delay. Finally, they were off again. They were told that they were to hike to the second – no, not the first, the first might be too dangerous – the second railroad station beyond the border.

The walk now was long and tedious. The ground was frozen solid, and the mud of a few days before formed uneven ridges and rails. Frost was on the ground, and in shady spots there was snow. The terrain had become more hilly, and their path now led through some woods. As they came to a clearing, there stood an old abandoned mill by a small half frozen stream, the wood on its large wheel half rotten. The Slovenes now halted and refused to go on, unless they were paid an additional handsome little sum, so much per person. It was no use telling them that Mr. Ruber had already collected their share; they wanted more, and if anyone didn't like it, he could go back and complain to Mr. Ruber. They warned that it was not a good idea to argue with them and lose time, because they might miss the next train to Ljubljana, and if caught lingering around the railroad station for a later train, there was always a chance to get arrested and thrown back over the border.

The Austrian couple moaned and begged. They did not possess the necessary sum, they claimed. The woman became quite hysterical, but the Slovene youths would not budge. After many tears and much pleading, the Austrian couple managed to produce somewhat less than the required amount, the small difference finally being made up by Saul and the other Austrian; this transaction, doubtless, left the Austrian couple penniless to face more years of exile, and who knew how many unforeseen crises.

The little stream by the mill was now crossed without further delay. Ljerka nearly sprained her ankle hopping from one partly ice-glazed stone to the next, protruding from the water. But luckily this did not happen, for Darwinian law was very much in evidence that day, and no one could afford the slightest disadvantage.

From then on, it was safe enough to take a country road. This was considered already the "hinterland," and patrols were not likely to be around. Rajko pranced along, obviously enjoying the whole trip.

"Oh, boy, now I'll have something to tell my old classmates in Grad when we get back," he told Ljerka. "This is adventure at last."

"Bend down and proceed quietly! Not a word from anyone," ordered one of the guides.

Saul caught a glimpse of a railroad crossing just around a bend, behind a low embankment, not more than twenty yards ahead. An Italian soldier was patrolling it, on his shoulder a bayoneted rifle, which seemed twice his size. The rifle was not so large, but the man was diminutive, and after seeing German soldiers parading in Grad, this one looked like a toy. He was apparently a newly posted guard, totally unexpected by the guides. Luckily his back was turned, and as he stamped his feet to keep warm and whistled a Sicilian tune, a little caravan of crouching figures slid past the low rise that separated them.

Some time in the early afternoon, the group arrived at a small railroad station. From there it was safe to take a train to Ljubljana, as all travel documents and visas were checked at the previous two stations on both sides of the border. The Slovene youths departed, and the Austrians separated themselves from the Kestners, disappearing somewhere within the station. It was best for everyone to spread out.

The stationmaster greeted Saul enthusiastically, invited the family into his small crammed office, and presented the Kestners with an assortment of boot brushes and shoe polish, explaining that

Italian officials were wary of muddy shoes, fearing that their owners might be partisans, even if there were children among them. Lately resistance units had sprung up in the surrounding hills and woods and were causing the occupation troops no end of trouble. Despite the freeze, Saul was surprised how much muck had stuck to everyone's shoes in the two days' trek.

Then the train whisked in with the screeching noise of breaks applied against the locomotive wheels and the characteristic swish of steam as the train came to a halt. The Kestners boarded at one end, the Austrians at the other, and that was the last that Saul ever saw of them.

It was already getting dark when the train arrived in Ljubljana, the capital of Slovenia, now officially renamed Emona by the Italians, though nobody seemed to call it that, claimed to be its ancient Latin name in an attempt to turn the clock back to the glorious days of the Roman empire.

Half a block from the station there was a decent looking hotel where Saul found an available room, and everyone collapsed into bed, without having had lunch or supper. Tomorrow he would have to report to the Italian authorities. As tired as he was, Saul was too excited to doze off. The first segment of their escape had come off well, and this was cause to celebrate. From the heavy rhythmic breathing he could tell that the twins were already asleep. Though he was not a religious man, soundless words unexpectedly formed on his lips: "Oh God, show me the rest of the way! Lead me out of the desert, as you have led my forefathers!"

And while his father implored the creator, Peter silently mouthed the word "Silvia" before he surrendered to an overwhelming fatigue.

CHAPTER 12

Saul awoke with a start. He looked around the large barren room and wondered where he was. He felt cold, freezing cold, and wiggled his toes, which seemed not quite to belong to him. The room was grey in the pre-dawn light, which seeped through the frost-laden window pains. There was something familiar about the ice-etched glass, but recognition still escaped him. Next to him in a matrimonial bed was Rajko, and on the other side of the boy slept Ljerka, snuggled up against Clara, who was on the far side of the bed, precariously close to the edge. At the foot of the bed Peter slept on a narrow sofa. Saul had a feeling that he had had a dream, but could not remember it.

Then memory returned. He was in Ljubljana in a rented room, and more than a month had already passed while he and his family were waiting for a refugee assignment; the Italian bureaucracy took its sweet time. The government preferred not to leave a high concentration of displaced persons on former Yugoslav territory, where political antagonism was seething, but chose to disperse them throughout Italy. Jewish refugees like himself were treated as Yugoslav citizens, and hence citizens of an enemy country. Technically the Kestners were now civilian prisoners of war. They would be assigned to a particular province by a governmental office in Rome, and the provincial authorities would make the specific selection of town or village of confinement.

Saul looked around the room again. He had been so relieved and delighted when a few days after their arrival he had found the room to rent from the old schoolmaster's wife. Ljubljana was swarming with refugees, most of them Slovenians from the northern part, which was being Germanized, and accommodations were hard come by. The apartment turned out to ooze material and spiritual frost and decay. When Clara had made a fire the first day in the corner wood-burning tile stove, the room became filled with smoke, so that the windows had to be opened, and in the end the room was colder than it had been to begin with. The landlady was very apologetic, but the chimney could not be repaired in the winter, and no, the Kestners could not have any of the other half a dozen empty rooms. Tearfully she explained that because the schoolmaster's pension was not keeping up with soaring prices, she had persuaded her grudging husband to rent out the two most remote rooms, one of which had already been rented out when Saul rang the buzzer. Neither Saul, nor any of his family, ever saw the old man; they only heard his grumbling voice behind closed doors. He periodically sent his embarrassed wife to complain that Rajko used too much toilet paper in the common bathroom.

Saul felt a pinch inside his abdomen and heard a gurgle as his stomach asked for food. The evening before, like many other evenings, Clara had cooked a small cauliflower for dinner – they did not have access to the kitchen, so Clara had cooked it in a small pot, despite the smoke, there was no other way, placed directly on the fire through the open stove door – divided the cauliflower into five equal parts, distributed the water in which it had been cooked, portioned out half of the daily bread ration, and that was that.

Once, Saul recalled, they had had extra bread for dinner. He and Clara had met a couple, whose eight-year-old daughter with a head full of Shirley Temple locks and a dimple in her right cheek, procured bread without rations by going from bakery to bakery and simply telling the bakers that she was a refugee, so Clara sent out Ljerka and Rajko to do likewise. The twins returned late in the afternoon that day, Rajko with something between a grin and an embarrassed grimace on his face, and Ljerka with flame red eyes and wet cheeks, hugging three small bread rolls.

"The baker gave me the rolls free," Ljerka sniveled and sobbed. "He thought I was a beggar." Tears poured down her cheeks.

"It's all right, you don't have to go again," said Clara pulling the girl onto her lap and hugging her.

"We are proud of you and we don't want you to go again" weighed in Saul, but Ljerka was inconsolable for the rest of that day. His little girl had been humiliated as never before. And that was the last time they had extra bread.

With the cold and the scarcity of food, Saul had devised a scheme for everyone to spend twenty-one hours in bed on most days, in order to stay warm and conserve energy. They would all get up at eleven, get dressed, and walk a considerable distance to a small inexpensive inn for lunch that was near the hotel where they had stayed when they arrived in Ljubljana. The servings were skimpy, but that was the best they could do under war circumstances and their limited means. Somewhere along the way they would buy bread with their ration cards, and by two o'clock they were back in their room, ready to go to bed to warm their half frozen fingers and toes under the warm blankets. At least once a week they deviated from this routine to go to the library, to visit, or shop for food if there was anything to buy.

In the absence of his practice, Saul spent hours on end calculating the required calories each would need to survive, and something to spare for the children to grow.

Saul's gaze now wandered to the Italian "potato cheese," which was sold without rations. That was not its name, but people called it that, claiming it contained more potatoes than milk curd. More light now seeped into the room, and he could see it clearly. There it was, a slab of cheese they had managed to purchase yesterday, the center of attraction of the entire room. It gilded a large plate set on top of an otherwise empty dresser, sitting there as if it were a famous actor dominating an empty stage; yet no one noticed the emptiness, for all eyes were on the star.

Something stirred inside his belly again, something wet and liquid seemed to slither and glide like a snake, followed by an angry growl. Soon Clara would be up to parcel out the remaining half of the bread rations, along with snips of the cheese. No, he would not wait any longer. He would hop out of bed and cut himself a piece, a big hunk of that ugly thing. Then he changed his mind. He had to stall a little longer, stretch it out, or the span between breakfast and lunch at the inn would be too long. He despised the constant preoccupation with food. The cold he did not mind as much. The cold he could stand, but not the hunger, nor the idleness.

A kick in the flank distracted Saul from his rumination. Rajko had stretched and wriggled, and with a noise half way between a yawn and a giggle, let it be known that he was awake. The room now came to life, as everyone seemed to be awake. Rajko and Ljerka giggled, as they tried to tickle each other's feet. Clara divided up the bread and cut chunks of the potato cheese for everyone. By silent agreement, anyone who was still hungry could cut himself another slice of cheese. Saul had noticed that Clara was the only one who did not go up for seconds, and she always gave herself the smallest slice. She had a remarkable ability for self-denial in the face of hunger. Tamara would not have done that, he mused. She was not as kind and generous, nor was she able to be stoic like Clara. How different the sisters were. He leaned over the twins, and planted a kiss on Clara's cheek.

"Today is Tuesday," Clara announced. "Today is our library day, so everyone collect the books that are due and think about what you want to pick up." They had to stock up on books to fight the ennui of long hours in bed.

"Yoopee! I want *Robinson Crusoe,*" Rajko piped up. "I saw it there."

"What book do you want, Peter?" Clara asked. The boy had been uncommonly quiet lately, and she wanted to prod him on.

"Last time I was looking for *Crime and Punishment,* but the librarian told me the censors had withdrawn most Russian and English language authors. I wonder whether they missed *Robinson Crusoe*?"

"After the library I am inviting your mother for a coffee." Saul decided in a flash to splurge, "and they might even have hot cocoa."

"Hurray," came from Rajko.

"Now get your books out, and read, till it is time to get up and dress to go for lunch," Clara instructed her brood.

January and February of 1942 were bitterly cold in Ljubljana, and the cold seeped mercilessly into unheated rooms. Local people claimed that there had not been such a winter in thirty years. Saul reminded everyone that the colder it got, the more Germans would freeze on the Russian front. And he knew what he was talking about, when he spoke of the impassable Russian snow blizzards; he himself had had a short tour of duty as a very young man during World War I. In fact, it was the news from the Russian front, which was sustaining him now. Hitler had failed to capture Moscow, and the Russians had mounted a successful counter-offensive, which many people had doubted they would be able to do. For the first time in several years of aggression, the Germans had encountered an obstacle, and for the first time they were forced to retreat.

Saul was not in a mood to read his book. He closed his eyes and recalled that when he woke up that morning, a dream had slipped into oblivion. He tried again to retrieve it from its nocturnal crevice. His effort paid off, and he realized that it had not been a single dream, but a nightly repetition, a rerun he had experienced for several weeks. He was inside an unfamiliar police station. On the other side of iron bars was a group of people staring at him. He recognized them immediately. Zvonko Adler was among them, and he asked: "Saul, how come you are not with us?"

Saul tried to answer, but he could not speak. He wanted to run, but his limbs would not propel him.

"Why am I here, and he is out there?" said little ten-year-old Ruben Kohn.

"Maybe there is a reason," answered a very old man with a long white beard and a skullcap, whose face seemed pliable, one moment looking like old Lichtmann, and the next transforming itself into several different people.

Saul became terrified. "What do they want from me?" he asked Clara, who had suddenly appeared at his side, but vanished before she could answer. He ran as fast as he could through unfamiliar fields, but Zvonko Adler had apparently gotten out between the bars, and was pursuing him.

"Wait, Saul, listen to me!" he heard Zvonko's voice behind him. "Please stop!"

But when Saul stopped there was no one there. A train passed by full of Christmas trees. A stranger said: "Bettina is on that train. It is going to Poland. It is colder in Poland, and there is less food."

"Who are you?" asked Saul.

"Have you already forgotten? I am your classmate Zvonko."

"What do you want?" Before Saul got an answer, Zvonko disappeared again, and Saul was running now through some woods. The people behind the bars were watching him.

"Look out, Saul," Zvonko's voice came from somewhere. "Run! Run faster, or the Germans will get you."

"Run for me, too," cried little Ruben.

"Do you think he will make it?" Rosa Steinberg asked.

"We hope he will. We are all rooting for him," said the multi-faced old man with the long beard.

A troop of German soldiers was right on Saul's heals. He ran faster, but still they got closer and closer, and as an SS man reached out to grab him, Saul woke up abruptly.

Ever since Saul had heard about the deportation of the Jews of Grad, they were constantly in his thoughts. "Why indeed is it I and not Zvonko who is here?" he asked himself. "Why my children and not his?" And a shiver went through his spine. "But I am glad it is my kids," he had to admit.

The Black Bear Café on the premises of a hotel, which had seen better days in the bygone years, was located in the center of Ljubljana, near the one and only high-rise. It had recently become a beehive of activity and a favorite gathering spot for refugees. Saul led his entourage, loaded down with borrowed library books, into the overcrowded main room, which was pleasantly warm and heated, but unpleasantly full of cigarette smoke, despite tobacco shortages. Fortunately a group of customers were just leaving, so that the Kestners could be accommodated, which was not always the case, as some people seemed to park there for the day, seeking information about friends and relatives from the milling crowd. Word of mouth was the only means by which one got news, and that was infrequent and often inaccurate.

On that day Clara and Saul met a woman with a large hat sitting at the next table. From her they heard about Zvonko Adler's wife Mariana, and their children Anika and David. The woman had been in the women's concentration camp on the mainland, near Stari Grad, and when she came down with typhoid fever, was transferred to an outside hospital. She was not expected to live, and lingered there delirious for weeks in a corner bed, burning up with fever. When she eventually unexpectedly recovered, she seemed to have been forgotten, and was discharged back to the outside world, whereupon she promptly escaped to Slovenia.

"We were some thirty of us, women and children, squeezed into a small room in the make-shift barracks, when a new group arrived, and more were crammed into our limited space," the woman began. "I had met the Adler family when we had vacationed on the Adriatic some years back. When they arrived at the camp, Anika was separated from her mother, and assigned to my barrack. I had remembered Anika as a gangly child, and was amazed how lovely she had grown, like a rosebud unfolding, though beneath the petals I saw a hard edge, and, of course, panic. I was not the only one who had noticed the girl. A young Ustasha guard who came to inspect our barrack could not take his eyes off her. She became aware of his gaze and returned a half-smile. The next day the young man spoke to Anika on some pretext. For an instant her dark eyes reflected fear, as she tried to turn away, but then she quickly looked back at the young fellow, eyes narrow and lids fluttering with feline cunning. I can't say that I blame her. Here we all were, engulfed by this furious storm, and here was someone who could throw her a life preserver.

"The camp was intolerable beyond anything I could have imagined. The hunger, the filth, the lice, the close quarters! The inmates fought tooth and nail over every morsel or a turn in the lavatory during the brief period when we were allowed to use it. In her mind we all became Anika's enemies, who took crumbs away from her, who suffocated her by our closeness, and who were using up the air she seemed to think was only hers to breathe. So it came to pass that Anika developed a greater hate for the women and children whose fate she had to share, than for those who caused that fate.

"The young Ustasha arranged to transfer our section to his command. The cook started giving Anika bigger portions for the evening meal, which was the larger of the two pittances we received, and which was doled out in the central kitchen. Breakfast, you see, consisted of bread and water, so to speak thrown into the compound for the prisoners to divide among themselves, resulting in a stampede, with first-come-first-served, and the last few often got nothing at all. The guards knew so well how to pit us one against the other, and how to give just a little less of the small allotment of food, so as to turn us into a pack of sharks.

"Soon Anika was exempted from the meanest tasks, and sometimes she would be sent to scrub the young Ustasha's office, so that he could see her. He apparently always arranged to have extra food for her there."

"And then what happened?" Clara couldn't suppress her curiosity.

"The women in our compound started to exchange nasty comments in and out of Anika's presence, and many accusations were pointed in her way. And just as she hated the women more than the people who were causing our misfortune, they began to despise her more then their tormentors. Several claimed that the traitress would be the first to hang, when the day of reckoning would come. It was bad enough, they argued, for the Ustashe to be what they were, but it was ten times worse for a Jewess to associate, no, to prostitute herself to them.

"One evening of heightened tension – a child had succumbed in our section, which was not a rare event, but this one had been more pathetic than most – Anika's return from the office was the required spark for spontaneous combustion. The women in the compound, without premeditation, came down on her like a thousand furies, and would have torn her to pieces, had she not run quickly to the guards. The compound commander then duly punished all the inmates in the section, with his justice meted equally from the three-year-old child to the elderly. As for Anika, he welcomed her into his arms and into his bed, and that is how it came to pass that Anika became the mistress of a collaborator." The woman paused. Saul looked uncomfortably away, and Clara winced.

"The story does not end there," the woman resumed. "The young Ustasha was truly enamored of Anika, and sought official permission to marry her, but I don't know if he eventually received it. But his love for a Jewess did not stop him from continuing to dispense his type of justice to the other prisoners."

"What about Mariana and little David?" Clara inquired.

"Mariana was assigned with David to a different compound," the narrator continued. "The boy was scrawny, but seemed to have a ravenous appetite, and he whined incessantly for food. After a time he developed fits of anger, you might call them violent tantrums, demanding something to eat, driving his mother absolutely insane. The poor woman scrounged around, but there was no food to be had. Then one day she somehow, nobody quite knew how, found her way to the forbidden kitchen garbage cans, from which she stole potato and vegetable scrapings to feed her little son. On one such occasion, however, she was caught, for which she received a terrible beating, after which she stopped stealing garbage. In fact, something within her crumbled, and from that day on she ignored the boy. Some claimed that she became demented and no longer recognized him, and others, that she abused him, consuming herself his food allotment. The boy went from outbursts of temper in which he pounded with his fists his unflinching mother, to turning entirely mute, until one day at the line-up, he was no longer there. No one knew exactly what had happened to him."

"Oh my God!" Clara could barely hold back the tears. Saul sat there without a word, glad that the twins were at the other end of the large café, looking out the window, and that Peter had joined a small group of young people his own age.

"No one who has not been in the camp," the woman sighed, "can possibly understand what pain and exasperation must have transformed Mariana into a demented woman or a preying beast."

Saul got up. He had heard enough and was ready to go.

"Papi," pleaded Ljerka, "can't we stay a little longer? It's so nice and warm and cozy here."

"Papa," Rajko added, "We hardly ever come here. We've only been here once before, and it's such a great place."

"This is not a place for children," Clara commented, "but they are really enjoying the liberation from their beds."

Saul relented. "Yes, darling," he told Ljerka, and headed for the reading room on the mezzanine, hoping to find a newspaper. At the top of the stairs he collided with an unshaven young man in a shabby coat, and an involuntary exclamation parted his lips before he had time to reflect.

"George!" Something in the way the forehead met the brow of the man made him say that, but as he looked deeper into the man's face, mentally shaving away the beard, he was certain that he had made a mistake.

"Saul? Saul Kestner?" The words came back hollow, as if they had come from a cave.

"So it is you!" exclaimed Saul and threw his arms around the man. "And where is Marta?"

Saul looked into George's eyes, and saw two pieces of steel instead. Momentarily a flash of fire enveloped the steely grayness, before George looked away. No wonder he had nearly failed to recognize him. That look was totally foreign and had a quality of violence. A moment later George suddenly put his head on Saul's shoulder and wept.

When George regained his composure, the two walked on together, Saul leading the way to two comfortable armchairs outside the reading room.

"I thought I had no more tears left," George said unceremoniously, and then plunged into his story without prompting, his words welling up under pressure. "We left Grad and returned to Zagreb after Easter. When the gravity of the political situation became clear to us, which did not crystallize till the fall, we made arrangements to cross the border into Italian territory, but Marta, who was pregnant, started to bleed, and our plans collapsed. She urged me to go alone, and promised to follow as soon as possible, but I could not bear to leave her and the unborn child. 'Life is not worth living without you, I had always told her,' and I reproached myself for her condition.

"In December, Marta gave birth in secrecy, at the house of an old and devoted Christian friend. As soon as it was deemed feasible, we were going to leave, but our escape contact had vanished, and I could not find another one. During our absence, our apartment had been searched and confiscated, so there was no going back. My friend obtained false identification papers and moved us to a nearby village, where no one was supposed to know us, while he continued his efforts to arrange for our escape.

"Not long after, someone apparently reported us; I have no idea who. On a dark night, I was simply dragged away from the doorsteps, without ever so much as saying goodbye to Marta. Several Ustashe marched me off with a group of Serbs, political prisoners, and partisan suspects to the local graveyard. There, in a barren part, they lined us up in the snow. When I heard the guns cocked, I threw myself quickly to the ground, one instant before the bullets whizzed by to fell the others. I had spied a freshly dug grave nearby, waiting to embrace someone recently deceased, and I quickly rolled into it. The executioners put several more bullets into the slumped forms on the ground, and then departed victorious, singing the new Croatian anthem, leaving the dirty work of burial to the local gravedigger, whose tongue they solemnly swore to cut out, if he breathed a word to anyone about such goings-on at the cemetery.

"I remained a long time inside another man's grave, till I feared it would become my own frozen tomb. I could see the row of still bodies cradled by the snow, which had partly melted as it became soaked with warm blood, and which I knew should be a halo of confluent crimson, but by the light of the moon, which finally broke through the clouds, appeared as a black rim. Turning my back on death, which in the darkness I succeeded to avoid – no, to postpone. I hobbled back to the little house where we had been staying, certain that it was going to be empty, but compelled to see it with my own eyes, to remove the last shadow of a doubt.

"The door was ajar, and Marta and the baby were gone. I fled into the wood shack and sat there for a very long time. For an eternity! I was numb, empty, frozen. My life was over.... 'Life is not worth living,' I had said, 'without Marta.' Then why had I saved myself? Why had I dodged the bullet, Saul, can you tell me that?" His voice cracked. Without waiting for an answer, George continued.

"It was Marta I loved and thought about all those months, and not the infant. The child had aided the enemy, and had stood in the way of our escape. When it arrived, it seemed a complete stranger, mercilessly howling at night, and I could not take to it the way Marta did. But I regretted that I could not offer it a better fate than an untimely death in a concentration camp. As I thought about the calamity that was about to befall the infant, through no conceivable fault of its own, my heart seemed to quiver inside my chest, a wave of tenderness gushed forth like a geyser, and with a painful twinge brought me out of my apathy. I felt for the first time love for the little one, arising from a crushing pain and grief.

"My numbing self-pity changed into anger. Dawn would soon arrive. I had died during that night. My former self had died. But a man remained, who had only one thing left from his past – his memory. A man who had only one thing to live for – revenge!"

The hard look of steel returned to George's countenance, and his jaw set menacingly. Saul could virtually feel a wave of hatred slapping him in the face, and he involuntarily shrank away from George. No, this was not madness, but fierce passion, which had completely taken possession of the unhappy man.

"I swore that day," George continued, "that a hundred Ustashe would pay with their lives for Marta and my son. I found an axe in the shed, and set out on foot across fields and through woods, avoiding roads, traveling mostly at night and sleeping by day, sometimes hiding in barns, sometimes revealing myself to peasant folks, who most of the time fed me and sent me on my way with their blessings, but occasionally quaked in their boots – the ones with a murky conscience – and their hospitality had to be coerced. Eventually, I made my way across the border. Now all I am waiting for is the day of revenge." There was an enormous force behind George's words, the pressure of almost inhuman energy funneled into a single purpose.

George leaned over and dropped his voice. "I took care of two already, in my travel. There are ninety eight left to appease the blood that is boiling in my veins." After looking around the café as if searching for someone, he added, "Perhaps we shall meet again after the war," then he quickly got up and walked away, leaving Saul glued to the armchair into which he had settled.

"After the war!" Would that ever be? Would that day ever come to pass? Saul squirmed, suddenly feeling very depressed, unable to conceive of the day when all this madness would be over. He tried to imagine what that world would be like, but all that he could think of was George, and Marta, and Mariana Adler, and little David whom he had delivered and had taken care of whenever the little boy had been sick. No, he could not visualize himself, nor the residue of the Jews scattered every which way. He could not even begin to glimpse the light at the end of the tunnel, which seemed infinitely far away at that moment.

There was George, for example. What will happen to him when he finds out that blood does not taste so sweet, and hate does not, in any case, bring back the dead? How will he ever be able to go back to his practice of jurisprudence, to sit at a desk, and in a detached manner preside over petty feuds and squabbles? And what about himself? He, too, might not get off so lightly before it was all over.

"Why so blue, Dr. Kestner?" a nasal voice interrupted Saul's cogitations. Saul saw before him the caricature-like face of Mr. Klumperdingel, with the funny pudgy nose, thick lips, bushy eyebrows, and earlobes drooping in canine fashion. Needless to say, Mr. K. was an uncommonly ugly man, yet not repulsively ugly, but somehow pleasingly and harmoniously so.

Mr. Dingel, as he was sometimes called, was a short, thin, lopsided man, his trunk twisted like a gnarled tree, due to a curvature of his spine. As if this were not enough, he was also afflicted, as he informed Saul, "by a mysterious and incurable malady, known as allergy," which sometimes brought on violent sneezing, reputed to have disrupted many a card game at the café.

Despite his various afflictions, and despite the immediate problems of refugee status, Mr. K. maintained a remarkable degree of equanimity. Perhaps his long-standing suffering had equipped him with a certain fortitude, which now stood him in good stead, and he always seemed to have a joke or funny story up his sleeve. He was a favorite with Rajko and Ljerka, and when the twins saw him with Saul, they ran over to say hello and ask the "funny-man" to tell them a new joke.

Of the various stories, Saul liked best the account of Dingel's escape. Since no woman had taken a fancy to him, Klumperdingel had had a housekeeper, Katica, to cook and clean for him. Kata, as she was usually called, a coarse-looking unmarried peasant woman of huge proportions, proved to be a devoted and dependable servant.

When one day, under the Nazi regime, two policemen came to fetch Dingel, she managed to hide him under her bed, and informed the officials that he was not in. The two men insisted on searching the premises. Kata then became very indignant, and used vile language, which she was good at. The officers seemed somewhat intimidated by this overbearing peasant women, and when they reached her room, the last to be searched, she became so abusive, that they hesitated, but orders were orders.

"And while all this went on," Mr. K. recounted, "I was under the bed, and if there was one thing I am particularly allergic to, it is feathers. And there I was, under a mound of down, with an excruciating urge to sneeze. I struggled and struggled to hold my breath, and just when it seemed that I would burst, Kata swept the policemen out of the room, still cursing, and slammed the door. And that is how I avoided deportation and escaped with Kata's help."

"And why so blue today, doctor?" Klumperdingel repeated the question as he sat down next to Saul.

"I just heard a story, in fact two stories. People I know."

"The things one hears nowadays is enough to lose one's faith in God…in men…in everything!"

Saul nodded in agreement.

"But somehow with me," K. went on, "the more I hear, the more I believe. The effect has been paradoxical." He stopped to blow his nose, and to Rajko's disappointment, did not sneeze, then went on. "Our people are suffering, yes, as we have suffered for two thousand years, but I think of the other side of the coin, of our philosophers, our poets, musicians, doctors, even tailors and carpenters we have contributed, and I am proud to be a Jew. That pride gives me faith and strength."

"There is a lot to what you say. We certainly have contributed, despite periodic slaughters."

"I am even glad we have thieves amongst us, or we wouldn't be human."

"I can't agree with that. Jewish thieves make us more vulnerable to scrutiny."

"Not at all. Anti-Semitism is not fed by our lower elements, but by our successes. Did I ever tell you the story of my competitor?"

"No."

"You know I had a hardware business in my town. For some reason, the farmers preferred to buy tools from me, rather than from my Croatian competitor. So he went around and told everyone, 'Look at the Jew, look how greedy he is. He sells his goods at twenty percent profit. Twenty percent, mind you! I, for example, buy something for one dinar and sell it for two or three.'"

"Ah, here you are," Clara's voice felt like a caress. I've been looking for you everywhere. Hello, Mr. Dingel."

Saul now wondered why half an hour ago he had felt so discouraged. He was so much better off than many others. Ah yes, the others – the Jews of Grad. He remembered them and his dream. "Run for me too," little Ruben had cried. Were they really, like in the dream, rooting for someone to survive, hoping to live just a little longer in someone's memory?

The winter was endless and that particular night was especially long and cold. It had snowed for two days, and when the clouds parted and no longer blanketed the earth beneath, a bone-chilling night engulfed Ljubljana. Saul could not go back to sleep, no matter how hard he tried after a cramp in his foot had awakened him. Perhaps the cold that had seeped into the room had brought on the cramp when part of his leg was uncovered by shifting due to Rajko's frequent gyrations in his sleep. It was difficult indeed, night after night, for four people to share one double bed! Saul felt his patience nearing the limit. He wanted to get up, but it was too cold in the room, and he couldn't very well turn on the light and read, because the only source was an overhead chandelier. All he could do was fret and remain trapped on a narrow strip at the edge of the bed while the minutes and hours seemed to have come to a standstill. Saul felt powerless, thrust into a state of suspended animation that seemed to rule much of his life these days. "Ah well," he told himself, "there is nothing to be done.... Time is such a strange dimension it defies the usual yardstick." He amused himself with the thought that sometimes it slid by so quickly, and at other times, such as at this moment, it crept ahead so slowly, that the hours seemed duplicated, triplicated, or even completely stopped.

Such metaphysical cogitations, however, did not occupy Saul for long. These days he always returned quickly, almost obsessively, to the conduct of the war, the to-and-fro movements of opposing armies, the battle lines, as best he could gather from unreliable sources eventually trickling down to him. He and Peter were able to reconstruct the larger brush-strokes, but crucial details often remained concealed. The Germans were in retreat on the Russian front, that was clear, and though many people at the Black Bear Café predicted that the German armies would simply collapse the way the French did under Napoleon, that did not seem to be happening. The tenacity of the Germans to regroup was remarkable, and the war continued on. The war effort sapped more and more supplies from all corners of Europe and food shortages were more obvious each month.

Several hours later, everyone was finally up, dressed, the appetites more or less calmed if not completely satisfied, and they were ready to leave the room. The world looked better to Saul now that he could talk to Clara and Peter, and the two younger children, especially Rajko, injected some vitality into the frigid room, which during the previous night had temporarily transformed itself from a shelter to a prison.

Clara had made plans for everyone to go on a shopping expedition. The previous week she had heard that a local delicatessen chain with two separate locations sold non-rationed cold cuts once a week and this was the day. The storeowners had apparently devised their own system of rationing, and gave the same small portion to each customer, no matter how large the family was. So the five Kestners went forth to do battle, just as most other people did, each member of the family queuing up separately. To survive one had to resort to such wily strategies. Saul and Peter went to one store and Clara and the twins to the second, the one in the old city, just in case only one of the two had supplies. After the successful purchase, the plan was to hurry to the other store and reverse the process, so that each one of them would be served twice. Everybody was doing that, but it usually didn't work, as supplies ran out too quickly. Ljerka almost missed out altogether. When her turn came to be served, after standing in the snow for more than an hour, the woman behind the counter let out a squawk, folded her hands on her hips, and in a loud voice exclaimed, "My, my, who have we got here? I just served your brother not ten minutes ago!" Her voice rang through the store and everyone stared at Ljerka. Rajko had indeed been there a little earlier. Ljerka's cheeks turned crimson, she shrugged her shoulders pretending ignorance, and denied any knowledge of a brother. She turned to leave, but the woman had already cut three slices of some non-descript minced cold cut, wrapped them in brown paper, and threw the small package on the counter in front of Ljerka. After a moment's hesitation Ljerka picked it up, paid, and ran out of the store. She ran for three blocks through the trampled snow, then crossed the river via one arm of the triple bridge, which seemed to be the pride of the local citizens. Normally she would have stopped to look at the swirling waters of the Ljubljanica below. And she would have turned around and looked back at the dome-shaped castle hill behind the quaint buildings in the old part of the city, the access to which was now barred to the civilian population for security reasons. On the other side of the bridge she slipped on the compacted snow covering the cobblestones and nearly fell. At the far end of the plaza, as planned, she linked up with the rest of the family in front of the Franciscan church.

"Next time I'm going before Rajko," Ljerka declared vociferously, then admitted: "I didn't want everyone on line to think I'm a thief or something, so I lied." This time there were no tears, only anger as she hopped from one foot to the other to fight off the frost.

"No, I won't go second," Rajko protested.

"You don't have to worry, either of you," Saul said as he patted Ljerka on the back. "Peter and I were told that the delicatessen is closing its doors permanently. They cannot get new supplies. But everyone did well today, and every little bit helps."

Rajko took off his glove, licked his index finger and held it up, pointing in different directions. "The Sioux Indians licked their fingers to tell which way the wind was blowing. I read that in my book."

"It is late," Clara said. "We better go for lunch straight away."

"Ouch, my hand hurts," complained Rajko.

"Put on your glove, silly," Peter told his brother, and tugged on his coat. "Come on, let's go! And I don't believe your story about the Indians."

With that they proceeded to the little inn, while Clara put all the precious little packages into a sack. When they arrived at the inn, it was closed and an official notice was posted that it would remain closed indefinitely. Saul and Peter walked around the building to investigate, and in the back ran into the distressed owner as he was locking up the premises.

"What happened?" Saul asked. "We were here yesterday and nobody said a word about your closing."

"Oh it was terrible," the owner replied. "Absolutely dreadful!" He stood there shaking his head.

"What happened?"

"Yesterday, you must have left already, an Italian officer came with his wife for a late lunch. He told me to bring them a bottle of Chianti with the food, as they were celebrating. In the middle of the meal two partisans burst into the inn, they seemed to have materialized out of nowhere, and shot the officer. It was awful! I'll never forget the expression on his face, a blend of fear, surprise, and pain! He fell forward across the table, his right arm thrust ahead as he tried to reach out to his wife. He bled profusely. Somehow the bottle of Chianti had gotten knocked over and the wine and the blood mingled and totally soaked the tablecloth crimson.

"The attackers vanished as quickly as they had arrived, and as far as I know, have not been found. The other customers quickly dispersed, and by the time the police came, the restaurant was virtually empty. I am lucky that they didn't arrest me, but now that the inn is closed, I have lost my livelihood. I have a wife and children to feed."

"Was the officer from an elite 'Black Shirt' unit?" inquired Saul.

"No he was an ordinary army officer. He had come here a couple of times before. Seemed like a nice fellow, rather friendly, but we could only use sign language. I don't know any Italian and he didn't speak Slovenian.... Oh, it was so awful! His wife went crazy.... I know the Italians are our occupiers, our enemies, but he didn't seem like an enemy. Anyway, I like a man to face another man on the battlefield and not in a dining room."

Clara and the twins came over. Saul was glad the twins had not heard the account. The innkeeper bowed to Clara and added: "I wish you the best of luck in the months ahead, and for today's lunch, if you hurry, you can still get something to eat at the inn run by my wife's cousin." He gave them directions and quickly left. After another forty-five minutes, the Kestners found themselves eating a smaller meal at a higher price, but they were glad to get something. On an impulse Saul ordered two glasses of red wine to share; even the twins were allowed to have a sip. Saul felt a pleasant warmth spread through his body, and for the first time that day every last of his toes felt warm. Clara sat opposite him, a broad smile on her face, her cheeks flushed, as she listened intently to something Peter was telling her. The twins giggled happily. Unfortunately this could not go on, Saul knew. He was afraid to run out of money. He had heard that a mess hall had just opened up for refugees in an empty building in Tivoli Park, a sort of soup kitchen, which served lunch. From now on that would be their daily noon destination. Even if it were very skimpy as people claimed, at least it was free and allowed them to stretch the needed money for other purchases – that is, if there was anything available to buy. But today he splurged.

Saul could not explain to himself what possessed him to order the wine. Was it a celebration, an accomplishment for them all to have finished a meal and the wine and still be alive?... No, he must not allow himself to lose heart. Every day that passed, no matter how difficult it seemed, was a victory over the enemy. He must redouble his fortitude, and whether by crawling or sprinting, he must reach that finish line.

CHAPTER 13

It seemed to Peter that the winter would never end, and that he would simply get smothered under his blankets. That might precisely have happened, had he not made a new discovery. It came to him as a revelation, an electrifying experience, making his stark existence more bearable. It was the world of opera. His parents took him and the twins to the opera house to see Rigoletto.

As the lights went out, the music burst forth, pervading every nook and crevice of the theater, radiating its magic from the orchestra pit and the stage. Peter hardly dared to breathe, except for periodic gasps, and he felt that not even a fibril stirred within him, as all his energy was channeled into soaking up that wondrous outflow of sound. As the plot unfolded, he marveled at the brilliant duets; and when Rigoletto sang his dramatic plea to the courtiers, he felt his hair stand on end. The magic spell continued through an incredible counterpoint of four voices, and an amazing blend of instruments creating an orchestral storm. It was all too soon when the velvet curtain slid down on a somber chord, and the music died out. For a little longer, the music reverberated inside him, warmed him, and then it was extinguished, as he walked out with his family into the late afternoon chill.

Peter went several times more, arriving in time to get a strategic place in the standing room section. He was grateful to his parents that they allowed him to go, though they denied themselves additional performances, despite the fact that the standing-room-only tickets were dirt-cheap. It made life a little more bearable, between the lengthy hours of confinement to the bed, the constant gnawing cold, the daily midday walks to and from the mess hall, where everyone got a plate of dishwater soup with a few overcooked chopped leaves of cabbage, an occasional cube of potato, a rare bean, and once a week a fragment of inedible leathery meat. But most of all, he yearned for Silvia. Sometimes he conjured her presence with such intensity, that it was hard to believe she was not nearby, but most of the time he acutely felt her absence, pondering the question of the finality of their separation.

As all things under the sun are subject to motion, even if time seemed to stay still for Peter, that winter too, that unbearably cold and dark and long winter, did pass. The thick white mantle of snow was wearing thin, and patches trickled away in minute streams, which the earth drank up, leaving bald spots of dark soil, till the entire coat was gone. White bells and yellow trumpets sprouted in Tivoli Park, followed by blades of green; Peter was finally able to crawl out of his cocoon, and go on lengthy solitary walks. Within a few days the trees and bushes became transformed, decorated with little flame-shaped leaves dancing gracefully in the breeze, like little ballerinas. And how many different shades of green! In comparison to the lush green leaves of yesteryear, the little crumpled and unfolding ones looked almost yellow, and for some reason reminded him of newly hatched chicks he had seen in the village near Grad at Easter time. Even the larger and older ones did not yet possess the deep green of summer, but retained the delicacy of youth and spring.

"Ah, what a delight," he told himself, as he greedily sucked in the fresh air. "Life after all seems worthwhile." And no matter how depressing some days had been lately, they all seemed to fall away, his chains shattered, at least for the moment, while his spirit soared.

When he returned to their room, everyone seemed rather excited. "Peter," his mother said as she planted a kiss on his cheek, "Papa finally got our assignment for Italy. We are leaving in three days."

"I wish we wouldn't have to go there," Ljerka whimpered. "I wish we could go home. I miss my friends."

"We will, we will, darling, but not yet," Saul added, caressing the head of his little girl, who suddenly was not so little any more.

CHAPTER 14

Early in May 1942, Saul and his family boarded the train for their assigned confinement. No sealed cattle-cars, not even a police escort, but five free days to reach the provincial capital of their destination, which he had learned was Como. There they would be assigned to a small town or village selected by the local authorities. The Kestners had stopped by the Black Bear Café to say goodbye to a few acquaintances, and everyone thought that the assignment was favorable, because it was in northern Italy, which was more prosperous than some of the poor southern provinces, but no one had any specific information or knew anyone who had been assigned to that area.

The first day Saul had arranged to stop in Triest, a port city on the Adriatic coast, where he visited an old acquaintance of Slavic stock, now under Italian repatriation. His host welcomed the Kestners, and a spirited discussion ensued with the adults sipping vermouth, and the children drinking hot cocoa.

"The war will be over soon," the host declared, "only a matter of months."

"Ah, if it only were so! But my reason tells me otherwise," insisted Saul. "After last winter's setbacks, the Germans have regrouped and are on the offensive again."

"The Allies will land soon in France, and then it will last only a few more weeks, you'll see."

How many times had Saul heard in the spring that the war would end in the fall, and in the fall that it would end next spring? It was the same old tune of optimism, detached from reality, the same thread woven into so many fabrics, which he had heard expressed in different languages, in different places, and by people who had very little in common with one another. In her inimitable way, Clara had asked how come no one suggested the war would end in the summer or the winter, only the fall or the spring.

"You are a pessimist, Saul. You didn't used to be that way in the old days," the host commented.

"No, I'm a realist, as always."

The following day the Kestners headed for Venice, a fairly short and comfortable train ride. The station and the train cars had prominently displayed posters of the Fascist version of " Hear no evil, see no evil, speak no evil," with a hand sequentially covering the eyes, ears and mouth. These seemed to create a reserve and chill in the atmosphere, and no one spoke in the train compartments. The long arms of the state intruded on the passengers; the Italians acted in the public space of the train as if the "Duce" kept an eye on them.

When they arrived in Venice, Saul and Peter had to lug their battered suitcases for some distance – the train actually stopped in the outskirts. When they were finally settled in a small hotel, they discovered that food was in very short supply in Venice, and they had trouble finding a place to serve them a meal. They did not possess the necessary ration cards to be served pasta or bread. Communication was difficult, and when Clara pointed to some dish a man was being served at the next table, the waiter nodded his head, and a while later brought them a platter of artichokes. The Kestners had never seen or eaten artichokes before, and when Peter tried to eat the outer spiny leaves, he nearly choked.

"This is yucky!" Rajko piped up.

"I'm hungry, Mami," Ljerka complained.

The waiter finally took pity on them, and brought each a steaming plate of minestrone, sprinkling onto the surface the tiniest amount of grated Parmesan, which he stingily dispensed, as if it were gold.

Their hunger partially satiated, the Kestners set out to explore Venice. Unfortunately the Palace of the Doges was closed, the interior lined by sandbags, mobile art objects already removed for protection against air raids, but Saint Mark's was open.

"Magnificent!" Clara was the first to break the silence, as they all stood agape, their necks extended. "Those are all tiny little stones set into the ceiling, called mosaics," she explained to her children.

"Where did they find so much gold?" Ljerka asked.

"You see, you are missing school," Clara added, "but you are learning other things."

"Oh, boy, will I have things to tell my friends in Grad, how they use stones in Venice to paint ceilings and walls!" Rajko, all excited, raised his voice so it seemed to reverberate within the immense space.

"Shhh" came simultaneously from Clara and Saul.

"Fantastic," sprang from Peter's mouth, though he had no intention to say it out loud.

The Kestners had the basilica all to themselves, except for two young women, kneeling in a pew, and an old woman dressed in black lighting a candle, her lips moving in a silent prayer.

The Piazza, too, was deserted, and even the pigeons were gone, either because no one fed them any longer, or because, as rumor had it, they had ended in people's ovens.

Two mournful looking gondoliers suddenly came to life by the wharf and vociferously tried to outbid each other, waiving frantically to Clara and the twins to come for a ride. Saul was hypnotized by a large camouflaged ship, which came partly into view across the lagoon, not far beyond the opposite bank of the Canal Grande. He felt a flash of anger and exclaimed: "Clara, the Italian Navy is exploiting the image of Venice and is jeopardizing its priceless treasures."

"Ah, wars and those who conducted them have no regard for culture or history; they are ready to despoil art and leave behind heaps of rubble."

After wandering around through semi-deserted narrow streets, they zigzagged back and forth between canals, narrow streets, and unpredictable passages that obligated them to choose unintended directions, or brought them to dead-end alleys.

"I'm tired," Rajko complained.

"Me too," chimed in Ljerka.

"My feet are killing me," admitted Clara.

"We were taught in geometry that a straight line is the shortest distance between two points, but that doesn't seem to hold in Venice," Peter added.

"Let's go back to the hotel," Saul said. "We are probably not far from it, but we seem to be going around in circles. I only hope we can find our way in this maze." Slowly, with Peter's assistance, Saul led the family back to the little hotel, and within minutes, everyone was fast asleep.

The next day, the train veered inland from the Adriatic coast and brought the Kestners to Milan, easily the second city in Italy. Milan did not depend on tourism the way Venice did, and it seemed much more alive and better fed. Saul could find little stores that sold yogurt, something they had not seen in months, and others that had nuts and raisins.

"This is great," declared Rajko, who had never seen such a bustling metropolis. "This is much better than the stinky canals."

"No it isn't," Ljerka protested, "It's more fun to have boats on the streets than cars."

Despite their skimpy funds, Saul was ready to treat his brood to an evening at the famous La Scala – after all, they had cause to celebrate – but unfortunately there was no opera that night, only a politically motivated program honoring contemporary Fascist and Nazi composers.

Saul's disappointment about the Scala was compensated the following day, when they arrived in Como. He, Clara, and all three children were intoxicated by the natural beauty of the city, partly nestled at the foot of a mountain, wrapping around the curving shore of the lake bearing the same name. With a cable car and a pleasant walk they reached the summit of a hill, allowing them to look further up the alluring and spectacular shores of the lake, which had taken a bend. And there, straight ahead, just a few miles away, Saul saw the snow-capped Alps in Switzerland. How many millions of people, himself included, would give anything and everything to be on the other side of that line which men drew on the face of the earth and called a border!

There had not been many refugees assigned to the province of Como when the Kestners arrived at the prefect's office, which sent several clerks scurrying around in confusion. With a bit of patience and a great deal of good will, the problem was solved, and the Kestners were sent in the company of a carabiniere in a spiffy dark uniform and a characteristic Napoleonic hat, to a small town called Fieno.

It was already dark when the Kestners stepped off the trolley, which ran between Como and Lecco, and they set foot on the pavement of the town, where they were to remain for the duration of the war. The moonless night enveloped the houses, and only barely perceptible threads of light outlined an occasional window, which had been paper-covered on the inside to comply with the mandated black-out. With faltering steps, the carabiniere led the way to a small inn, where the Kestners were warmly welcomed, being the only guests. A modest spaghetti dish, reflecting the constraints of the war economy, was prepared while two rooms were readied. The carabiniere bade everyone good night, and departed.

When Saul and Clara woke up the following morning, they looked inquisitively out the window and were greeted by blue skies extending from East to West and North to South, limpid and unmarred by a single cloud. Everything sparkled in a glorious sunburst, and Clara exclaimed: "This looks like heaven on earth."

After a meager breakfast, Saul set out with his family to explore the town. At the end of the block the street opened onto a cobble-stoned piazza with a fountain at its center. Two- and three-story houses surrounded the square, an occasional one with a store on the ground level, all of which were closed, except for the bakery, from which emanated the most delicious smell of freshly baked bread, and a store that sold milk and ice pops. A rather plain small white church with a disproportionately large tower dominated the scene. A woman who came out of the bakery nodded a greeting to Clara and Saul. The scent of flowering acacia, which hung in white grape-like clusters from a number of trees, perfumed the whole town.

"What a place for imprisonment!" exclaimed Clara enthusiastically. "It is fit for a king!"

"Yes, and kings too have had their exiles," Saul said out loud, and added to himself, so the children would not hear, "and have also had to dodge the executioners." Then he added, "Fortunately for us,

Mussolini, whatever his inclinations or exploits are, does not share with Hitler an intense desire to torture or kill us." But how strongly Mussolini felt about his autonomy, or how determined he would be to resist deportation, especially of the foreign exiles, if pressure were applied from Berlin, was anybody's guess. Nor did Saul know how keen Germany would be to interfere in Italian sovereignty over a handful of "undesirables" like his family.

"The contrast between Italian and German occupation," Saul continued, "is incredible. Since we are in free confinement, and not in that large camp in the South, we will actually get a small allowance, quite insufficient, but it will help us pay the rent."

The church bells were now tolling, reminding everyone to come to the morning mass, and groups, mostly of women in their Sunday best, with their children in tow, little boys in short pants and little girls dolled up in pretty dresses with bows in their hair, hurried to the main church.

The path the Kestners had taken intersected the paved street with the trolley tracks that had brought them the day before, and continued as a side street that meandered upwards and away from the main thoroughfare, no longer flanked by sidewalks. Ljerka skipped along, playing imaginary hopscotch, and Rajko found a few little stones, which he stuffed into his pocket, claiming that he had found diamonds and rubies. The road now wound around a small green hill, and beyond that Saul could see a larger hill, the top of which had been eroded to its stony core. The street narrowed and at that level seemed hemmed in by two stucco walls. "Wow!" exclaimed Peter, who was walking a few steps ahead of the others, and a gasp escaped Clara's lips as she caught up. The wall on one side was partly interrupted by a slightly recessed wrought-iron gate, and between the metal bars a magical vista opened up, an enchanting garden with lush green grass gently sloping downward. At its center presided a little stone cupid over a fountain encircled by large balls of flowering pink and sky blue hydrangeas, and beyond was a semicircle of cypresses. Over the sloping edge they glimpsed the main church, and to the left, a portion of the square with its squat little church and oversized "campanile," from which bells now tolled chaotically. A bit farther another magic garden opened up on the other side, as a small gate breached the wall, which up to then had hidden the little green gem of shrubs and spruce from prying eyes. In the direction of Lecco Saul saw a little splash of water, a small lake, and on the horizon beyond, hovered a mountain shaped like the teeth of a saw.

A young man whizzed by on a bicycle singing an Alpine song in a thin falsetto voice. Clara smiled, obviously delighted. Saul glanced at his watch.

"It is time to go to the police station to report. I inquired at the inn, and it is not far from here." He carefully took out a piece of paper on which the innkeeper had drawn a map for him, and he felt his breast pocket for the third time, to reassure himself that he still had the assignment papers he had gotten at the prefecture in Como. "Tomorrow I will also have to go to the mayor's office, just to check in."

"Will the children have to report to the police station every day?" Clara inquired.

"At least at the beginning. But we'll have to do something about Rajko and Ljerka, so they won't giggle during roll call. Fortunately our escort last night had a sense of humor."

"Saul, even I find those Napoleonic hats the carabinieri are wearing extremely funny."

"Indeed they are. How different from the goose-stepping Germans!" Even the police here, Saul thought, had an air of unreality, an air of theatrics. It felt at the moment as if he were in a fairyland.

After the initial novelty of Fieno wore off, Saul began sorely to miss work. He wondered sometimes what deficiency, what inner defect, he possessed not to be able to simply sit and wait. Could he not for once stay idle without a sense of guilt? Did he have to prove himself every day anew, to justify the daily bread he consumed? He reflected, as he paced up and down the floor of the small apartment they were able to rent, that in the rare instances when he was asked for his opinion, which was mostly in the realm of the spirit, he was totally ineffectual. This situation arose shortly, when several other Jewish émigrés arrived. Perhaps because he had come there first, or because of his profession, he became their adviser and unofficial leader, and his life became intertwined with theirs more than was to his liking.

It was old Ben Lieberman, who called on Saul most often. His only son had perished with group D, and just like Friedman, whom Saul and Robert had met on a street in Zagreb, Lieberman constantly concocted new theories about the whereabouts of those boys. He and his wife were immersed in an aura of despair, which virtually exuded from them, sometimes stifled, but mostly overt, with periods of frank depression enveloping the wife, and brief periods of mania possessing the husband, as he discovered a new harbor for their son.

"I have the latest information," words would sprout under pressure in disorderly sequence from Lieberman as he cornered Saul, leaving the old man quite short of breath. Saul had to calm him down and agree that the whole incredible story, the product of the man's confabulation, was not only possible, but quite likely. Within a few hours Lieberman amplified, rearranged, and polished up the story, which was then ready for presentation to his wife. Perhaps he invented such tales to counter his wife's depression, and ended up believing them himself.

"Please come and see my wife," he often begged Saul.

Mrs. Lieberman was a meek little woman, looking much older that her years, spending most of her waking hours crying. To soothe her, the husband would continue repeating the last version of his salvation stories, but his word rang hollow with repetition. The less she believed, the more adamant he became, and he yelled at her when she did not stop crying, despite the "good news" he had brought her. His frustration stemming from his helplessness to console her and his anger that she demolished his own illusions, prodded him stubbornly on, and seemed to poison his mind. His patience had been stretched too far, his balance made precarious. And so he yelled at her, criticized, quarreled, insulted, tormented, and embittered the only loved human being he still possessed, till all that remained between them were memories and mutual misery. Instead of consoling each other as they walked in the twilight of their lives, they became hostile partners kept together by force of habit. Saul could readily diagnose depression, but there was nothing that he could do to alter the quarrelsome, irrational old man, or help the grieving old woman, whose main joy in life had been her son.

Nor could Saul help Stella beyond an ice pack for her eye. The young lady in question was a striking looking redhead with hazel eyes and a finely chiseled face, whose arrival in Fieno led to a small commotion among several male internees. Just as she had never noticed that people in the streets of her native Zagreb would turn their heads to stare at her when she passed by, she was now unaware of the stir she caused. Stella, a budding actress at the repertory theater in Zagreb, had been engaged to Boris, a journalist, who shortly after the German occupation was arrested and was never seen or heard from again. Had it not been for her married sister, who from the Italian-occupied Dalmatian coast bombarded her with messages, Stella would not have left Zagreb. Out of loneliness and a desire to join her sister, rather than any inkling for survival, she drifted to the occupied coast, but the Italian bureaucracy denied her the soothing companionship of her sister's family, and sent her to Fieno, a tiny leaf blown by the wind, landing when the wind momentarily ceased to blow.

Stella often came to the Kestners, not for advice, but for support. "Some days I have hope," she would say, tears flowing from her hazel eyes like water from a fountain, "But today I feel that Boris has perished…or perhaps is dying this very moment." She seemed so small and vulnerable, so childlike. Saul felt utterly helpless to console her, and on more than one occasion he found himself holding her in his arms, as if she were Ljerka, and stroking the shimmering copper in her hair. And down deep inside an old wound seemed to reopen ever so slightly. No, not Ljerka. Tamara.

Among the various refugee arrivals were a group of five young men from a village in Serbia. They gathered around Stella like bees around honey. For a few days she accepted their attention as a bit of harmless distraction, but she soon tired of their company. One of the five, Alfred, was totally smitten by Stella, and after a brief pursuit by Alfred, Stella put an end to it.

"I wish I could learn to love Alfred," Stella told Clara during one of her afternoon visits to the Kestners.

"Alfred is an attractive young man," Clara said, trying to promote a romance.

"For me this has been just a superficial flirtation, meaningless repartees. There is no substance, no involvement of the soul. In fact, the contrast with Boris is making me more miserable." Two large tears poised momentarily on the edge of her lower lids, before they slid down her cheeks. "There is none of the magic I felt when Boris and I found each other. I remember it so well. I had known him for some time before, just another acquaintance among many, until that fateful Sunday picnic, when he stood up and made a plea for some villagers in Macedonia he was writing about for the newspaper. His words struck a chord, which echoed inside me, and that instant I felt my heart leap out of my chest and fly to him." She paused, gulped, and a fresh crop of tears streamed down her flushed cheeks. "There will never be anyone else for me!"

"A beautiful young woman like you," Clara persisted, but Stella cut her off.

"It's no use! I tried. Alfred just increases my agony, and I find myself irked by his presence. In my mind's eye, I keep seeing Boris. Somehow the illusory man seems to have more flesh and blood and substance than the real one standing next to me." She dabbed her face with a handkerchief. "How long had that moment lasted when Boris and I looked into each other's eyes at that Sunday picnic? It was just an instant, but in my mind I have lived it over and over, days and nights, and I will live with it for the rest of my life." Then turning from Clara to Saul, she added: "Tell me, Doctor, how long does a moment last that has been captured in one's heart and stretched for a lifetime?"

When Stella left, Saul felt exasperated and looked to Clara for sympathy. "I am a black bag and stethoscope doctor, not a miracle worker. I can't bring the dead back to life."

"She is being over-dramatic. An actress, you know. And you have been more to your patients than just 'the doctor.'"

It was true. No one could accuse him of shunning the spiritual or personal problems. On the contrary, the farmers flocked to him to discuss what crops to plant, how to deal with a shrewish spouse or a straying scion, and a whole spectrum of human dilemmas, tribulations, or consequences of ignorance and poverty. He was far more comfortable dealing with any of the problems that the generally stoic, often illiterate, peasants presented to him, than these more complicated, sophisticated urbanized men and women, who now seemed to assail his competence.

Saul thought again about Stella, how different she was from Olga, another one of the internees, also from Zagreb, who had arrived right after Stella.

"How ironic life can sometimes be!" he told Clara, shaking his head.

Olga's husband, Leon, had been swept up into the officers' corps by the general mobilization in March of the previous year, just before the war began. During the brief clash between the German Panzers and Yugoslav bayonets, his unit was captured somewhere in Bosnia. It was cumbersome for the Germans to imprison all the captured men, so they allowed the soldiers to disband, but they detained the officers in makeshift field camps. This measure proved sufficient to break the backbone of the Yugoslav army, separating the foot soldier from his leadership.

After the initial detention and questioning, Leon was sent to Germany to a prisoner-of-war camp, not as a Jew, but as an enemy officer. After that, the trail grew cold, and Olga no longer heard from him.

Olga was one of those tiny fragile creatures whose pale face made her look like a porcelain doll, whom men had the impulse to protect. No sooner had she arrived in Fieno, than a champion presented himself wishing to shield her from any mishap, and offered her his broad shoulder to rest her little head on. It was Milan, the oldest of the quintet of men from Serbia, a rather virile looking man of thirty-eight who had narrowly escaped marriage on several occasions.

Olga unabashedly told Clara and Saul, "I need something or someone concrete, not just a hope that I might last out the war, that my husband might survive against great odds, and that someday we might pick up the threads of our lives where we had left them off."

Under more normal circumstances, Olga might have weathered the separation, but in those days, when the present was oppressive and the future unfathomably remote, a man of flesh and blood who could caress her troubled brow was much more real than the memory of one who perhaps was already dead. Shortly after Olga's arrival, Milan moved in with her. "The present is too frightening to be borne alone," she declared. "I need someone to love me." Despite the condemnation and scorn that sometimes came her way from the other internees, Olga insisted that the world had gone berserk, and that she and Milan needed "an oasis in this world of chaos."

Gradually Olga's lover came to totally eclipse Leon, who receded into a reservoir of past memories she was aware of but could hardly believe were ever part of her existence.

"My life with my husband seems to me like an episode in a movie I have seen, or a minor sub-plot in a novel I have read," she tried to explain to Clara.

Clara shook her head as she later commented to Saul, "Olga's past with her husband is like an isolated bar of sand in a bay, or a small mountain lake with no connection to the mainstream of her life. He neither belongs to cherished memories of her past, nor to the struggles of the present."

"Life is so ironic, as I've been saying over and over lately," Saul added. "Olga's unwanted husband might survive, keeping himself alive by fanning cherished hopes through the long years of military imprisonment, only to find out that for him his wife is dead. And on the other hand, Stella is remaining loyal to a young man who will never return."

"Olga and Milan are shutting their eyes and pretending the fiery world in clashing arms does not exist." They – Adam and Eve – lived alone in a timeless misty world, drinking deeply from the pools of love.

Clara added, "Even those who survive may be losers."

Saul found his forced idleness demoralizing. Clara somehow managed better to occupy her time, after the morning report to the police. Purchasing food and preparing meals for her family was often time consuming and a challenge, and it provided her with a worthy cause. On many afternoons she would take Peter and the twins to a small nearby lake for swimming, along with some neighbor Italian children, who readily attached themselves, prattling in lively Italian.

On cooler days she would take them on hikes in the neighboring hills, respecting the distance limits imposed by their internee status.

Saul's mind kept wondering, as he tried to look into the future, beyond the struggles and turmoil of the war. It was clear that they would all be scarred by it, but he suspected that there were some whose wounds would never heal, whose lives would be so shattered they might never be able to put the pieces together again. And these things happened because their great grandfathers happened to be Jewish, and in turn their great grandfathers had been Jewish, for who knows how many generations back. He felt a pain, not as if it came from a wound in his flesh, but a general grief, a painful sadness, as he had not experienced since his teens.

It was a mad world, and all the internees seemed to be swept along by the current. Everyone, except Rajko; the boy was the only one who did not brood like Peter and Ljerka, or despair like the adults.

Without having his time occupied by the symptoms and ailments afflicting the citizens of Grad, Saul struggled to preserve his equanimity. He was particularly fond of Stella, the sad and beautiful Stella, who now was avoiding Alfred as best she could. When it finally dawned on the young man that she was neither honored nor overjoyed by his amorous advances, which according to him, she should have been, he turned his resentment on her.

"She is putting on airs," he told everyone, "because she came from the big city, and I, a Jew from the provinces, am not good enough for her. She has listened to my declarations of love, only to mock me and make a fool of me. At roll call she converses endlessly with that old fool, Lieberman; not that she can possibly find him entertaining, but because she knows that he and I are not on speaking terms, since that silly affair about a few pounds of black market potatoes."

When weeks later Stella and Alfred came face to face on the dark stairway to the town dentist's office, she greeted him with a slight nod and tried quickly to pass him by. To her dismay, he grabbed her arm and yanked her towards him. A moment later he had his arms around her and was kissing her. An exclamation of surprise peeled off her lips, and she instinctively pushed him away, which kindled rage and unreason in Alfred's simple mind. He suddenly gave her a shove. She veered to one side, lost her footing, and rolled down half a flight of stairs. A few Italian youngsters, who were kicking around a soccer ball, interrupted their play and helped the "bella signorina" to her feet. And that was how Saul came to treat Stella's black eye with ice packs from the ice cream parlor, an eye that she camouflaged with dark eyeglasses for a week. But for her intense loneliness and increasing isolation he had no remedy.

"We all seem to be unraveling," Saul complained to Clara.

"It is the gains Rommel has made in North Africa, and the advances of the German generals on the Russian front after they regrouped from the winter losses, that have set us all on edge...and on a collision course with each other."

It was just the other day that Lieberman and that queer Mr. Ungar had made a scene in the street. Ungar, originally from Germany, was the last refugee to arrive in Fieno. He was a strange man with rodent like teeth and cavernous eyes, well on in the middle years of his life. There were two discrepant stories about him, neither of which he confirmed or denied. Depending on the season, or some other rotating denominator, he fostered one or the other of these, cloaking a definitive answer in mystery.

According to one version, Ungar was a widower. He had married an exceedingly beautiful young girl who fell victim to leukemia and died in a matter of weeks – a rare flower plucked in the prime of life, a loss he could never replace, never forget – the Cinderella, the Snow White, the Sleeping Beauty without the happy ending.

The other and more prevalent, though less romantic version had it that Ungar was still bound by matrimony to a middle-aged Amazon of pure Teutonic extraction, who did not feel the necessity to follow her husband into exile, and had remained in the Fatherland. At this juncture there were two further subplots: namely, that Brunhilde had remained behind at great sacrifice, to help from within if possible, while preserving their nest for the future, cut off ultimately from any communication with her husband. Or alternatively, that she was glad to be rid of him, denying valid legal ties.

Saul believed neither. The man seemed to concoct stories for personal aggrandizement. Seemingly Ungar had been alone, rootless, and jobless as he escaped from Germany to Austria, and thence on to Italy after the "Anschluss." He was allowed to travel unimpeded, but not allowed to take up residence in Italy, and for lack of alternatives, he tried to reach Palestine, which had led him to Libya, an Italian colony since its conquest in 1912. There he joined a handful of Jewish families, who like himself, were looking for boat passage to the Holy Land. Such a boat was eventually found in Tripoli, and it cost dearly to hire, for the risk was great, and not many boat owners were willing to undertake it. At the appointed time in the middle of the night, when the passengers arrived at the prearranged quay, the boat, the captain, the crew, and the money were gone. Ungar was eventually sent back to the mainland, where he was confined to central Italy, and later was transferred to Fieno.

"What seems most remarkable to me," Saul commented to Clara, as they walked to their daily report, "is how much Ungar needs to magnify himself." Whenever this puny little man was addressed as "Mister," he would correct the speaker, "Dr. Ungar, if you please," claiming to have doctoral degrees, both in law and philosophy. "I am certain that his education has not gone beyond secondary school. Not that that would have stopped him from becoming successful, but he claims to be what he is not."

"And what difference would the degrees make in the present circumstances, if he had them?"

"You would think that with all the troubles and toils of long exile, Ungar would at least have learned some humility.

"At least Ungar's deceptions are harmless," Saul continued. "I have heard about another man, alas Jewish, who posed as a physician, when he was only a dental technician. In this false capacity, facilitated by the crisis of war, he provided medical care, but fortunately it was only for a very short time."

"Apparently persecution and suffering are not soul cleansing, and the victims do not emerge ennobled. At least not from what we have seen!"

"On the contrary, sometimes the worst is dragged out of people, with fate and misfortune shattering the character, stretching morality, and forging deceit."

On that particular day, Ungar made another scene in the street, threatening to jump out of a window, or drown himself in the lake. "It looks as if the Germans will win the war after all," he said hysterically. “Last year’s British success in Africa all came to naught, the Germans have taken Tobruk, and will surely not stop now till they cross the Nile and reach Suez. They are not even meeting any resistance; they are simply waltzing through North Africa.... The whole African campaign has been nothing but a farce, and the long hoped for third front seems never to materialize. It is just a dream for us, and propaganda for the BBC. What is the use of remaining alive in Italy, if the Germans are going to win? Even in Russia they are winning again.”

Saul tried to pacify him, and calm down the others, who also were shaken by Ungar’s predictions.

“These are difficult times,” Saul argued. “Another front will surely open up in France, and once it does, it will gain momentum like an avalanche.” But Saul, too, felt not entirely convinced that the landing would be soon enough for people like himself and his family, whose sand seemed to be running out of the hourglass, but this doubt he kept to himself.

CHAPTER 15

As the weeks went by in Fieno, steeped in seemingly endless sunshine, Peter lingered indoors. The twins played outside, befriended by neighborhood children, but he kept busy reading the Italian newspapers "between the lines," as he called it. He spent hours on end copying maps of the Russian front, and only once in a while, in the worst heat, did he treat himself to a swim in the nearby lake. The beach was empty most of the time, and that was the way he liked it. Local people considered swimming unhealthy, and some, particularly older women, furtively whispered about hidden enemy submarines at the bottom of the waters. Lake Como, especially, was considered to be infested by submarines, which according to the believers, had been launched from nearby Switzerland, but even smaller satellite lakes and ponds were viewed with apprehension. And so the people of the town avoided the waters, just as their ancestors had done centuries before, fearing that dangerous and evil spirits lurked at the depths.

Sometimes Peter would join his family and a few of the fellow internees, most two or three times his age. The group would gravitate in the hot dry summer evenings past the Jesuit school, where a low brick wall marked the end of the grounds, providing comfortable seating. They would thrash out old and new fragmentary news, speculate what military moves might, would, or should the Allies undertake the next day or next week, repeat the same old stories they had told each other before, and dreamt of better days – and of liberation. They sat there, welcoming a refreshing breeze, which set the evening apart from the scorching day, falling silent as the evening progressed. A myriad of stars flickered above them, and every so often one would inscribe a slender silvery line across the sky as it burned to dust.

"One, two, three," Rajko counted, the bright streaks. "Seven, eight…twelve, thirteen, fourteen."

“If you make a wish on the falling stars,” Ljerka told her brother, “it will come true.”

“Shush, I’m counting! Eighteen, nineteen.”

“I’ve never seen so many stars,” Clara declared with obvious awe. “No wander Galileo was Italian.”

Peter felt a pang. He remembered the evening two years ago, no, a century ago, when he and Silvia had gazed at the stars in Grad, and into each other’s eyes. He thought a great deal about her, the Silvia he had once known, not the one she might now be. He saw her now in the moonlight under the magical carpet of stars, as a beautiful goddess bearing the image of the girl he loved, but having become a deity, she eluded him, and he was becoming resigned that she was unattainable. Though he had relinquished almost all hope to possess the girl he loved, he had not relinquished his love for her.

On some days, when his mind played tricks and eliminated the distance that time had placed between the past and the present, he still grasped for her, filled with incredible longing and torment, but such moments were becoming less and less frequent.

Then one day a face pulled Peter away from his maps. He had stood in the street alone waiting for his family to go for the daily police report, when he heard a clip-clop of wooden shoes against the pavement. A girl, maybe sixteen, looked at him boldly and smiled – or perhaps laughed at him – as she passed by. She walked slowly, swaying her hips, and disappeared into a shop down the street, leaving him in a state of utter confusion. There was something about this girl, Peter could not put his finger on exactly what, something in the way she carried her head and the way her lips pouted, that was reminiscent of Silvia. He felt as though Silvia’s phantom had walked by, although in fact there was little genuine resemblance between the two.

The next day Peter came down early, hoping to catch another glimpse of the Italian girl. He could not conjure up the girl’s face, and all that his mind’s eye saw was Silvia’s face, and yet he could not put the girl out of his mind. “Ridiculous,” he said out loud, kicking a small pebble against the stoop. There was no question that he waited in the street only to return the mocking stare.

As if by appointment, the Italian girl came at the same hour, a basket over her arm, weaving her way slowly, and brazenly locked her eyes onto his, holding on to his perplexed gaze until she was well past. Peter was furious and promised himself not to go out so early, but the following day he was in the street even earlier, impatiently pacing in front of the house, anxious that she should come before he had to leave for roll call.

Within a week Peter became acquainted with the girl – it was she who broke the silence – and learned that her name was Marisa, a contraction for Maria Luisa, that her mother had died a few years ago, and that she no longer attended school, for lack of interest and necessity to keep house for an eight year old brother and a semi-alcoholic father.

At closer range Marisa seemed as bold as she had appeared initially, and her haughty manner and provocative smile made the blood rush through Peter's veins and his heart pound. Attractive, though not beautiful like Silvia, her face nonetheless seemed to bewitch him, and there was this amazing quality about her looks which seemed to superimpose on Silvia's image and blend into a composite, which Peter had trouble separating. He was utterly confused, wondering whether he still loved Silvia, or Marisa, or was he so fickle that he loved both?

After many months of pain, Peter felt warm and alive, and the world around him, which had been flat, seemed to become full and round and acquire a new dimension. Marisa's pouting lips beckoned invitingly, and for his part, Peter was willing to follow wherever she might lead him. She took him away from his maps and the Russian front, and after a few evening strolls and passionate kisses, she led him on afternoon hikes into the hills and woods where she taught him in out of the way spots, behind bushes, to do things he had never done with Silvia. From her he learned of a sweetness he had not known existed.

Peter could not tell how much Marisa really cared about him – it seemed more spite and rebelliousness on her part than love – but he did not dwell on this. With their growing familiarity, Peter no longer wondered in Marisa's absence which way the outlines of her face curved, and he might have drawn a reasonable facsimile of her. He had more trouble now calling up Silvia's face. But somehow the abstract physiognomies of the two girls still overlapped and fused into one. His feelings, too, seemed to fuse, and he continued with his predicament of not knowing which of the two he loved. Sometimes it seemed one, and sometimes the other. If the two somehow blended into one another, were one and the same, then he could carry in his heart the same love for both. He hungered for the heat of Marisa's body, of which the more he partook, the more he desired, but when his thoughts led him into the past, he could still exhume his old feelings for Silvia, as if nothing had happened in the interim; as if a hypnotist had mesmerized him back in time, and the more recent months were erased. Were he confronted simultaneously by both girls he had no idea what would have happened. He was annoyed with himself, and full of guilt. There was something utterly stupid in the confusion between the two girls. Why couldn't he possess the clear-sightedness his father had? If he only were a little older and wiser, no not older – older people could also be quite foolish – but somehow wiser, to reach a rational solution.

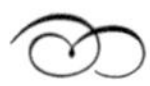

When the rainy season came up, the radiance of the little Italian town faded into a chilly drizzle. Food shortages, which everyone had supplemented with seasonal fruits and vegetables, became painfully evident. The small refugee colony grew more restless.

One day Ungar and one of the quintet, as Peter referred to the group of five, had come to blows on the main town thoroughfare, like two little schoolboys, over a non-existent secret tunnel to Switzerland. After that, Ungar and Comforti carefully chose different hours to visit his parents, lest they should run into one another. His father was, like the secretary of a league of nations, receiving different warring factions and acting as a peacemaker. Lieberman and Alfred were still not on speaking terms, and Stella avoided all of "The Five."

Even his parents, Peter felt, showed increasing signs of tension. His father, who never so much as cut a deck of cards before, now spent hours playing solitaire, asking the cards to answer the riddle, as if they were a sphinx, such as "Will the war end next fall?" or "Will it end the following spring?" If the same answer came out three times in a row, he would try to convince Clara – and probably himself – that the statistic was valid. His previously handsome face now bore several corrugating lines of weight loss, and he did not hide his disappointment that a new front had been opened in North Africa, instead of France. Clara remained silent throughout these mumbo-jumbos, and only shook her head.

Peter could sometimes feel his mother's probing and anxious eyes resting on him, but as soon as he looked at her, she would pretend to be doing something else. Occasionally he could see her lower lip tremble, and once he thought he saw a tear well up in the corner of her eye, as he felt her gaze caressing him. At other times she stared at the twins or would exuberantly hug and kiss them, and contrary to her usual outspokenness, kept her thoughts to herself.

The gloom of the adults spread to Peter, and he and Marisa quarreled. It started quite innocently, when she asked him how come he never went to church. The question of religion had not surfaced in their earlier conversations, nor was she a devout worshiper, participating only episodically in confession and communion following attacks of stricken conscience. When Peter answered that he was Jewish, she looked at him in amazement. "You can't be!" she blurted out. "You don't have horns and a tail!" Her words had been so simple and unaffected, that he could not help but laugh. He had heard Jews accused of a thousand and one things before, but of such an allegation he had never heard before.

"You are making fun of me, telling such preposterous lies. I know better than that." She quickly crossed herself.

Peter, stung by her persistence, took refuge in retreat, and they temporarily broke off their affair.

But with all the gloom and dampness of the 1942-43 winter, as the weeks went by, his father declared that the turning point in the war was finally at hand. The Germans were once again suffering tremendous losses on the Russian front, and the colder it got, the better. Despite the German propaganda claims to the contrary, the defeat at Stalingrad had broken the backbone of the German army.

CHAPTER 16

Clara looked under the bed. There were so few potatoes left to feed her family. How was she going to stretch them till the spring, when the street vendors would be selling peas, and a little later other vegetables and fruit to supplement the meager rations. Last week she was lucky to be able to buy some cornmeal at the store with the ration cards. She cooked the cornmeal till it was quite thick, and when she turned it out of the pot, it had a perfectly round cake-like shape, though it was rather thin. She had also bought a small packet of powder to make chocolate pudding, but since she had never succeeded in buying milk in Fieno, she cooked the powder in water and then spread the watery pudding on top of the corn mush. There it was, she was proud of it, a golden cake with a chocolate topping for the twins' birthday. It was meant to last for two servings, but everyone looked at the remaining half so longingly that she let Saul and the children finish it off.

"This is the best birthday cake I ever had," Rajko declared, and as usual, was seconded by Ljerka.

Clara looked at her hands and massaged them. They were supposed to be the hands of a pianist and not kitchen hands. She had no access to a piano and had not played since her piano had been requisitioned about a year and a half earlier. At convenient moments the dining room table became a keyboard as she played imaginary scales to keep her fingers nimble so that one day she would still be able to reasonably play Chopin – these fingers that one of her teachers had predicted would some day play in great concert halls. No, she was not suited for that; she did not have what it would take to climb that ladder. She yearned too much to share her life with Saul and the children, perhaps because as a youngster she often felt alone. Her parents were good honest people, but as ordinary as the grass and the daisies that pushed up from the ground in the park. She felt she had little in common with them and that they did not understand her. Nor could she bring herself to tell Tamara about all her inner thoughts, dreams, and longings, Tamara who seemed so clever and who thought Clara hopelessly romantic and silly. When she was growing up, Clara buried her loneliness in music lessons, longing for a companion who would share her thoughts, who would value her strengths and tolerate her shortcomings. Perhaps no one existed like this imaginary soul mate she had created in her daydreams, but she could not get away from a feeling that she was not whole, and was searching for the missing portion of herself – the proverbial other half. Perhaps that was the real meaning of Adam's rib, and maybe the Good Lord had taken a rib out of Eve and given it to Adam. Her parents and friends had tried to marry her off to candidates who were as conventional as the matchmakers. Clara insisted she would sooner become a nanny, if she did not succeed at the conservatory, than marry one of them. With that she plunged herself even deeper into the world of etudes and nocturnes.

When Tamara brought Saul to meet the family, Clara instantly fell for that little twinkle in his left eye, which sadly she realized was rarely evident these days. When she met him she immediately decided that he was much more appealing than the imaginary companion she had yearned for, and after she heard him talk with great compassion about one of his patients, she discarded the mythical model she had created in her mind for the real man of flesh and blood before her. Of course, this particular one belonged to Tamara – Tamara always won out – but at least Clara became convinced that there could be someone who would capture her imagination. With all her heart she hoped that one day they would find each other.

When Saul proposed to Clara, she knew that she would have to live for some time under Tamara's shadow, but she was absolutely convinced that she was better for him than Tamara had ever been, and besides, she never quite got over that heart-warming infatuation she had experienced when she first met him.

"Enough of dreaming about the past," Clara told herself. "I have to scrape together a meal." She decided to extend the potatoes by mixing them together with cabbage. No one liked it, but nobody complained about it, not even Rajko. The children seemed to sense the difficult situation. She had planned to cook some of the spaghetti she had succeeded in buying the previous month with the ration cards, but she had no meat, no sauce, nothing to embellish it. She would drizzle a little olive oil over the pasta, but there was not a speck of the grating cheese left. Perhaps there would be a new shipment at the store tomorrow, she was desperate to buy some, but somehow with each passing month there was less and less on the store shelves. Even last year's shortages seemed a feast to her now. Perhaps Saul could ask their Italian neighbor, the bicycle shop owner, to help him buy more black market potatoes.

Clara could not resist escaping from the daily chore of scraping together meals and returning to her daydreams, to the glorious day when Saul had asked her to marry him. Whether it was a rational conclusion, instinct, blind faith, or even sheer madness, she had an unshakeable conviction that the marriage was the best decision for both of them. And indeed, there followed several happy years in Grad, where Saul established his medical practice, eventually being appointed as county physician, and she gave piano lessons to a handful of willing and unwilling children. Peter and later, the twins, blossomed out. As roses have thorns, so beautiful things in life may have their stings. From time to time Clara could not repress a feeling of jealousy that Saul had once loved someone else as much or possibly more than her. On the other side of this painful coin was the feeling of guilt that Tamara had had to die so that she could marry the man for whom she had fallen.

Clara's thoughts returned to those happy days in Grad. Saul had established himself as a dedicated practitioner, respected by the local population, and loved, yes loved was the right word, by many of the simple warm-hearted villagers in the outlying areas. He had worked too hard, Clara was convinced, but he obviously enjoyed the challenge, and somehow, no matter how busy he was, he found the time to discuss his daily activities with her, to play with the children during free intervals, and to chat with his patients and their families. It was this constant ebb and flow of predictably unpredictable activity that had filled Saul's and Clara's lives with a feeling of accomplishment and satisfaction.

The war and the displacement had disrupted the normal pulse of their life, and she was worried about Saul, though she tried not to show her concerns. He needed his work, his immersion in other people's concerns. Or was that all? Somehow Clara felt that he had distanced himself from her lately; he no longer shared his daily thoughts with her the way he had done in Grad, despite the fact that he had been so busy. Was it because they spent so much time together in the same two rooms day in and day out that he found less and less to say to her? Were their lives falling victim to circumstances, as did the lives of several other refugees in Fieno? Was that all, or had their marriage become mired in stagnation and estrangement? Everything in life, she believed, grew and evolved, or there was a danger it might wither; but now their lives were static, on hold, and there seemed nothing that she could do to countermand the situation. Or was it all in her imagination? By instinct Clara recoiled from such ruminations. It was useless to dwell on conjectures or possible self-recriminations. She had to look ahead, and not look back to risk being turned into a pillar of salt.

And then there was Peter. The boy, no, the young man, had turned nineteen, had become taciturn, and often seemed sad. Clara guessed that he still pined for Silvia, though for some reason he never talked about her either to her or his father. As an adult Clara had always viewed herself as a caretaker, a mender of hurt feelings, a dresser of scraped knees, the tireless guardian of her family. When she married Saul, she could soothe his and Peter's lives. Now Peter had grown up and she and Saul seemed to have drifted apart. Only the twins still needed her.

As she stirred the Savoy cabbage with the potatoes, she wished she had a smidgeon of bacon to add to the mixture. When Peter and the twins walked in, the twins went to the bedroom to play a game. Clara noticed Peter's handsome figure, his bearing lately resembling his father's, and he had Tamara's beautiful eyes.

Peter came over to Clara and asked, "What was my mother like?" Clara was taken aback. She had not expected the question. He had never asked about Tamara.

"She was very beautiful. Like most beautiful women, she was pampered…but she always knew exactly what she wanted. She loved you and Papa very much, and I am sure that she would be very proud of you."

"I wish so much that I could remember her." He went over to the window and looked out.

Clara couldn't help feeling a little slighted; was it jealousy? Was Peter, too, estranged from her? She went back to stirring the pot so that the potato-cabbage mixture, prepared with very little water not to waste precious vitamins, would not stick and burn. Peter swung around from the window and came over to her. Though their facial features were quite different, there was something in Peter's expression at that moment, especially the way he smiled, that was so reminiscent of Saul.

"I know you are my real mother and I love you," Peter said as he gave Clara a big hug and a kiss.

CHAPTER 17

Saul stared at the rows of cards on the table. The kings, queens, and knaves seemed to mock him, and he threw the rest of the pack in their faces. He was bored with solitaire, with the penetrating wet cold, and with the war, which continued to drag. He always thought that once the turning point would come, the Axis would implode and the war would rapidly end. But such did not seem to be the case. Outside the trees had begun to renew themselves, but inside their small apartment, the winter chill hung on. It was spring, the spring of 1943, and he had resided in Fieno for nearly a year already.

Carefully he set down the wooden spoon, picked up the glass of herbal tea, and tiptoed into the bedroom, where Ljerka was well on the way to recovery from dysentery. Clara, sitting in a chair at the head of the bed, interrupted the reading.

"Papa, the children are safe in the desert. They found an oasis with water. Look here how they are drinking." She pointed to a picture in the book Clara was reading to her.

"You too, darling, need to drink a bit," and he handed her the glass. The girl's face looked a bit pinched and paler than usual, but he was relieved that the symptoms had subsided.

Saul returned to his chair and looked away from his demolished card game. Peter stood motionless at the window, stretching his neck to look up and down the street, hands in his pockets. From the backyard, where Rajko was playing, happy shrieks emanated from youngsters at play.

Saul shuffled the cards, cut the deck, and started again. What else was there to do till tomorrow ten A.M. – till roll call? Of course, some people like Lieberman and Comforti would probably stop by, and if Ungar and Alfred arrived before the others had left, there would be another row.

The refugee colony grew ever more tense. The gnawing hunger had become more constant and intense, and despite Allied victories, tempers grew shorter every day. Minds were bending reality, fostering suspicion if not frank paranoia, and if anyone found a new source of contraband food, he was certain to keep it to himself.

Olga clung more than ever to her new man. Fate had thrown them together, and she would not let it tear them apart. Alfred had grown taciturn, embittered, and vengeful, and on more than one occasion anonymously reported Stella for black marketeering, but a midnight search of her tiny flat turned up only stacks of un-mailed letters written to Andrej.

"No. No one is the same any more," Saul told himself, "not even Clara." She who used to give opinions about everything has now fallen silent, her probing eyes settling on his cards with disapproval.

Damn it, what was she thinking? What else was there to do? The five of them all day long in two small rooms! He missed his privacy, the privacy, for instance, to have a good fight with Clara. And privacy to be with her alone. Soon the afternoon visitors would drop by, but they were no more amusing than the cards. Everyone, except Stella, that is; she was not like the rest. She seemed like the adult version of his Ljerka, and he felt a special sympathy for her.

But was that all? There was something about Stella that reminded him of Tamara, and gave him discomfort. Tamara still seemed to cast at times a shadow on his life, and at unexpected moments her spirit seemed to rise within him like a phoenix.

Stella had not come to visit for several days, and at the morning roll call she looked very pale – not the usual pallor of a redhead, but a waxy transparency of something amiss. He was certain of that, though the exact diagnosis eluded him. "A sixth sense," he used to call it in his medical practice.

No, it was not just intuition, and Stella was not an ordinary patient. He could not see her in proper perspective. Involuntarily he sighed.

"What is the matter?" Clara asked. He had not even noticed that she had returned from an errand.

"Nothing," he snapped. He saw a tear roll down Clara's cheek before she turned her face. Without a conscious decision, Saul found himself on his feet, his arms wrapped around her, as his lips rained kisses on her face. "There is no fool like an old fool," he murmured. He had tried hiding his feelings from her, his restlessness, his boredom, but all it created was a distance between them. She smiled, and something within him seemed to melt.

"Ha, ha, ha." Rajko entered noisily into the room, applauding the domestic scene.

Having regained his normal composure, Saul was reminded again how much he needed Clara, and how their lives were intertwined to help build a fortress within which they resided. Tamara was just a mirage, an occasional subterfuge. Clara was his real companion, his other self, his source of love and comfort and strength.

"Without you I am nothing," he blurted out. How could he possibly have compared Tamara's histrionics, the self-absorption with her exceptional beauty, and the pain she sometimes caused him with her flirtations, to the soothing calm warm relationship he shared with Clara!

"Don't exaggerate, darling. You're just having battle fatigue, like the rest of us." She smiled broadly and mussed his hair.

"I am going to look in on Stella," he announced, totally at ease with himself that he had shaken off any shade of unwanted attraction to this young woman who reminded him of Tamara. "Will you come along? I just have a feeling that there's something wrong."

"Good idea," she replied. "I've been worried about her, and I'd go with you, but I don't want to leave Ljerka just now."

As he approached Stella's apartment, Saul suddenly felt foolish; he partly retraced his steps, but then reconsidered, remembering Clara's encouragement. After all, wasn't it the physician inside him who had taken over and who bade him to follow a hunch?

Stella's tiny apartment was on the second floor of a dilapidated old building. There was something depressing about the pungent musty mousy odor on the landing. He had never been inside the building before. He paused on the steps for a minute, as a strange thought entered his mind. Then he raced up the remaining steps. Yes, he was right, there was no doubt about it. It was the odor of gas he smelled. He rapped on the door. No answer. He turned the doorknob. The door was locked. He smashed his fist against the door, than kicked it hard, and the central panel gave way with a creak. In a flash he was inside, flung the windows open, and shut the flameless burner. Stella lay on the floor nearby, and as Saul carried her to the landing, she gave a faint moan.

"Ah, still in time," he congratulated himself.

Stella opened her eyes and looked somewhat dazed. The pallor in her cheeks turned into a flush. She whimpered, as her whole body was shivering. She indicated that she had a headache and was nauseated, but she would not respond to questions. Was it an accident, or more likely, Saul feared, self-inflicted? And what now? Clearly, she could not be left alone. He did not want to seek official medical help, as she would be harshly dealt with by the authorities, and most likely sent to the camp in Calabria.

"You will come home with me." He had to sound firm enough to be persuasive, without being harsh. He wrapped her in a coat he found in the closet. Then he gently raised her to her feet, as she hung on his arm, her steps somewhat wobbly as they slowly walked down the steps and into the street. Stella's teeth dug into her lower lip, and a few tears rolled down her cheeks. No, he had not expected this from Stella; Mrs. Lieberman yes, but not Stella. As he thought about Mrs. Lieberman, Saul had an idea, and instead of making a left turn at the corner, he turned right, slowly winding past the schoolhouse, past a bicycle shop and a little restaurant, till he reached the Lieberman apartment.

Saul found Mrs. Lieberman sitting in the darkest corner of their small dingy appartment, and after explaining to her what had happened, the old woman sprang to her feet and embraced Stella.

"You must not do that, my child. You must not help our enemy, who wants to destroy us."

"My enemy is within me and all around me," Stella replied. "It is emptiness, and most of all loneliness."

"Then you must stay here with us."

Stella buried her face in the bosom of the older woman, and her agitation seemed to ease a little. It momentarily reminded Saul of a picture he had had in his office of an infant at her mother's breast, the little one taking in the nourishment, the other giving sustenance. He hoped that this arrangement would remain mutually beneficial to the two women, and he had a momentary sense of accomplishment.

“Come, come my dear, you must lie down and rest, and I’ll make you a tea from the chamomile flowers I found near the park.

As he stood there, Saul realized how drained he had become by the rash events of the day. He took leave of Lieberman and the two women, promising to look in on his “patient” the next day, relieved to be leaving her in good hands. When he got out, he could not wait to hug and kiss Clara again.

CHAPTER 18

It was on a crystal clear balmy spring night in 1943 that Saul was awakened by a strange and distant thunder-like rumble. Something sinister seemed to be happening in the silence under the veil of curfew. The left half of the double bed creaked as Clara stirred next to him, and a whimper from Ljerka's corner blended with the purring sound of Rajko's light snore. Saul strained his ears, but he could hear nothing – nothing but the little sleeping noises of his family blending in with a background of nocturnal chirping of insects flowing into the bedroom between the slats of the window shutters – and he wondered whether he had heard anything after all.

Several nights later, Saul again was roused from sleep by a rumbling almost rolling sound, this time accompanied by distant sirens.

"Daddy, what's that?" Rajko shouted as he bolted out of bed.

"I don't know. It's an alarm."

Ljerka slid into the double bed between her parents and snuggled against Saul's arm. Something was happening in the middle of the night, he wasn't just dreaming, he now had witnesses. There was something exciting and yet ominous in the air, but he wasn't sure what it was.

In the morning Saul and Peter scoured the newspapers for any clues, but found none. Without success, Peter hung around the door of the nearby tobacco store in the hope of hearing a customer's comment or of snatching a fragment of the newscast from the tobacconist's radio.

"This is intolerable," Saul kept repeating, "This lack of communications! Something is happening; something is changing in the course of the war."

"But there is nothing in the news. Not a word," Clara retorted. "Local people are going about their business as usual."

"No, just look at the Italians! They are no longer smiling, no longer stopping to chat. They are looking at their feet now when they walk, in order not to look each other in the eye."

"Come let's go out and see who can jump further," Rajko gave Ljerka a tug, but she shook her head.

"You always win anyway."

"Maybe those were drills," Clara suggested, wrinkling her forehead.

"No, no! This thing is too big to lie about. They are simply suppressing official bulletins.... Perhaps preliminaries to a landing. Right now I'd rather be in the midst of pandemonium than be isolated in a rat hole like this."

Clara winced. "Only a year ago this town was a beautiful perfumed haven."

It was not till some days later that Gian Carlo, the owner of the little bicycle shop who lived on the first floor, whispered to Saul on the stairway that Genova had been attacked by sea, and Torino subsequently by air.

Surely no one could have heard the explosions from that far away. Even the bombardment of Turin was hard to imagine, but certainly not Genoa!

Then came yet another clear night in which there was no mistaking. This time not only did the local sirens go off, but the stillness of the country night was broken by the humming sounds of flying fortresses. The sound was so clear and sonorous, it made Saul jump out of bed and run to the window. As he carefully opened the shutters, he thought that in the bright moonlight he could see moving shadows cast on the ground by those mighty airplanes. His heart seemed to race, this time not with the heat of anger or the flutter of fear, but with joy and excitement as if he were on the wings of a bird. At last he could feel the front lines advancing. It was no longer a newscast about battles fought a thousand miles away, which would surely influence the balance of the war – he didn't mean to detract from its significance – but the action was finally here!

Within minutes distinct multiple simultaneous and overlapping explosions were heard.

"They are bombing Milan," Saul concluded, and with rising exhilaration added, "they are going to beat the hell out of the Axis," barely able to hold back the tears of joy which were forcing their way to the surface. The day that he had been waiting for so long – the day of liberation, the day when the war would be over – was finally in sight.

After the first moments of exhilaration had spent themselves, Saul remembered the day they had spent in Milan, and how they had strolled along the wide boulevards, forgetting momentarily the emptiness within their stomachs. And he recalled that Gian Carlo's sister lived there with her husband and two little children. He was delighted that the ring was constricting around the Fascists, but he had gotten to be fond of the Italians. He felt a strange mixture of joy and sadness.

Clara and the children crowded around him at the window. The sky lit up southward with the glow of a thousand distant fires, as if dawn were arriving. Then the explosions died down, and the planes apparently took a different route of return.

"I wonder if my favorite green marble building is still there," Rajko added wistfully.

After the first air strike, Milan suffered several further raids, and the Milanese fled in droves to nearby towns and villages. Saul saw many of them in the streets and shops in Fieno. Lodgings for rent, which had been over-abundant, became extremely scarce, and food even more so. A general atmosphere of uneasiness crept into the entire town. The few loyal Fascist members quaked in their wooden shoes and made themselves inconspicuous. One local opponent even dared with alcoholic courage to parade up and down the main street on a Sunday afternoon belting out anti-Fascist songs. In the old days such behavior would have earned him a sojourn in the jail, and the almost legendary castor oil treatment, which the Italian Fascists used to toxic levels to torture political prisoners.

Even church bells, which were so bountiful in Italy before, ringing chaotically every hour, half hour, and sometimes in between, could no longer be heard; nor did they ring out for mass or vespers. The whole countryside had been silenced, uneasily awaiting doom. Months before, the bells – and there certainly were many of them – had been converted to cannons. Saul and his family, along with a silent crowd of local residents, had witnessed the sad scene in the market place, when the largest of the town bells was removed from its tower and pushed out the steeple window. It came down from the height with a big thud, like an enormous sack of potatoes, followed by a vaguely metallic after-sound. And there it lay cracked in the dust, dishonored, and quite dead, ready to be carted away to a new and different life.

The only things that remained unaffected in the town were the sunshine and the blue skies during the day and the innumerable stars at night.

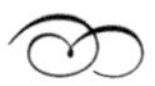

On one of those tense and chaotic days of flying fortresses, distant thunder, and city folks flooding the rural areas, Peter became ill. When Clara and Saul had returned from the daily tally at the Carabinieri station, they found Peter still in bed, his legs drawn up. Saul examined the boy, and as much as he wanted to deny it, his well-trained fingers told him that it was not an ordinary intestinal flu, but an early stage of appendicitis that afflicted Peter. There was no alternative, Saul realized with a funny sensation in his own abdomen, but to have Peter sent to Como for surgery. For this he had to obtain a special permit from the mayor, following medical certification. Though he had not had any personal dealings with the local physician, Saul knew him by sight, and he set out straight away to fetch him.

Dr. Carbone was a rotund little man with a pointed beard and small dark eyes, given to excessive gesticulation with his small chubby hands as he spoke. He seemed absolutely delighted to be called by Saul, exuding his pleasure in a cascade of superlatives. "It is an honor to assist a colleague, who I am told studied in Vienna," he declared at least five times. His examination of Peter had the air of theater, punctuated by several "benissimos" and "bravissimos."

When he was done, he bowed to Clara and Saul, declaring that there was no cause for concern. "Just a little indigestion!"

Saul, taken aback, emphasized the location of greatest tenderness, but the doctor shook his head. Saul argued, and when that failed, he pleaded.

"A man ought not be the doctor for his own family," declared the Italian, imperiously waving his right arm. "A purgative will do. Arrivederci!"

Saul felt his blood draining away, his knees simply folded under him, and he landed on the edge of Peter's bed, the jarring motion eliciting a moan from Peter. Saul remained sitting, his thoughts racing furiously ahead, not in a straight line, but like a merry-go-round, spinning in circles, coming around the bend, only to find himself back at the starting point. He was trapped in a corner of pompous ignorance, and wondered how the devil he could get out of it. As was often the case when he met such adversity, his past life flashed back to him, in a compressed three-second version. As a medical student or young graduate physician he had tackled life with vigor and optimism. There was little that he could not do, when he set his mind to it, even against overwhelming odds. Ah, those were the days of glory, the days when he could rely on his own energy to steer his destiny in a world that had emerged from a war to end all wars!

Then disaster had struck, to humble him, to show him his own limitations. He had grown too confident, and he was punished for his arrogance and presumptuousness. Tamara had fallen ill, and neither his efforts nor his anger at his Creator, whom he suddenly engaged in one-sided conversations, changed the inexorable course of the disease, or the rapidity with which he lost his beloved. It was not for some time, with Clara's support and Peter's flourishing, that he regained his confidence. Then madness erupted again in Europe, spouting fire and ashes, which he was so desperately dodging, driving him into an enormous sea. And now he was a mariner adrift in a small boat in uncharted waters, tossed aimlessly hither and thither.

Saul's glance came to rest back on Peter. No, he could not let things go, he had to continue the fight. He felt another wave of anger sweep over him, which lifted him off the bed, and he swore to break that pompous little doctor's neck, if he did not send Peter to Como.

After searching the town high and low, he located the vain little man, and was surprised to find the doctor meek and deflated, amenable to suggestions. One look at Peter now, hollow-eyed, cheeks flushed as if two circles of rouge had been dabbed on, and lying immobile with legs drawn up, left little doubt as to the diagnosis or seriousness of his condition. With newly found energy, accompanied by several huffs and puffs, Dr. Carbone seemed to transform himself into a veritable steam engine, and with great speed – for local standards – made all the necessary arrangements. Saul was given permission to accompany Peter under police escort.

The sun had already set as Saul and a Carabiniere lifted Peter in the semi-darkness onto the trolley. The cars were virtually empty, and they deposited Peter stretched out on the bench. Saul sat next to him, and took the boy's hand in his. Peter lay still, consumed by fever, moaning faintly with every jar, as the tram threaded its way on narrow tracks through the darkness. The red spots on his cheeks had faded, and his face was ashen and wet with perspiration. Saul dabbed Peter's forehead with a handkerchief, and as he touched his son's cold wet skin, a chill went through his body. Peter seemed to be slipping right through his fingers.... And there he was adrift again in the middle of an immense ocean.

By the time the trolley reached Como, Peter had become delirious. Two orderlies carried him on a stretcher to the infirmary. A small woman in a nun's uniform opened the door.

"You are in luck, Signore," she addressed Saul. "Dr. Fiorelli is still here. He was just about to leave. He is the best!"

Dr. Fiorelli was a man of medium height, his handsome face reflecting weariness, but his dark eyes were bright and alert, and his voice kind and soothing. He was one of those rare people who Saul felt inspired immediate confidence. Saul wondered how come the man had escaped the military draft. Perhaps his graying temples explained that, or the slightest hint of a limp.

Without further delay, Peter was taken to the operating room. Saul remained behind in a whitewashed corridor on the main floor of the surgical building, a long corridor in what seemed like an endless night. He had not brought his watch – it had not been running for months – so he tried to count his steps, as he paced up and down, to have some tangible measure of the passage of time. With repetition he counted faster and faster, till the hall was spinning around him. He tried to divert himself by inspecting the cracks in the walls, and the shallow gullies worn in the tile floor by decades of footsteps. But nothing could calm his nerves. Oh God, he had not been so scared since he had been half buried in the trenches in 1916! It was that ashen transparency that had settled on Peter's face that frightened him. He had seen it before. He remembered the first time he had seen it as a medical student, at the foot of the bed of a dying young woman. The professor's ominous words rang in his ears. No, no! It need not be that way! Why was he haunted by such thoughts? He had lost all objectivity.

Saul noticed a wooden bench at the far end of the corridor, where it opened into a small foyer, and where another corridor intersected at right angles, leading to the sick rooms. Saul sat down. Occasional muffled voices and spasmodic coughs reached him from the patient rooms. He vaguely noticed a young woman in white gliding noiselessly past him, carrying a pitcher of water. He wanted to ask her if she knew anything about the new patient in surgery, but she had already disappeared before he collected his thoughts.

There was no way of letting Clara know what was happening. Internees had not the right or the means to send messages, and she would not know what had transpired, till he was able to return. She must be awake in their tiny apartment, wringing her hands in the dark, probably pacing as he did.

Saul got up and paced again, counting his steps by rote. They must be done by now. An appendectomy does not take that long. He inspected the foyer. Someone moaned in one of the sick rooms and a bell tinkled, followed by barely audible shuffling of footsteps. Saul's eye caught on a finely carved column and an elaborate doorway at the end of the intersecting corridor. "This hospital must have seen better days," he told himself, and wondered what the operating rooms were like. Perhaps ornate theaters; that's what they used to call them, "theaters." They ought to be calling him soon. He paced for another infinitely long period then sat down again.

Saul was startled when Dr. Fiorelli tapped him on the shoulder. He must have dozed off for a moment. The surgeon's face looked somber, the fine lines drawn tight.

"The appendix was already ruptured," he said, "but at least it was retrocecal and the infection was contained. Not an easy access, but I am optimistic. You may go stay with him now. The next twenty-four hours are critical."

Fiorelli led Saul into a ward shared by several patients. Peter's bed was on the right-hand side, next to the door, partly shielded by a wobbly white screen. The boy was sleeping quietly. Some color had returned to his cheeks. Saul sat down on a chair provided by one of the nuns, his eyes searching Peter's face to gather up all the good signs he could possibly extract. He had not noticed when Fiorelli left, and wondered whether he had thanked the Doctor properly.

The ward nurse, a stern-looking elderly nun who reminded Saul of one of his school teachers, appeared from around the screen. She touched Peter's forehead, checked his pulse, and fussed for a moment with the pillow.

"That was a nasty one," she mumbled, before departing. Saul could hear her rapid little staccato steps, as she hurriedly went from bed to bed.

Peter stirred, and Saul was already at his side. Yes, the boy looked better – that transparent pallor had disappeared – and he seemed to be waking up.

"Papa," Peter whispered, "Will I be all right?"

"Of course you will."

"I am not so sure, Papa."

Saul hardly dared breathe. Panic hovered at his elbows, like some hungry vulture.

"Remember, one day we're going to work together, after you finish medical school." He tried to remind himself as much as Peter of their one-time dream.

"I'm not sure that I'll…that I'll…."

"Just rest quietly now."

"Perhaps you and Rajko…"

"No, no, you and I."

"But, Papa…"

"Yes, yes! Just keep telling yourself that."

"Just in case...in case I don't..."

Saul shuddered. Pessimism was not a good sign.

Peter dozed off again with the deep rhythmic respiration of restful sleep. Saul watched over every breath, relieved that it came evenly and easily. Nature made young bodies strong, resilient, ready to mend and heal. He had seen youngsters on the brink one day, and virtually up and jumping the next.

The nurse returned to check the patient again, her face drawn into a guarded smile. For a moment she fussed with the bedding, then laid a hand withered with age on Peter's forehead, hesitated as if weighing something, and went off without a word.

As if conscious of the activity around him, Peter stirred, a faint sigh accompanying his movement. A moment later his eyes opened and roved around the room, till Saul caught them in his gaze. They were big and dark and sunken, but inside the darkness was a flash of light, a spark that bespoke an alert mind. How fragile the boy looked!

"Just rest quietly," Saul whispered, caressing Peter's hand. As the boy drifted back into slumber, Saul noticed how much Peter's large and sunken eyes were reminiscent of Tamara's as she was dying. "Oh God!" He panicked. "Twenty-four hours, another twenty-four hours!" He remembered that he had sat similarly beside Tamara at her bedside, and that she suddenly seemed to be slipping away. He had gotten his arm around her shoulders and lifted her. He gripped her hand and held onto it with all his might, imagining that somehow if he held on to her, contrary to all his medical acumen, she would not leave him. He had looked at her gaunt face, into those beautiful hazel eyes, sunken by that time but still looking back at him. He remembered that the day before she had cried and begged him to take good care of Peter after she was gone. Her tears were pink and bloody, he recalled.... He must not, no, he must not lose Peter now. "Oh God, have mercy! I am a proud man; I do not often ask for favors. But grant me this precious life. Do not take her son away from me."

The elderly nun stopped by again and felt Peter's forehead and his pulse. She went away shaking her head, and returned shortly with a cold wet towel which she applied to Peter's forehead, and a small glass of milk with a piece of stale bread for Saul, which he accepted gratefully.

"Tonight and tomorrow are crucial." She repeated Dr. Fiorelli's assessment. "For the moment he is holding his own. His young body is strong, and with God's will and blessing he will walk out of the hospital in a week. You too need strength. We had to transfer out the patient in the next bed, so you can use it for the night. We will say that you are a new patient for observation, so they will bring you food from the kitchen tomorrow."

"You truly are a Sister of Mercy," said Saul respectfully and bowed his head.

He was getting tired and his mind fuzzy. His clouded thoughts wandered back to Tamara, to her last hours. To those sunken eyes, which had looked back at him pleading. With a shudder he recalled the almost imperceptible wave that had passed over her face, extinguishing the light within the darkness. So gentle and ripple-like was the change, so imperceptibly had it cast its shadow, that Saul could not tell the moment when life was and when life was no longer. A violent cough from someone at the far end of the ward brought Saul back to the present. His mind was confused, and he thought he had had a dream about Tamara. Only half awake, with his limbs aching and body sore, Saul virtually collapsed on the empty bed and fell asleep instantly.

Two melodious voices reached Saul, first as a distant melded sound, and shortly thereafter as a man's and a woman's voices conversing in impeccable Italian. It was Dr. Fiorelli and a young nun making rounds. Saul had not slept long, but his sleep was so deep that he felt refreshed. Beams of sunlight poured into the ward, and little dust particles danced merrily within the rays. Peter stirred and seemed to wake up.

"I am Sister Aurelia, the day nurse," the nun introduced herself. She checked Peter's temperature, while Dr. Fiorelli listened with the stethoscope to Peter's abdomen around the bandages. "The temperature is still up," she said scowling.

"He is coming along, but he needs fluids. He can start small sips of tea and broth," said Dr. Fiorelli, as he gave Saul a pat on the shoulder. "We are very short of help, so would you try to get your boy to take two or three sips every ten minutes. If that goes well, increase the amount gradually."

"And if there is a problem, call me," said Sister Aurelia, as she gracefully slid away to the next patient, catching up with Dr. Fiorelli.

Saul now dedicated himself completely to nursing Peter back to health. The boy was feverish and drowsy, and fell asleep again before Saul could persuade him to have more broth. Framed by the pillow, Peter's face looked so thin and gaunt, the stubble on his face creating such deep shadows, that it reminded Saul of a painting he had seen in Vienna at a museum; it was that of a hollow-cheeked young man lying in bed, surrounded by members of his family, as Death hovered above to claim his victim. That was his enemy, the faceless phantom with a scythe whom he has been battling for so many years already, sometimes winning, sometimes losing. Saul shuddered. How easily he was flung these days from the heights of optimism into utter despair. He did not used to be that way. He wished Clara were by his side; he really needed her to steady his nerves right now, to keep him on a more even keel, to make him keep his balance. She seemed to have this magic power to soothe his discomforts, to buoy him at critical moments. "Oh Clara, how much I need you, and how much I miss you!"

Peter awoke and asked for tea. "Papa," he said, "I am very thirsty. Can I have the whole cup?"

"No, you need to go slowly," and with trembling fingers Saul held the cup. Peter's responsiveness was a good sign, but intense thirst could be a warning. As the afternoon went by, Peter seemed to rally, and by the time Sister Aurelia and Dr. Fiorelli made the evening rounds, his fever had abated. A flood of elation swept Saul up and loosened a tightness in his chest that only now that it had dissipated he become aware of. In an instant he was buoyed by renewed hope and he felt totally at peace with the world around him. The sudden reprieve from the accumulated tension and physical activity of the last few days made him lightheaded, and before long he fell asleep in the chair, well before his bedtime.

Nearly three days after Saul went to Como he found himself on the trolley heading for Fieno. He had to go back to Fieno as soon as Peter was out of danger and return to his daily police reporting; and, of course, Clara and the twins needed to know what was happening. He was physically drained though cheerful now, and as the trolley wound its way, Saul barely noticed the stops along the way. It was late, and it would have been pitch dark had it not been another moonlit night. The tram slid past twisted and gnarled trees flapping their limbs in the breeze and casting strange shadows that promptly dissolved into the darkness. Of course, he would have to go back to Como to fetch Peter. Saul closed his eyes and sleep briefly overtook him. Clara appeared to him in their garden in Grad in a lively print dress, with two-year old Peter in her arms. He had taken a snapshot of them, so he could always cherish that moment, but the picture had been abandoned in Grad, and was probably now at the bottom of a pile of rubbish.

Someone pulled the cord to request a stop, and the conductor announced Fieno. Saul barely had time to rouse himself and jump off the tram. Hospitals were not places for rest. His knees felt shaky, the legs sluggish and unwilling, as he crossed the road, but the rebirth of hope lifted him, and he climbed the stairs to their flat with renewed energy. He let himself in with the key, barely controlling the stagger of exhaustion.

Clara was alone in the front room, which served as their living room, dining room and kitchen, needle and thread in her hand, mending Rajko's shirt. For once he was glad the twins were already asleep. The moment Saul entered, Clara put down her work and raised her dark eyes to meet his. He could see her lower lip tremble. He opened his mouth, but for a moment no words came from his dry throat. "He's all right, he'll make it," finally sprang forth as he hugged Clara and Clara hugged him back. They stood there a long time, each unwilling to let go of the other. An enormous pressure gripped Saul, till he felt that something would burst inside him, and he found himself weeping like a little child in Clara's embrace.

"We almost lost him," he said, then added: "He'll be home in a week…. I missed you so much." He felt Clara's soothing hand caressing his cheek, and the tension of the last few days seemed to melt away. "I love you," he whispered in her ear.

"I love you too," was the reply.

Oh, how unfair he had been to Clara continuing to fan smoldering feelings for her sister, when in reality all that was left from that past was cinders and memories! Clara had raised Peter as her own, loving him no less than the twins. Saul's guilt continued to fester.

"Clara," he finally managed to get out, before his voice failed him again.

Clara seemed to sense his thoughts, and put her hand over his mouth. He could see through his own tears her wet cheeks and the sheen of moisture in her dark eyes, as she fought back the tears. Then with a gentle motion she placed his hand on her shoulder.

"Lean on me," she whispered. "Lean on me now, for all the times I've leaned on you."

Clara's words echoed inside Saul and reached into a remote recess of his forgotten self. He stumbled in the darkness of a primal magma for a shadow, a shadow of an illusive memory, for something familiar, perhaps a déjà vu – a breakage of chains, a spiritual liberation.

"The trick is," his voice now seemed steadier, and he felt surprisingly calm, "to lean on one another."

CHAPTER 19

Peter was awakened by Rajko shouting: "Hurray, Peter is back," as Rajko noticed his brother in the bed which had remained unoccupied for more that a week. The twins had been asleep already when Peter and their father returned from Como.

"I missed you, Peter," said Ljerka, as she sat up in bed.

"I missed you, too," replied Peter yawning.

"We all missed him," said Clara, "and are lucky to have him back. Now let's see who will get up and get ready the fastest. Papa is already up."

"Me, me," yelled Rajko, jumping on his bed, literally tearing his nightshirt off and tossing it in the air.

"No, me," said Ljerka as she tried to challenge her twin.

"I really missed you guys," Peter repeated, "more than you realize."

"Were you scared?" asked Ljerka.

"No I wasn't," Peter answered, but he knew he wasn't telling the truth. He just didn't want to admit it to others, especially to his little sister.

After breakfast Peter was back at his maps, but it was difficult to concentrate. He had lost precious time to chart the Allied progress. It was very hard to follow events from the contradictory news that eventually trickled down to him, even if he was at it every day, and his extrapolations were always several days behind the real events. Now after the gap it was especially difficult, his eyes wandering farther West than the Russian front and settling somewhere in Southeastern Hungary. "Oh Silvia, where are you? If I only knew exactly where, I'd put my finger on the spot. If I close my eyes now and inhale deeply, and if I concentrate very hard, perhaps you will hear me. And if I send you a kiss, maybe you will feel it, will you? Old Darinka claimed that some people had the power to do that. Oh Silvia, do you still care for me, or have you found someone else?" Peter became hot and giddy. Maybe he would lie down again, till his parents returned from the morning report. The world seemed better when he talked with them, even if for some strange and incomprehensible reason he never talked to them about Silvia. They had other concerns more serious than his infatuations. He could talk to them about many things, but this was one area he intuitively or perhaps mistakenly felt he could not share and had to keep to himself.

A knock at the door interrupted Peter's cogitations. Who could it be? Nobody ever came to look for his parents till the afternoon. The twins were out romping in the courtyard. He opened the door, and there was Marisa standing in the doorway, her usual brazen expression gone.

"Pietro," she always used the Italian version of his name, "I heard you were very sick. The cyclist downstairs told me you nearly died. I am so glad that you are well again." Two tears rolled down her cheeks. "I prayed for you, Pietro. I love you in my own silly way." She sniffed and more tears rolled down her cheeks. "I hurt you, Pietro. I am just a stupid girl. I do silly things, and sometimes I do things just for spite. I spoke to Sister Margherita at the cloister. You know they have a school there. She will give me a chance to study there. I want to become a schoolteacher. You will like me better then. You'll see!" She sprang forward, and with an innate quality she possessed, that Peter could best describe as some sort of mysterious animal magnetism, she threw her arms around him, gave him a searing kiss, and a moment later fled bare-footed, cradling her wooden shoes in her arms.

Peter remained at the door, his lip still burning and his heart pounding. Now which one is it, is it Silvia or Marisa? And now Marisa too is gone. At least for now. She didn't say it in so many words, but Peter knew that's what she meant. If he transported himself into the world of the previous year, his feeling for Silvia was as intense as it had been then. But if the flight of his imagination went back only a few months, he would experience the intense feelings he had for Marisa before they quarreled. How could that be? When this crazy war was all over he would look for Silvia and see how they felt about each other. He would have to do that before he could seriously think about Marisa or about anyone else. For the moment he felt something inside him churning, a restless energy bubbling up that made him giddy.

Peter was still struggling with his confusion and restlessness when his parents returned from the police report. The twins followed a moment later. Rajko must have seen Marisa, and in a teasing singsong voice started to chant, "Peter li-ikes girls, Peter li-ikes girls."

"So what's wrong with that?" Ljerka asked.

"Peter used to like Silvia. Now he likes Italian girls. Girls, bah!"

"Oh shut up!" Peter snapped at Rajko.

"In a couple of years you too will like girls," Clara said to her younger son.

"Girls are silly," Rajko persisted.

"What about me?" Ljerka protested.

"Other girls are silly all the time. You are silly only half the time."

This was too much for Peter. He had just come home from the hospital, and though he still felt weak, he began feeling an inner energy driving him on, and he just simply had to get out of the confining little apartment. He rummaged in the bin behind the little stove where scraps to light fire still remained from last winter. His prize was a piece of cardboard, to which he added a pencil and a few sheets of white paper that he fished out from under his bed.

"Papa, I'm going out for a while," he said.

"Won't you have lunch with us first?" Clara asked.

"No, Mami. I'll have lunch later. And please, don't worry about me." Then he stepped out and slammed the door.

Outside the sun was blazing, but in the shade it was comfortable. Peter had to collect his thoughts. Somehow the world looked different today. Everything looked brighter, the sun was more dazzling, the green leaves on the trees and shrubs were greener. The sky in Fieno was a more intense celestial blue on sunny days than he had ever seen it in Grad, but today it was even more magnificently blue. Without any plan he walked around wherever his feet carried him and drank in the sights of the beautiful partly hidden gardens he and his family discovered the day after they first set foot in Fieno. Then he walked some more till he felt a little calmer. He looked for a low wall he had seen along one of the streets opposite a villa he liked, and sat down where a tree had spread out its branches, unfurling a leafy canopy over his head. The villa was built of rosy-red brick, with ornate windows under the slanting roof reminiscent of but not as elaborate as the ones he had seen in Venice. The windows sparkled in the early afternoon sun, and the reflected rays seemed to reach out to Peter and welcome him. It was his favorite building in town, sumptuous for Fieno, probably the summer home of a wealthy Milanese, or so he imagined. Today the bricks of the villa seemed brighter and rosier than usual.

Peter wondered why he was feeling so restless. No, that was not the right word. About two weeks ago he was at death's door. Now he felt as if he had a new life that was bursting inside him, that gave him this restless energy, despite the fact that his body had been weakened. Even the colors around him were now brighter. He unfolded the sheets of white paper he had been carrying, placed them on the cardboard, and started sketching the villa, the wrought iron fence in the foreground, which encircled the villa, the bushes in the front yard. He didn't even know until last week that he could draw. He had never tried beyond the geometric compositions he was required to do in his gymnasium art class. When he was recuperating in the hospital, a middle-aged Italian occupying a bed in Peter's ward befriended him. He was an artist, the man told Peter. Not a good one, he claimed, but a third-rate one, or perhaps even a fifth-rate one. The economy after World War I was disastrous in Italy, and he could not make a living selling his art, so he made posters for the local Fascist bureau, not out of conviction, but out of convenience, just to survive. And of course, he was a member of the party, he had to be, there was no other way. Often when he made the posters, especially lately, he spat on them. Peter was shocked to hear his new friend make the last statement so publicly; that could be dangerous.

"Ah, Pietro," the man replied. "What can they do to me? I am a dying man. I have only a few more months to live. And I don't have a wife or children for them to take revenge on."

The last three days at the hospital, the Italian convinced Peter to sketch with him outdoors in the hospital gardens and from their ward window. Peter discovered that with a little guidance he could passably manage to transfer something of the three-dimensional world onto two-dimensional paper, and that it was fun and immensely soothing. A panacea. With great fanfare the Italian presented Peter with a drawing pencil and a few sheets of paper when Saul arrived to pick him up.

"Don't become an artist," he said shaking his index finger. "It is not a good living, but draw or paint for yourself. It will heal your wounds. Good luck, Pietro," and he threw his arms around Peter and gave him a big hug.

A small cloud had drifted above the villa, and Peter quickly sketched it in. He added more vertical lines in the garden to fill in some shrubs. Then he fussed with the birdbath to make it look round rather than flat. While he was thus occupied, hours flew by that seemed like minutes. His nerves felt soothed. He looked at the villa again, and up and down the street. The vegetation definitely was a brighter green than he had noticed before, and the bricks too were more vibrant. He felt as if there were a new life bubbling inside him since his recovery. He looked at his sketch, looked at the villa, and down again at the sketch. "Not bad!" His villa was weightier and lacked the grace of the real one, but could pass muster. It was the cloud that displeased him because it looked like a stone up in the sky, no matter how much he tried to make it look light and wispy. The few lines he had put on the paper looked dense and heavy rather than vaporous. He could give the cloud its proper shape but not the lightness; he simply could not capture the essence of the cloud. But the garden in the foreground was inviting, and altogether not a bad beginning. No, not bad at all, in fact very good! It had brought him respite from the seething conflict inside him, and the throbbing in his temples, as if the sketching had sucked out venom from his wound. So immersed was he in his picture-making that he even forgot about lunch.

Peter carefully folded up his papers. He hoped he would not be scolded for staying out so long – he had lost all track of time – and now hurried home. Now he was ready to face the crowded apartment, Rajko's teasing, the dancing of bright colors that his recovery had awakened, and a yearning for a lasting love in his fractured life.

CHAPTER 20

The events in late spring and early summer of 1943 absorbed Saul so completely that he no longer experienced the pangs of hunger despite continued weight loss. Even Clara's fretting about the ever-decreasing food supplies did not dampen his spirits. The campaign in Africa was concluded, and in July, Allied troops landed in Sicily. Rumors circulated in Fieno that even high-ranking Fascists now felt that the war had been lost. It was Mussolini who had lost the war for them, or had gotten them into the war on the wrong side, whichever way one wanted to look at it. When Saul and Clara ran into Gian Carlo, the bicycle shop owner, on the stairway he informed them, with glee, that Mussolini had been apprehended, and that Marshal Badoglio had taken over the reigns of the Italian government, with the approval of King Victor Emmanuel III.

Despite these radical developments, there was no immediate change in the situation of the refugees in Fieno. They still had to report daily to the police, still were civilian prisoners, and the war seemed to continue, at least for the moment. The threat of German invasion now became a reality, just as liberation got closer, and Saul, overwhelmed by anxiety, had trouble keeping the inner agitation at bay.

The war was finally brought to the Italian "terra firma" the first few days in September. The Italians, who never had the stomach for the battlefield, wished to preserve as much as they could of their historic land. On September 8th it became known that Marshal Badoglio had signed an unconditional surrender, hoping to buy Italy as favorable terms of defeat as possible and avoid further destruction.

Once the armistice was signed, the hope was that the Allied troops, already present in the South, would sweep right up the Italian peninsula. Saul was certain that Germany would try to fill in the gap, but where the two opposing forces would meet was anybody's guess. He thought it might be in central Italy and the province of Como would certainly fall to the Germans. As for the Italian army, it just simply disbanded, initially of its own accord, and later with the blessings of the Germans, who did not want their former allies to turn against them. With the armistice in effect, the ordinary Italian foot soldier considered the war over, and he could think of nothing but going back home to his sweetheart or his "Mamma." In the meantime, over the Brenner Pass came German reinforcements. A few Italian officer groups tried to organize resistance to the invading Germans, but such attempts were for the most part unsuccessful at their very inception.

The moment the armistice was concluded, Saul felt that it was urgent to leave Fieno, feeling certain that Northern Italy would come under direct German occupation. Because of the daily 10:00 A.M. report, he did not want to disappear and leave the remaining thirty and some internees in a compromised position. He therefore called a "secret" meeting following the morning report – secret, because the internees were not allowed to congregate.

"We need to leave immediately and inconspicuously – no luggage, just what we have on our backs. I am not going to be a sitting duck here and wait for the Germans. Escape is risky, but we have no choice. I suggest that we disperse and make our way to Como. There we can get on the train and go South. As far South as we can, till we reach the Allies."

"I think Switzerland makes more sense. It is so close, and only a few miles from Como," Alfred suggested.

"Unless you have a guide, crossing into Switzerland is too dangerous. The Swiss guard their border tightly, and anyone who gets caught gets thrown right back," said Comforti. "Otherwise we would all be there already."

"We should not make any rash decisions. For the moment we should wait and see what happens," said another internee. Because he had a feeble elderly father with him, he hoped to remain right there, and didn't want anybody else to leave.

And so followed deliberation, argumentation, and above all, procrastination.

No agreement was reached that day regarding the course of action, nor on the next, despite continued deliberations. The day after that, while the Kestners were in the middle of their noon meal, a scurry could be heard outside through the open windows. An indeterminate shout emanated from someone who had just heard the newscast: "The Germans have just entered Lecco," which was only ten miles away. The food dried up on Saul's and Clara's lips. Time had run out.

Instantly they all got up, leaving behind the table with five half-empty plates. Saul collected what few papers he possessed. Clara, totally shaken, took an inordinately long time to locate her gold watch and a couple of rings, which they might have to trade for food and shelter. Ljerka bit her nails and shivered, but for once her parents took no notice of her. Peter rifled through his few possessions. If he only had something – anything – from Silvia, perhaps a photo, he would take it along, hide it in his shoe or sock. He looked for a leaf Marisa had found on one of their walks; she had pressed it and given it to him. He had placed it inside the only book his family owned, an Italian dictionary, under the letter "M." In the intervening months the leaf had withered in its lexicographic sanctuary and it crumbled as Peter attempted to extract it. There was no photo, no leaf, no pebble or seashell; he would have to take the memories with him, inside his head, or even better, inside his heart. Only Rajko, in his semi-ignorance, semi-superstition, remained calm enough to fill his pockets with a few cans of sardines and bars of chocolate, which Clara had put aside for an unforeseen emergency.

It was shortly after noon when the five Kestners tiptoed out of their apartment with their only possessions what was on their backs. Ljerka wondered who would discover their disappearance, and Rajko tried to imagine the expression on that person's face when he still saw food in the plates. Saul felt a mixture of frustration and anger, the first because he had no time to notify the others that he was leaving, and the latter, that he had delayed his own departure by two crucial days on their account, and thus had drastically reduced his family's chances of eluding the Germans. He marched his family for about a mile, till they came to the outskirts of Fieno, where they were less likely to be recognized, and then they all got on the trolley for Como.

The jarring of the tram reminded Saul of his recent trip on that line with Peter and all the anguish and uncertainty that had accompanied it. And now with a tiny bit less of anguish and a bit more of uncertainty he was traveling that route with his whole family.

"Good-bye, Fieno," he told himself, "I'll come back to visit one day…if." There was still a big if, a big unknown future that stood between the five of them and the end of the war. Life was always full of ifs.

As the trolley approached the city of Como, the Swiss Alps gleamed in the September sunlight and appeared invitingly close. Saul dismissed again any thoughts of Switzerland, fearing the efficient Swiss border patrols, nor was he certain that Hitler might not invade Switzerland to consolidate his defense lines. He was sick and tired of the cat and mouse game, to be pounced upon time after time. Despite the enormous risks, he would lead his family southward and not stop till they were free.

In Como the Kestners boarded the next train for Milan, which happened to be an ultra modern electric train, an example of the technological superiority and achievement that Mussolini, as an empire builder, strived to attain. Nobody asked questions, as long as Saul paid for the tickets, and in less than an hour, they were in Milan.

The Kestners arrived at a subsidiary railroad station. The city had been badly bombed, and in the aftermath there was no public transportation, so they had to walk to the main station. Milan was a sad reflection of empire building, with many bombed out buildings. There was a general air of hurry and scurry as people strode silently down the streets. Nobody talked, and the easygoing smiling people Saul had seen on the streets of Milan only sixteen months before now were enveloped in gloom and appeared to be carrying the burden of the world on their shoulders. Crossing the main piazza he saw the beautiful lace-like Duomo intact and had a fleeting feeling, he did not know from whence it came, that that was a good omen. But a few steps beyond the piazza, he saw a bare interior wall of La Scala, and beyond that wall, he could not tell how much, or perhaps, how little of that legendary music palace had remained. He remembered the many theories and fanciful explanations the people of Fieno talked about, to account for the opera house's phenomenal acoustics, particularly praising the peerless aged timber in a perfectly proportioned structure. All attempts at reproduction elsewhere resulted in inferior copies, they claimed, for no one could find such unique timber, and Saul feared that perhaps this enchanted theater could no longer be reconstituted.

The only southbound train from Milan was sitting on a track at the main station, beneath the beautiful arch-shaped glass roof Saul had admired on their first arrival. It was bound for Rome, with stops in Bologna and Florence. The Kestners encountered no problems in boarding the train, and nobody bothered to question them. After a lengthy wait, the train made a totally unscheduled departure late in the evening, but somewhere before Bologna, it halted at a small railroad station and remained standing for a very long time. No one seemed to know what was happening, and there was a great deal of noise and speculation among the passengers, who mostly were disbanding Italian soldiers. Some claimed they could see an enormous fire in the distance. After several hours, the train slowly set into motion again, and Rajko and Ljerka fell asleep, despite the din. Shortly the train came to another stop at another inconspicuous little station. This time the stationmaster came on board and announced that the train could not continue, as a stretch of the tracks had been knocked out by an air raid. Bologna was not too far away, and perhaps some other train might depart from there, or more likely, from some station beyond.

It was five o'clock in the morning, and the day was just beginning to break as the passengers poured out of the train, and en masse, like a big procession, headed for Bologna. The Kestners melded with the crowd of disbanding soldiers, which after a time separated into faster and slower moving units snaking their way forward; occasionally small clusters of men took completely different routes. At one point, just before a bridge crossed a small stream, the procession stopped. The ground seemed to tremble, accompanied by a roaring noise. From the opposite side approached enormous camouflaged tanks, still retaining the desert colors of the African campaign. They were a small platoon of German Tigers. Ljerka gulped as she saw those enormous tanks, her limbs frozen to the ground; she remained immobile, swallowing the dust. Even Rajko was unnerved for once. Saul saw the children's agitation and whispered some words of encouragement, which they could not hear over the deafening noise, but his hands on their shoulders were a comfort. He was delighted that the Tigers and their crew were going in the opposite direction from which he and his family was traveling, and he was satisfied with his calculations, that the Germans would consolidate along a defensible front line in the North. Hence they were retreating. After the tanks roared by and the ground stopped shaking, the marchers continued. A couple of hours later they reached the outskirts of Bologna. Following a lengthy wait at the trolley car depot, which would normally have taken them across town, it became apparent that the service was not stopped just for the night, but had completely broken down. The remnants of the original crowd had thinned out, and now a maze of alternative streets presented itself to the tired trekkers.

The sun was high overhead when Saul and his family reached the center of the city and crossed the main square, which they all recognized from picture postcards. A number of streets converged on the piazza, and disbanding soldiers poured in from all sides, but they exited through one particular street. Several German soldiers were standing on guard in the center of the square. Saul, adhering to his newly developed policy of "following the crowd" and of steering as far away from the Germans as possible, soon left the piazza behind with his family. On one of the side streets, Saul noticed a circle of people with backpacks surrounding a large straw-filled wagon to which was hitched a remarkably muscular horse. He halted, like everyone else, to find out what was going on. The owner was having a loud public discussion, which ended up with him inviting everybody to ride, for a small fee, to some God-forsaken little railroad station from which he claimed there would be a train in the afternoon.

It was a boon to sit down. Clara fished out a piece of chocolate from Rajko's pocket, split it in four, and distributed it to her family. Surprisingly, no one was as hungry as one would have expected. They had been underway for nearly twenty-four hours since their interrupted lunch, and the only food they had consumed since was a small can of sardines they all shared late the previous night. One of the disbanding soldiers, a young Sicilian, burst into "O Sole Mio," and suddenly everyone's burden seemed just a little lighter.

Ljerka turned around to imprint in her memory the silhouette of the mountains in the background, the Appenines, about which she had read and parts of which were now receding in the distance. Saul also contemplated the mountain range, but for a different reason. He experienced relief to leave behind this terrain, which with his World War I strategy he considered would soon become the battleground.

As promised, the farmer, for such he was, delivered his human load to a small railroad station. A train awaited the passengers. It was the northbound train for Milan, but due to disrupted tracks, ended at this local stop South of Bologna, just as their previous train had ended North of the city. So the trains became shuttles, running back and forth along the isolated stretches, until they could no longer run at all, or until the tracks were repaired.

Saul found out that the train they had boarded was going to the coastal city of Ancona, rather than to Rome, as he had hoped. But wherever it went was fine, as long as it was down the Italian boot and not up. After all, these days one never knew whether there would be more trains departing from any destination. He hoped they could ride as far as possible, and the rest would have to be negotiated some other way. One had to take advantage of whatever possibilities presented themselves. With any luck, in Ancona one could transfer for Rome.

When the train arrived in Ancona, it made a full stop in what looked like a railroad yard just outside the station, though the station did not appear bombed or damaged in any way. The yard was occupied by a group of young Italian officers who wanted to organize resistance against the Germans. They did not allow trains with disbanding soldiers to depart, and were forcing everyone off the train. Any male traveler became a suspect deserter, and so Saul's family suddenly and unexpectedly encountered an obstacle from an unforeseen quarter. They had passed themselves off as Italians for the last two days, the children doing most of the official talking, for their Italian by now was fluent and without accent, but just as a precaution, they claimed to be from Istria, the Italian territory near the Italo-Yugoslav border with a significant Slavic population. With so many different dialects in Italy, no one questioned this further, and no conductors appeared to check papers or tickets. Suddenly, to Saul's consternation, they were taken for genuine Italians, and Saul and Peter found themselves shoved to one side with a number of the disbanding soldiers in order to be pressed into the army. Ljerka nearly hysterical ran after Saul shrieking "mio Pappa, mio Pappa!" and with great tenacity wrapped her arms around her father and would not let go. She was followed by a tearful Clara, with Rajko in tow, pushing her way between the men. One of the Italian lieutenants tried to calm Ljerka, stroking her head and muttering, "Che bella bambina." Italians had a soft spot for children, and perhaps he had a daughter Ljerka's age. The lieutenant ordered Saul and Peter released immediately as "innocent" passengers, traveling as a family.

"I love you, Papi," said Ljerka, drying her last tear on the sleeve of her dress.

"Here's a handkerchief I found inside my pocket," said Clara. "It's the only one we have now, so we'll have to share it."

For the moment the crisis was averted, but as no trains were leaving, there was nothing to do but linger in Ancona. It was around noon when the Kestners found a restaurant that was open. With all the food shortages, many restaurants had gone out of business, and with the latest developments, others simply remained closed. The only food Saul was able to order for his family was a meager soup, but even that was spoiled by the arrival of three German officers, who were accommodated at a nearby table in an otherwise empty dining room.

"Let's get out of here," whispered Saul, and they did so in an unobtrusive manner. Upon their return to the railroad yard, there was no trace of the rebellious Italian officers, and the Kestners were able to board the next, perhaps last, departing train of the day. It was to go South along the Adriatic coast to Pescara, again steering clear of Rome, and departed after a considerable and unexplained delay.

Clara, Peter, and the twins dosed off in the crowded stuffy compartment. Saul rested his gaze on the sparkling Adriatic, but the blue waters and the impeccable sunshine aside, he saw signs of a desolation he had not seen further North. Towns flew by with empty streets, deserted beaches, and the vegetation, excepting dwarf-like trees, had assumed the same color as the dusty soil.

As the train approached Pescara, it halted at the northern perimeter, and the passengers were unloaded, with the promise that another train would be departing from the other side of the city, a story that was becoming boringly repetitious.

As the trekkers made their way through the city, they discovered a ghost town, with some buildings still smoking from a recent air raid. Most window panes were broken, and Ljerka hopped to avoid the strewn glass shards with her skimpy sandals. A large railroad yard had obviously been hit badly, and variably mangled locomotive skeletons bore witness to the ferociousness of the recent attacks. Saul urged his family to walk faster and leave this target area quickly behind.

The train at the other end of the city was mobbed, with ex-soldiers hanging out the windows and standing on the entry steps. Young men crowded the platform, and it was apparent that not everybody would be able to get on. When the Kestners approached, somebody murmured, "a woman and children," and those words were echoed on other lips. "Make way for women and children!" In their inimitable way, the young Italians stepped aside, making a path for the Kestners to board. A few helping hands reached down and pulled up Rajko and Ljerka, then made room for Clara, Peter, and Saul. There were no conductors, nobody paid, and it was a miracle that there was an engineer.

It was late in the day when the train finally left. This time they would hopefully reach Rome. It was always easier, Saul felt, to get lost in the crowd of a large city. After a time, the train came to a grinding halt at a station. Night had fallen, and it was dark outside. Word slowly spread from one train car to another, that the train would go no further, and general confusion ensued. Eventually word seeped through that they were in a small city called Sulmona, that the center of town was uphill, and that tomorrow there might be a train for Rome. The information one obtained was only hearsay, as official word no longer existed.

The crowd dispersed rapidly. Although there was no street lighting due to the curfew, it was a clear enough night to follow the path into town. Suddenly, coming around a bend, a half a dozen British soldiers appeared, and Saul, overjoyed, ran up to them. This was so much better than he had foreseen. He had not expected that the Eighth Army would so quickly sweep up on the heels of the retreating Germans. But he had not heard any news or seen a newspaper to know what was happening, and this seemed to him to be a small reconnaissance patrol. What luck to finally be freed! The German resistance had obviously completely crumbled in the last two days. He could no longer contain himself, and tears of joy simply poured out of him. He threw his arms around the British soldiers, and hugged and kissed them. In the ensuing confusion he prodded the twins to do likewise. Ljerka seemed half-flustered, half-bewildered, and half – if there was to be another half – enormously ridiculous, as she kissed a surprised mustachioed Englishman. Rajko declared that the whole spectacle was rather odd, this business of war and fighting and killing and now kissing. The soldiers must have found the spectacle as ridiculous as Ljerka, and were certain that "the Italian" who was virtually attacking them with kisses and embraces had gone mad.

Communication with the Englishmen was difficult, as Saul did not know more than three words of English, and the Englishmen knew even less Italian. Soon it became evident that one of the men was an Italian gendarme who also did not know what was going on, and who carried a large bottle of Chianti, from which one of the Englishmen took frequent gulps. All that wine had gone to the soldier's head, or perhaps his legs, and he wobbled rather distinctly in the moonlit night.

Eventually the situation was clarified via one of the Britons, who knew a little French, from whom Saul found out that they were runaway prisoners of war, their Italian captors having disbanded, permitting them to simply walk out of the unguarded campgrounds. They remained in uniform, because if caught in civilian clothing, they could be executed as spies. They, too, had no idea where the current front line was, and headed South to rejoin their troops.

The remaining portion of the walk uphill was short, but a tremendous letdown for Saul. For a brief moment he thought that he had reached the peak and could finally look into the valley of freedom, but all that he could see was another mountain range that his tired spirit would have to surmount.

Sulmona was completely shuttered up. Saul and Clara wandered around aimlessly with Peter and the twins, till they found themselves in a small park. Mercifully there was a fountain with a water pump and several unoccupied stone benches.

"This is the best water I ever drank," declared Rajko.

"Me too," added Ljerka. "I don't even feel hungry any more."

The water blunted their hunger, and overwhelmed by fatigue, Peter and the twins fell asleep instantly on the stone slabs. Not so the adults, whose bodies were less malleable, though they were just as weary as the youngsters.

The following day, more British soldiers and officers could be seen in the streets. There was no longer any confusion about their status; the only confusion was whether there would be any trains departing, especially for Rome. Saul and Clara, exhausted from the hard stone benches, and hungry, decided to spend another day in Sulmona, "till the dust settles," Saul declared. Somewhere they got ersatz coffee and a tiny piece of bread for everyone for breakfast. Somewhere else they bought some grapes, which were in season, and had those plus a ration of chocolate. A room was readily found in a virtually empty hotel, which turned out to have a view of a large piazza, an old Roman aqueduct in the background, and mountains beyond. Though it was only midday, they all went to sleep, totally overcome by exhaustion. A church bell, announcing the evening vespers, transiently awoke Clara and Saul, a particularly sweet tempered and enchanting sound that had miraculously escaped the fate of so many other church bells, before they were lulled back to sleep.

Sometime after midnight, Clara and Saul were awakened again, this time by noises from a stream of motor vehicles. The Germans had taken possession of the city.

"It is all my fault," Saul whispered. "We should have left yesterday."

"We were too exhausted. We didn't even know if there was a train."

"Everywhere we turn, the Germans are right on our heels."

As soon as it was daylight, Saul shepherded his family downhill to the railroad station. No one knew whether there would be a train that day, or whether there had been one the day before.

When the Kestners reached the station, a number of disbanding Italian soldiers were milling around. No uniformed Englishmen were to be seen. A short train was standing on the nearest track, with a locomotive hitched to several cattle cars. Word had it that it would leave shortly for Rome, and Saul herded his family to the platform. He did not realize that the Germans had occupied the station, and by the time he became aware of that, it was too late. Unexpectedly, he found himself stopped by a uniformed German, a representative of the army, and not of the Gestapo, demanding identification papers.

Saul gulped. Any hesitation meant disaster. In profuse Italian, he explained that he would presently let the man have his papers, and after fumbling around several pockets, he fished out a booklet. It was the identification he had received from the Italian government, in which, boldly in black and white, it gave his name, nationality, and worst of all, in the appropriate place, it said "Ebreo," the Italian word for Jew.

The German put on his eyeglasses, looked at the booklet, looked at Saul, and then looked at the booklet again. He seemed irritated with Saul's verbal cascade, scowled, narrowed his eyes, and for what felt like an infinitely long time to Saul looked him up and down. Finally, with an expression of contempt the German returned the booklet and waved the Kestners on.

Only after Saul settled himself and his family on the crowded floor of the cattle car did he notice that he was shivering. At the moment of confrontation with the German he had remained surprisingly calm. Perhaps it was the suddenness of the encounter, which did not give him sufficient time to panic. There was no chance to withdraw, and the only option that remained was bluff. He thanked his stars that this soldier was middle-aged, presbyopic, and a far cry from the twenty-two year old, alert, tall, voracious Bavarians who arrived in Grad in 1941. The Reich was obviously scraping the bottom to keep the ranks filled. Fortunately the identifications issued to the internees by the Italian government resembled in all outward aspects those issued to their own citizens, except that, of course, the incriminating information, namely birth place, nationality, and religion, was all there. Had the man looked only at the picture, were his glasses poorly fitted to easily decipher the inserted information, were his senses blunted by weariness from the desert battles, or was he only familiar with the German word "Jude" – Jew? This clearly was the closest call since that night in jail in Grad.

Shortly the train rolled slowly out of the station, and as it gained momentum, it became obvious from the position of the sun that despite a well know saying that all roads lead to Rome, the train was not heading that way. Rumor spread through the train – there was no conductor to corroborate this, and no one knew the source of the information – that the Germans were blockading Rome, and no trains were allowed to proceed to the metropolis. The mood aboard the train was somber, and for once the disbanding soldiers were silent, tired and frustrated by the frequent interruptions in their homebound journey. The countryside became stark, befitting everyone's mood, as the train rolled on into the Abruzzi, only to come to a halt in a small town. The stationmaster told everyone that several hours later there would probably be another train, but its destination was still unknown. The passengers jumped off the train and wondered aimlessly through the town.

Not far from the station was a small square with a well and a pump. Clara chose some randomly distributed large stones to settle down and portion out the last can of sardines and chips of chocolate to her family. Along with water, this was their lunch and the first, and possibly the last, meal of the day. The midday sun was scorching, and there was not a tree anywhere to offer some shade. Rajko and Ljerka whimpered that their limbs ached, perhaps from being huddled in the crowded train.

A small gray truck pulled up, and several German soldiers jumped out. They sat down on the stones on the opposite side of the square, unpacked their rations, filled their canteens at the pump, and appeared too absorbed in their own immediate needs to pay any attention to the few "local" people sitting on the other side of the well. Even so, Saul took precaution to get rid of the empty sardine can on which was stamped "Made in Yugoslavia," and to withdraw his dusty and weary family whose clothing was obviously different from that of the villagers who came for water. It was just as well to return to the station, because the train on which they had arrived was getting ready to depart. Characteristically, nobody knew why the train had been detained or where it was going now. Speculations were rampant, but all that mattered to Saul was that they were continuing South, and that much he could tell from the position of the sun. If the train went, Clara declared that trains were supposed to go, and if it stopped, she insisted that they were meant to stop sometimes. And so when the train stopped again, no one was surprised, only irritated, as the traveled stretches were becoming progressively shorter and the stops more frequent. A few young Italians got off to find out what was happening and where they were. For some reason, supposedly strategic, the plaques bearing the names of the towns had been removed from all the stations. Various reports soon started circulating. The train had stopped so that the steam engine could be watered and would be continuing shortly for Benevento, and thence on to Avellino. Thereafter no one could tell what transportation would be available, if any, because the front line as of several days prior was somewhere South of Avellino, but nobody knew just how far South.

"This means," Saul whispered to Clara and Peter, "that the Allies may be only forty miles from here." This was good news, and the first of any kind of demarcation or line of confrontation that he heard about in nearly two weeks, when the Eighth Army had landed somewhere near the heel of Calabria.

"Benevento has been extensively bombed," reported one young Sicilian, "and railroad trains and stations are special targets, so if you hear planes approaching, jump off the train, which I am told will be moving very slowly, and run for cover."

Suddenly a wave of excitement swept through the cattle train. A northbound train was being watered on another track, and it included several carloads of Italian army blankets confiscated by the Germans. This incensed the disbanding soldiers, who swarmed over the other train and helped themselves to the blankets. Under other circumstances this might have been regarded as plunder, but the young men were outraged that Italian property was being sent to Germany and felt that they were merely retrieving Italian property for Italians. They felt no loyalty toward their previous allies and comrades in arms. Anyway, they had been mislead by their former dictator, and presently their centuries' old antagonism to their Teutonic neighbors to the North came to the fore.

Fortunately no Germans accompanied the requisitioned shipment, because they would have been certain to open fire on the raiders. The incident, however, had repercussions. The stationmaster fearing for his life because he was held personally responsible for the goods, refused to let the southbound train proceed until all the blankets were returned. Reluctantly, and after some delay, the men parted with their newly acquired blankets, as that was the only way to depart. This cost them a delay of nearly an hour.

The train now proceeded at a turtle pace. The tracks had been sadly neglected and had fallen into disrepair, making faster travel hazardous. Several particularly rough bounces gave Saul the feeling that the train was derailing. Obviously this less-traveled North-South route had been decaying for some years, and now it could not cope with the augmented traffic. Once or twice the train practically stopped, but then it gained momentum and rolled onward. It took an inordinately long time to cover about two dozen miles, at the end of which it came to a complete and final stop. Word spread that they were at the periphery of Benevento, that once more rail disruption prevented the train from entering the station, and that another train might be available at the other end of town, going on to Avellino. Benevento, some claimed, had been bombed some thirty minutes prior. Lately there had been several air strikes every day, sometimes massive, sometimes involving only two or three planes.

"Such tactic suggests that Benevento is just next to the front lines," commented Saul.

Everyone got off the train, and like a herd, followed the main dirt road toward town. The September afternoon southern sun was blistering. The countryside was parched, barren and clay-colored. Rajko and Ljerka could not keep up with the soldiers' pace, and the Kestners, being the only non-military people, lagged behind. The road led past a field of tobacco plants, growing in regular rows. It was a relief to see something other than the grey soil, even though the plants were not truly green, but rather grey-brown.

"I think I can hear the hum of airplanes," Clara said nervously.

“Mami, look how large the tobacco leaves are,” Ljerka commented. “Do you think, Papi, we could curl up under them and hide from the airplanes?”

“No, darling, we have to rush and get away before the planes come again.”

“Hurry up, you two creeping snails,” Peter scolded his siblings.

But the hum either receded or had not been there in the first place. A few deserted farmhouses stood along the roadway, one of which was still smoking from the last air raid.

“There’s something funny up ahead, something white,” announced Rajko, who had been exceptionally quiet for some time. As they passed by, they saw that it was a young dead Italian soldier, whose body someone had covered with a white sheet, perhaps while he was still alive, leaving the head exposed. Above the sheet was a round, pallid, terrible face with open eyes and bulging white eyeballs that greeted the passers-by. The twins quickly looked away, but it was too late.

“Why is he looking that way?” Ljerka half asked and half complained.

“I wonder where he is from,” Peter added. “Most of the disbanding soldiers are either from Calabria or Sicily.” Perhaps the dead one had done battle in Africa or Russia, and had escaped many dangers, only to be felled by the wayside off a dusty road on the last leg of his way home.

“Come, come, children, hurry up” Saul prodded on.

“When the train was delayed over those blankets, everyone grumbled about departing late,” Clara commented. “But had we departed sooner, we would have arrived just in time for the air raid. You can never tell ahead what’s best.”

“There is no time to speculate now!” The living had to go on living. Saul urged everyone again to hurry, as they were very vulnerable on that road if the planes were to return. It would be doubly tragic to be killed by friendly forces whom one is trying to reach. Intervening foothills and bluffs shut out Benevento from view, but smoke was clearly visible, rising upwards from behind the hillocks.

Up ahead the road intersected a railroad track, and Saul saw that a new group of trekkers, who had caught up with them, turned in to follow the rails. He decided to do likewise. Then the tracks disappeared into one of the hills and the Kestners found themselves inside a tunnel.

"This is the best way to find the next station. Just follow the tracks and duck if a train should be coming," Saul explained. "And here there is no danger from the airplanes."

The entire city of Benevento had come to the same conclusion. Thousands of people had moved in and set up households in the tunnel. This consisted of entire families huddled on a bit of straw or a blanket, with a few miserable possessions, a couple of cooking utensils, and small supplies of rice and beans. At first, people used it just as a shelter, coming and going with each attack, but the last two weeks Benevento had been bombed so intensely and so frequently, that the most sensible thing was to just remain there for good. Many no longer had a home to go back to, and just went out between attacks to look for water and food, and to use the hillside for toilet facilities. But sometimes they did not even do that, and the tunnel stank of human habitation and excrement. Water dripped along the tunnel walls, adding a musty odor, and Saul noticed that some people licked off the drops.

Inside the tunnel there was total darkness, after the cone of light entering its mouth had become extinguished. Sometimes someone would light a fire to cook, but there was very little food to cook, and even less firewood or matches to get the fire going. Nobody seemed to complain about the smoke; it neutralized some of the stench.

"Mama, Papa, I can't see you," whimpered Ljerka.

"We have to stay together. The passage is narrow, and we will proceed in single file," Saul instructed. "I will lead. Mami will hold on to me, then Peter will hold on to Mami, and you, Ljerka, will hold on to Peter; the last will be Rajko. Yell if you lose your grip."

"I like that! I'll hold up the rear," said Rajko, finally sounding like his old self.

"All right, here we go."

Saul stretched out his arms, and felt his way along like a blind man. In this manner they snaked their way, sometimes stepping on people who had established themselves in the tunnel, young people, old people, sick people, maybe even dead people that no one yet realized were there.

Progress in this black underworld was slow. Rajko tripped once over something that moved and moaned in a feeble voice, losing his balance and his grip on Ljerka's dress. He experienced a moment of panic, but quickly righted himself and noticed that he was still holding on to Ljerka, though he had partly ripped her only dress. It was obvious that no train had passed through the tunnel for some time, and that the track interruption had not resulted from the most recent bombing. The tunnel inhabitants confirmed that a small railroad station was located just beyond the far end of the tunnel, and yes, trains have occasionally departed from there for Avellino.

Finally, a trace of light appeared in that eternally dark tunnel, and the Kestners could see a bright archway through which sunlight was pouring in. The darkness had been so thick that it did not merely seem to be the absence of light, but a tangible palpable blackness, which gave Saul the illusion of being immersed in a black slush. And now the light, too, seemed to acquire a substantive quality and seemed to be materially flowing in.

In the semi-darkness, near the exit, a ghost-like woman perched on a rock asked Saul whether he had seen Arturo, a small boy. She asked the same question of Clara, and of all the other people making their way through the tunnel. Saul gathered that she had been separated from her child when they were briefly outside the tunnel and caught by a surprise air attack, for which even the sirens did not have time to sound. The only question that was not clear was whether that severance had occurred earlier that day, a few days ago, or some weeks before. The local dialect was so difficult to understand, that in the end they could not tell whether the woman was simply inarticulate, or had gone completely mad, having lost all concept of time.

As Saul had been told, a small railroad station lay just beyond the tunnel. The sun by now was inclining to the West. There was not a trace of a train, and so for want of anything better, the Kestners, along with a handful of disbanded soldiers, settled down to wait for the train. A number of the tunnel inhabitants walked about, to stretch their limbs and breathe some fresh air. Suddenly there was a scurry and a few shrieks of "airplanes, airplanes," and most of the people ran back into the tunnel. It was dangerous to remain at the station, and two Italian soldiers shouted, "Follow us, follow us."

"Run, children; run, Clara," Saul instructed his family to run into the brush, away from the tracks. After a while they all stopped to catch their breath and survey the station. The planes did not come, and there was no audible hum.

"A false alarm," one of the soldiers said.

"I guess we'll go back and wait some more for the train," Clara said.

"No, Signora. We're not going back. My pal and I don't think there'll be more trains. You see, people here say the front line is just outside Avellino, so we think this is the end of the line."

"Si!" added the pal emphatically.

"We know a little village up in the hills, a little Southeast of here, and we're going to go there," continued the more outspoken member of the pair. "You see," he turned to Saul, "going straight to Avellino wound be dangerous. Right here is a narrow valley where the train runs," and he swung his arms to emphasize the point. "This is where the battles will be fought, in the valleys, so my friend and I, we're going up into the hills, and we'll wait it out up there. Come with us."

"Si, si," said the quieter Italian.

Saul recognized the wisdom of the suggestion. He had had a vision, more like a dream, of walking through the front lines, not resting till he and his family were freed, and on the other side. That was when, according to his calculations, the Germans would withdraw and regroup in the North, the Allies would advance without much resistance, and somewhere in between, the front line would gently pass over his family as they advanced to meet it. But under the circumstances of considerably more fighting and confrontation than he had expected, it would indeed be wiser to head for some out-of-the-way little village up in the hills, and he immediately accepted the offer.

"First of all," said the young man, "we'll have something to eat." That suggestion was unanimously and enthusiastically accepted.

The seven of them followed a narrow flat plain between parallel hills, trampling down some brush and sparse dry grass that happened to be under foot and had more the appearance of hay, though it was still attached to the ground by its roots. On the way they passed through a vineyard, with aromatic clusters of fully ripe grapes hanging from the vines. Everyone helped himself generously, as this was the only meal of the day. Normally this would be designated stealing, thieving, or a number of other uncomplimentary words, but these were exceptional times, and everyone was caught in the same net of imminent danger and pending disaster. Many of the farmers had fled their homes in the wake of the bombardments and battle. Others could not find help to harvest their crops, and beyond their own needs, they could not even find a market for their surplus, if they had any, in the midst of this scourge. And here were these grapes, bursting their skins, begging to be picked.

Local farmers were stoic, accustomed to periodic losses, disasters, governmental seizures without compensation, a hardy impoverished lot tilling an infertile soil, facing the inevitable with a shrug of the shoulder and a tightening of the belt. Perhaps some of them had sons in the service and hoped that in turn, nobody would deny their own hungry boys a few mouthfuls off the land. In those days of shortages and war ravage, many permitted the disbanding troops to feed themselves…and then there was always the threat of the Germans taking their food away in the name of the Reich, which might have been defined as robbing or plundering, but in such perverted times, definition of words and rules of conduct had lost their proper meaning.

As they were leaving the vineyard, the sun dipped below the horizon, and the wooden stakes with the grapevines spun around them, forming delicate black lace-like silhouettes against a red and blue sky. The shadows gradually deepened, the blue vanished, the red darkened, and in the end, only shades of blackness remained.

During the twilight, the young men led the small group onward, but the rapidity with which total darkness descended was amazing, without the slightest streak of moonlight, so that the only thing they could do was to stop right then and there. Everyone was actually exhausted, and it being a late summer night, they simply lay down on the ground and went to sleep. Rajko, in fact, was already asleep as he hit the horizontal. Under any circumstances the boy slept like a log, but with the great fatigue and a low calorie diet, he slept like ten logs, or even a hundred. His sleep was not disturbed, like that of the adults, by the waxing and waning sounds of motorcars as a retreating German convoy passed nearby. Nor was he awakened when American airplanes passed overhead and dropped bombs on that convoy, one of which exploded some hundred yards away. Much to the adults' surprise and dismay, the main South-North road from the current front in central Italy ran some dozen yards from where they had settled for the night. They had not been aware of the proximity to a road the evening before, and it was too dark to move on. The Germans utilized the cover of darkness for their retreat, and the air raid aimed to forestall effective withdrawal and regrouping.

At daybreak everyone was up. The two young Italians went to reconnoiter. The main road was a short distance downhill and westward. It was to be strictly avoided, both because of the threat of encounters with the Germans, and because it was a target for the Allies. Some three hundred yards ahead of their camping ground, the hill slope abruptly ended, opening into a deep ravine. Had they walked on in the darkness of the previous night, someone might have perished. The quieter Italian crossed himself and mouthed a Pater Noster. The two young men lead the group first into a vineyard for breakfast, and then eastward into bigger hills.

The young Italians were good company. The more extroverted one was always ready to be gallant and offer help uphill. He talked warmly about Sicily, his and his friend's home, though they were from opposite ends of the island. He had a thin but pleasant tenor voice, which he exercised readily, without much coaxing. Presently they found a steep path, and eventually a dirt road that wound around the hillside. After they crossed a small bridge they ended in a God-forsaken little village on the slope of a barren mountain, the one the young Italians were looking for. Facing them across the narrow gulley from which they had ascended was another winding road, ending in another small village clinging precariously to the mountainside.

The two ex-soldiers scouted around and found two old spinster sisters who were willing to rent out some rooms for the night and also cook a meal straight away. It was mid-afternoon already, so it served as lunch and supper. When the food was ready, it was brought out into the street and served on the house steps. There was very little room inside the house, and the sisters scurried around to rearrange the floor space for the night. The meal consisted of some sort of homemade pasta with tomato sauce, within which floated a few miniscule chips of something that may have been meat. Whether it was the herbs or the hunger, everyone partaking of the meal thought it worthy of a royal banquet. Rajko unceremoniously licked his plate clean, while Clara pretended not to notice.

After a good night's sleep, the world looked brighter, and particularly, after a corn mush breakfast, which in the old days the twins would not have touched. Saul, Peter, and the two soldiers held a lengthy conference. Although nobody knew exact details about the battle line, everyone seemed to agree that it was just outside of Avellino, as had been rumored before. The young Sicilians had definitely decided to remain in the village and would lodge with the sisters. The Kestners could stay there another night, but then they would have to find other accommodations. Initially the spinsters were eager to get their hands on some cash, but it soon became apparent that their meager larder supplies were more valuable than a rapidly devaluating currency.

In the evening, right after dusk, and without any forewarning, there was an exceedingly loud bang and a quiver of the ground while everyone was still sitting around the remains of the fire which had been lit for cooking supper, and now was the source of light. For some months already there had been no oil for lamps or tallow for candles in the only village store, and the sisters had run out of their supplies. Everyone ran out of the house, thinking that it was some sort of explosion, and saw the sky lit up by multiple, often simultaneous, rather spectacular flashes of lightning, briefly followed by crashing thunder. Lightening had struck the side of the mountain, and then across a narrow gorge, the next mountaintop, beneath which the other forsaken village seemed engrafted into the stone. The sisters crossed themselves and audibly said several Ave Marias while they fingered their rosaries, which they had extracted from their long skirts. Such a storm was an omen, they insisted, as in all the decades of their lives, they had never seen such a violent storm, and they redoubled their prayers. It now was apparent to Saul that in such terrain, with so many crests and troughs, they might not hear ground fire, even if a battle raged, so to speak, around the corner. He had hope that the fine weather they had been having so far would continue, because rain would impede the Allied offensive. The storm disappeared as hastily as it had arrived, and Saul had his wish, for the next morning the sky was clear, without the faintest trace of a cloud.

CHAPTER 21

Saul and Clara parted company with the two Sicilians and the spinsters. Saul decided it was wisest to remain in that forlorn, out of the way mountain village with a dead-end road and no electricity as of yet. Troops would obviously not march through there, and heavy armored vehicles would not negotiate the slopes or the dirt road. The battles would be fought, as the young Sicilians had pointed out, down in the valleys, between the mountain ranges, with some defense forces entrenched in accessible hills; steep and high places like this one were islands, or oases, where one could wait for the tide of the war to pass. Up until now they had advanced, but now was the time to just sit and wait – and stay out of the way of the waves. He wished he could hear the rumble of distant gunfire, but all was quiet, making him occasionally doubt that the front line was by Avellino.

Saul and Clara now had to find lodging for their family, which they readily did, and transferred a few houses down the street, to the last and poorest house in the village. There dwelt a grey-haired widow of indeterminate age, with her brood of illiterate, shabby, bare-footed children, excepting her oldest, a gaunt young woman in her late twenties, well on her way to spinsterhood. For years this devoted unattractive daughter, whom life and fortune promised to pass by, had been wearing her fingers to the bone sewing, mending, ironing. She had been the sole bread-winner in the family, but lately people had no money for new clothes, and even if they had, there was no cloth or thread to be bought; and so the young seamstress could no longer provide for her mother, her mentally disabled teen-age brother, and several other school-age siblings, who looked so much alike that Saul was never sure which was which, or how many there were altogether. In better days, the daughter might have ventured to look for a job in Benevento, but now this alternative was denied her. She was desperate to get a few lire and was delighted to accommodate the Kestners.

The widow's house was made of raw bricks and was of the same dull clay color as the entire mountainside. It was built on the edge of the slope, a crude structure with a small, unfenced backyard. The downstairs was a barren, bleak single space, with a front door left ajar from dawn till bedtime, and a tiny window close to the ceiling, meant for light to enter, but too high for the eye to see the street. The large fireplace on the far wall opposite the entrance, served as the kitchen stove, with pots to be set directly into the fire. A crude table, a few chairs, and a wooden bench were the only furnishings, and the space served as the living room, dining room, kitchen, and if needed, an accessory bed room. A second floor partly subdivided the interior space, with a shelf-like partition sitting on stilt-like wooden pillars over the kitchen area, creating an open space bedroom. A ladder led to the upstairs sleeping quarters, which contained a narrow double bed, a small table, and two wicker armchairs. The upstairs room was much pleasanter, as it had windows at eye level, allowing one to look outside and fresh air to seep in at night; Saul had arranged for the use of the upper floor. Even without the Kestners, there were fewer beds than souls in the house. As a result of the slope and the stony terrain, a small cave-like space, which did not communicate directly with the interior, was accessed via a separate entrance around the far side of the building. It was essentially a glorified crawl space under a portion of the house, up to four feet high, though considerably lower in some spots. The owners called it "the grotto," as it resembled a cave. In normal times the grotto would have been used as a cellar, but in those days of deprivation, there was nothing there but straw, and the disabled boy often slept there.

Food must always have been scanty in the widow's house, but now it was especially so. Everyone received a piece of bread and some water for breakfast, and the Kestners were included equally in the meager distribution. Besides this, only one other meal was served in the late afternoon. One day that consisted of beans – but that was the last of the beans. Another day it was an unrecognizable mush, and once it was a thick semisolid pea soup full of pebbles. The only butcher in the village had closed his shop for good some weeks earlier, as he had nothing to sell. The grocery opened only once a week for a few hours, mostly for gossip, as there were no supplies with or without rations that Saul and Clara could purchase for any amount of money. For a few days Saul found a supplier of grapes, but that also soon dwindled.

Ljerka met a girl her own age from Benevento who was staying at her grandmother's house in the village. The girl invited the twins to go reed hunting with her down the hill, where a stream would run during the rainy season. The stream had dried up months ago and left behind a white bed of sand and scattered stones. Wisps of dry grass, brush, and scattered skinny reeds were irregularly strewn along the edge. It was the reeds that the children picked and sucked on. On their way down they talked and dreamed about finding something sweet and juicy to suck on or chew, but the sun had extracted the last drop of herbal fluid, and all the sap was gone. The tasteless woody stalks stuck to the children's lips, and the southern Italian post-meridian sun beat down on them mercilessly.

On the way back, the trio passed in back of the spinster's house. There the two Italian soldiers were busy skinning a scrawny rabbit carcass so the sisters could make them a stew. Apparently the soldiers had some dry food rations in their knap-sacks, which they could now share with their hostesses.

"Wow, I'd like some of that!" Rajko said, drooling at the thought of some meat.

"Yuck," declared Ljerka. "Earlier today I saw the quiet guy carry a live rabbit," and she made a motion as if she were to throw up.

"Look what I have." The Italian girl pulled out a mysterious red nearly globular thing out of her pocket. "My grandmother gave me this pomegranate."

"What is that?" the twins asked in a single voice, never having seen one before.

"It is a fruit, and when you open it, it is full of rubies." Rajko and Ljerka hoped the girl would offer them some of the rubies, but she said good-bye, skipping on home to eat it alone.

As evening approached, several neighboring families gathered on the front steps of their houses on the street where the widow and the spinsters lived and engaged in lively talk and some sort of a strange activity. It consisted of women and children arranged in rows or circles, playing with each other's hair. It was Clara who figured it out.

"My goodness! They are picking nits." And indeed, when forming a circle, a person would pick nits and catch lice on the head of the person ahead, and in turn, would have that service performed by the person behind, and so on down the line or around the circle. Saul marveled at the inefficiency of this manual treatment, but then an effective substance like kerosene had not been available to the local public for some time – it all had been channeled into the war effort – or perhaps was not even known as a remedy in this forgotten little corner of the world.

In the beginning, Saul, Clara, Peter, and the twins tried to sleep together crosswise on the narrow double bed, but only Rajko seemed to manage to get enough sleep. The mattress seemed to be made of forty percent straw and sixty percent bed bugs. It was the crawling and parading of these beasts that kept awakening Saul, Clara, Peter and Ljerka. The next night, Clara and Ljerka chose to sleep in the wicker chairs, slumped over on the table, but it was one thing to doze off for a while in a chair, and another to sleep every night slumped over the table. Saul finally persuaded the seamstress to let them have the grotto, which she considered unbecoming of such well-spoken people. There they had a little more space to stretch out, though no one could stand up straight with the low ceiling; the main advantage was absence of insect cohabitants and somewhat cooler nights.

As the days went by, the food shortage went from bad to impossible. The slices of bread for breakfast had gotten thinner and thinner, and there was not much left of the original round loaves the widow had when the Kestners arrived. There was no prospect of getting more, or of buying flour to bake some. The mountainside was barren, and little could grow out of the stones or the dry clay. Even where something might have grown, nothing had been planted for lack of seeds, lack of manpower, lack of tools, lack of fertilizer, and above all, lack of will. Why should a man plant if he will not reap? And why should he reap if most of it would be sent to feed a man on the Russian front today so that he could be killed there tomorrow?

For Saul and Clara, who had lived most of their lives in the midst of plenty, it was difficult to imagine what nooks and crevices shortages could creep into, and to what extent these could influence the routine of daily life. In a land with few forests and a large war effort, not only firewood to cook meals was scarce, but also lumber products, such as paper, were vanishing. In a place like this mountain village, the last newspaper that had reached it was many weeks ago. For illiterate people, as many of them were, the most valuable uses of a paper were wrapping groceries, starting the fire, and wiping one's behind. In the last instance there was some poetic justice, considering the bold lies printed in the papers by the Fascist press.

Most houses in the village did not have an outhouse, not to mention a bathroom. Baths, when and if taken by the villagers, were sponge baths in a basin. But soap was so scanty that people hardly dared waste it on anything but hands, or laundry. The other function of a bathroom could not be as easily eliminated, and for that specific purpose, a portion of the backyard was set aside, which meant that it was an open area behind the house and away from the street. This allowed people to squat down without being seen from the street, but there were certainly many opportunities to be seen from several neighbors' backyards. As everybody on that street used the same type of facilities, nobody paid much attention to one another, despite the lack of fences or shrubbery. One always turned one's back toward the house next door, though surely neighbors could recognize one another from the backside, but one always fancied that they might think it was someone else. Since the widow's house was the last on the street, one did not have to worry about the far side; there were advantages at times to being the poorest and the last. Actually, the first thing that one did, after ascertaining that no other member of the household was using the backyard, was to locate a desirable spot between other dunghills. Depending on the time of day and location of the sun, one might even get a shady spot near the house, but in general, there were fewer fresh heaps swarming with flies farther away. While deciding which piece of ground to fertilize, one picked a few weed leaves, preferably broad ones, that grew between the stones and the clay, and in the absence of newspaper or its facsimile, these leaves served the purpose reasonably well. It was surprising that the stench did not pervade the whole village, but apparently the sun baked the mounds rather quickly into odorless cakes.

The days passed by in indistinguishable monotony, each day more blisteringly hot and dry than the previous one. Fortunately the well in the center of the village had been dug deep enough that there was sufficient drinking water, which the widow, just like other womenfolk, carried home on top of her head in a large crude-looking clay urn. Saul had to stop worrying about its cleanliness; he could not worry about everything. He and Clara sometimes watched the procession of the women returning from the well, which took place, as if by appointment, at the same time every day, even if no one had a clock. This was always early, before the sun got too oppressive. The silent figures passed them, often barefoot, each wrapped in long, dark, colorless homespun clothes, their faces prematurely wrinkled, burdened by poverty, childbirth, and rigid tradition of village behavior imposed by their men-folk, the last of which did not extend to either the house of the spinsters or of the widow. In fact, the widow's family seemed to be outside the demands and expectations of the other villagers, outcasts in their own town. Saul was told that there were a few others who were outside the limits of village justice, but these were at the other end of the spectrum and had liberated themselves by relative prosperity or education.

In those dreary days, each day seemed to be the very last in which a few more mouthfuls of food could be scraped together in the widow's house; but something always seemed to turn up each day, meager as it was. The twins, especially Rajko, developed dark circles under their eyes. Saul almost lost his trousers one day, and finally dug up somewhere something that could pass for a piece of rope, which he tied around his waist. But one day that inexorable moment would come when the dwindling supplies could no longer be stretched. Bread could be sliced thinner each day, but how could one divide it after the last crumb was gone? The race was now on between the vanishing food and the delayed Allies. Not a sound seemed to penetrate that stagnant wait in which the very pulse in one's blood vessels seemed to have slowed.

There was only one being – perhaps half a being – in the whole village whose pulse had quickened. It was the mentally impaired boy, and he acted very strangely indeed. His distressed mother was constantly walking the streets, looking for him, because he had suddenly taken to disappearing. She explained to Clara and Saul, somewhat apologetically, in the local dialect, which for once they could understand, "He is in love." And that is indeed what had happened to the half-witted, half-child, whose bodily development lacked nothing, but whose mind and speech could only be understood by his mother and older sister. He had been stung by love, and the object of his affection was a young village girl, supposedly beautiful, but neither Saul, Clara, Peter, or the twins had ever seen her, and Saul wondered whether anything of real beauty could have sprung from that stark mountainside. But whether she was beautiful or not, the boy thought so, and it was pathetic to watch him slink and groan like a wounded animal, uttering guttural incomprehensible animal sounds, as he suffered the pains of unrequited love.

On the thirteenth day after their arrival in the village, something out of the ordinary occurred. It started out just like the other dozen days that had preceded it, but shortly before noon a wave swept over the village, and even those women who were kept eternally in the house and away from the gaze of strangers, now emerged into the sunlight. No one quite knew how to interpret the occurrence, or how the word had spread so rapidly from house to house, but on the winding dirt road coming up to the village advanced three clouds of dust, totally obscuring the vehicles that produced them. It was obvious that they were vehicles – only vehicles produced that much dust – and no civilians were motorized in those days. The two spinsters crossed themselves and fingered their rosaries. When the puffs reached the tiny wooden bridge just outside the village, the dust momentarily settled, revealing two motorcycles and a car. It was a small contingent of Germans, who for unknown reasons had come up to the village. They split promptly into groups of two and began searching at gunpoint every single house.

Rayko and Ljerka were back in the house when two sweaty robust German soldiers made their entrance, shoved the seamstress aside, and started to search for food. But that moment had finally arrived when the last crumb of bread had disappeared, and there was not a bean or a grain of sugar or salt on the shelf, not a potato in the sack, nor a fragment of pasta, nor a drop of oil anywhere. The soldiers stood there, bewildered, staring at the barren walls and the scant shabby furnishings, wondering for a moment where the tricky Italians would have hidden some food. Then one of the Germans, rifle in hand, swooped down on something he had spotted on the wall in the poorly illuminated area beneath the ladder. It was a wreath of garlic which none of the Kestners had noticed, braided according to local custom and hung inconspicuously on a nail, the last edible item remaining in the whole house. And lucky for the seamstress, for now the two Germans swiftly made their exit, triumphant with their garlic wreath, or otherwise they might have wrung the signorina's neck instead.

Since the grotto had no direct connection to the widow's house, and the Germans did not walk around to the far side, the house being the last one on the street, they did not discover its presence. They simply walked back to their vehicles the way they had come, and thus missed Clara, Saul, and Peter who had gone back to the grotto. The Germans were primarily looking for food, not for people, but had something aroused their suspicion, such as a crouching able-bodied couple or a young man in the grotto, the consequences might have been dire.

The Germans, who had fanned out through the village in groups of two, reunited back at their vehicles and departed. The rumbling of motors was heard briefly, and for a moment the three vehicles could be seen through the dust, which promptly swallowed them up and transformed them again into three moving clouds, slowly receding down the tortuous mountain road. The villagers swarmed into the streets to consult each other, commiserate on their food losses, and speculate on the meaning of this brief and unwelcome visit. They spoke agitatedly in their staccato dialect. Clara, Saul, and Peter were there too, having emerged from the grotto after Rajko summoned them, as soon as the Germans left the widow's house. Suddenly there was an explosion causing everyone to spin around on his or her heels and look down the road. They all focused their gaze on a fourth cloud of dust, much larger than the other three, which as it settled, left a gap in the road. Several people exclaimed: "They've blown up the bridge. The bridge is gone." "The bastards mined the bridge!" And the villagers turned their back again on the road to consult each other, but this time they frequently glanced back to see whether the little wooden bridge, which had been there for as long as they could remember, was indeed gone.

Elated, Saul exclaimed, “The Germans are withdrawing. They are blowing up the bridges behind them.”

By the afternoon, detailed accounts surfaced about the German seizures, all food items. From the richest farmer in the village – the only one considered by the others to be rich, but in reality only less poor than the others – they had taken his remaining livestock, meaning two chickens and a sow: the latter they found in the pen, shot, and loaded into the car. Rajko heard with disbelief that somewhere in that village there had yet been a mouth-watering pig.

The widow, with some money from Saul, was able to buy some dry legumes and grains from the “rich” farmer, who no longer needed them to feed the animals, so once again there was food on her shelf for a few more days.

A feverish quiet settled now on the village. No one knew exactly what was happening, and speculations filled in the gaps in knowledge. Later that day came word – three minutes after he had set foot in his mother’s house – that a young villager, the only son of another widow, had come home from the war, having made his ascent around the other side of the mountain, and had brought with him a glimpse of the world beyond. He was one of those many disbanding Italian soldiers the Kestners had traveled with, like the two Sicilians who had brought them to the village and were still staying in the spinsters’ house, or the ashen one who lay by the roadside, staring his white stare over the white sheet that had incompletely covered him. But this young man made it back home, had surmounted all the dangers, and now was the hero of the day. His mother laughed and cried and prayed and opened the door to her little house to invite everyone in, to see the miracle of her son returning from the wars.

When Saul heard about the young man, he could not resist the impulse to go see him. The two talked at great length, while the mother fluttered around and wept. The young man found more kinship with this foreigner than with the villagers whom he had known since his cradle. The two talked about the world beyond, from which this village had been severed, even when the little bridge was in place. They talked about the retreating German tactics and the advancing Allies. But above all they talked about the dreaded Russian front, on which they had both nearly lost their lives in two separate World Wars one generation apart.

Saul found out from his new young friend that the Germans had retreated toward Benevento, and that Avellino had finally fallen. Monte Fusco, a small town a few miles Southeast, which had been occupied by the American Fifth Army, was their northernmost outpost.

"Now that the Allies are on the move again, by tomorrow they will probably be much farther North," the young man opined.

Saul had no more patience left. The time had come to finally emerge out of the shadows of oppression and into a free world, to connect up with the Allies. There was no longer any reason to tarry in this forsaken village. Life as he knew it had stopped several years ago, and after so many trials and tribulations he could not wait one second longer. He simply had to start living again. He invited the two Sicilians with whom his family had come to the village to come along to Monte Fusco, but they declined, preferring the relaxation and safety of the spinsters' house for a bit longer.

The following morning, fourteen days after arrival, Saul was ready to lead his family out of the little mountain village in search of freedom. The Kestners were up early, to avoid the scorching midday sun. Several villagers had enthusiastically explained to Saul which little paths and roads he had to follow. A small crowd gathered in the street by the widow's house to see them off, escorted them to the ridge where the path began, and remained there waving, as Saul and his brood descended down the steep and tortuous path into a narrow rocky crevice, and up another path, till they reached the other village nestled into the next mountain spike directly across. The group included the signorina, the two soldiers, the young villager who had just returned home, the younger of the two spinster sisters, the girl from Benevento, several other neighbors, and a few unidentified curious barefooted village children in tattered clothes. Somewhere in the sister village across the ravine they lost sight of the Kestners and slowly withdrew to their domiciles.

The route now took the Kestners along a typical country dirt road, winding around mountain ridges, zigzagging alternately East and West, with a southward progression and a definite southeastern inclination. Progress was slow, and Rajko had a difficult time keeping up, complaining that his throat was parched and that his limbs ached. They had had some unrecognizable mush for breakfast, but there was no food to take along. They did not even carry water, as they had no canteen or appropriate container, and in any case Saul figured on drinking from mountain streams, but they were unable to find any along the way. The sun was more intense and oppressive than ever, and had already dried up all the little mountain trickles. It was suddenly Ljerka who did not whine or complain and prodded her brother to exert himself.

The road was interrupted in several places, where small bridges had been blown up. The Germans had obviously withdrawn, but where were the Allies? Saul expected them to be in hot pursuit, and right on the heels of the retreating enemy. But there was not a soul anywhere, not Italian, not American, nor Prussian, no one but the five of them, five wandering Jews, meandering their way in no-man's land. Those tortuous mountain roads had a way of being endless, even when air distances were ridiculously short; tortuous indeed was the road to freedom.

From a distance, the Kestners appeared as five little insignificant dots against the white dust of the road, at first glance resembling stationary black specks of dirt, but if observed closely, more like five slowly crawling ants. Such they appeared to the German sergeant through his field glasses as he peered over his trench, situated on a mountaintop, to command the view of the neighboring hills and several mountain roads along which advancing Allies were expected to travel. This was an ideal spot to hold with only a handful of soldiers and a few long-range guns. He would be able to annihilate any American reconnoiter units and deal a ghastly blow to the main force as it came into perfect range around the bend. The road would be totally destroyed, slowing down progress of American trucks and troops. He had been impatiently waiting for the advancing patrol, which apparently took its sweet time. Now on the road there was some movement that was advancing in the opposite direction and did not fulfill a number of his expectations. Nonetheless, although he did not wish to reveal his position or full capacity till there were bigger fish in the net, he could not let those specks get by altogether. When the Kestners came to a bare straight stretch, where they were most vulnerable, the German opened fire. Saul heard the all too familiar whistling sound of shells and yelled to everyone to duck into the shallow ditch by the road. In a flash he realized that he had once more underestimated the efficiency of the Germans, and that it would have been far wiser to have remained in the village. But now it was too late to retreat. In the same instant, he grasped the entire situation, realizing that the straight stretch was in full view of the Germans, but that it was fairly short, and that just around the bend they would be safely behind the hill, as the road virtually bent upon itself. The first round was way off, but there was no time to lose, because there would be more. He shouted to his family to crawl a little further in the ditch, and then make a run for it, but Rajko's feet were so heavy they kept dropping to the ground, and he could barely drag himself. Clara pleaded with the boy to make one more great effort, promising to rest as soon as they were around the back of the hill. Saul, exasperated, resorted to reprimands and verbal lashes, so unlike his usual self, but Rajko seemed unable to generate more strength. Something had happened to his legs and he could not go on.

The second round of gunfire was closer, but still too low. The next one would be on target. Clara tugged on Rajko's arm, while Ljerka pushed from behind. Suddenly Peter sprang forward, lifted his brother over his right shoulder, and darted ahead at amazing speed, with everyone else on his heels, till he rounded the curve, no longer in view of the German outpost. Then all five collapsed along the roadside, and remained there for a long time, speechless, panting, their energy drained. They were still in no-man's land, with the sun still high. Rajko shivered despite the scorching heat. Ljerka turned her face away so nobody would see the tears streaming down her cheeks, mingling with the salty, greasy sweat rolling off her forehead. Clara seemed completely withered. Only Peter seemed energetic, and to have finally regained his strength. Saul noticed that the path ahead was facing entirely southward, and they would no longer veer back to face that or any other German entrenchment. The road took a steep downward course, and he knew, from what he had been told, that at the bottom of the hill, hidden by a bluff, lay Monte Fusco, some half an hour away.

Saul closed his eyes, which were burning in their sockets. His head seemed to be swimming, and inside the buzzing in his ears, he could still hear the whistling noise of the shells.

"We are safe now," he announced. "Let's have a good rest." He stared ahead into the barren rock and clay of the down-slope and the irregular markings of the sun-glazed terrain. Outlines seemed to evaporate into dancing vertical streamers, mingling with the stagnant air above. Within the swirls of this boiling cauldron under the sweltering sun, he fancied he saw for a moment the face of Zvonko. Where were they now, the Adlers, and the Kohans, and the Steinbergs, and all the rest? In the tightrope-balancing act he and his family had been engaged in over the past two months, he had not thought about Grad, as if it had never existed. The long forgotten strange dream he had had after his family escaped into Italy now suddenly resurfaced: Zvonko prodded him on to run from the Germans and little Ruben yelled to him, "Run for me, too." He had run for his family and for himself, but perhaps just a tiny little bit for Ruben, and the Adlers, and all the other Jews of Grad. Even if he hadn't intentionally run for them, he would from now on carry just a little shred of each of them on his back for the rest of his life.

Saul was vaguely aware that Clara said something about a stream just ahead, which might have water, but his mind still lingered on Grad. Then he heard Clara's joyous exclamation: "There is water, there is water here!"

Everyone sprang up and ran over to Clara, even Rajko, whose legs seemed wobbly, as she stood astride a thread-like trickle of crystal clear water, so thin that its flow was inaudible as it slid down the mountainside. Clara cupped her hands to catch a few sips and splash her sunburned face. Everyone else followed suit.

"Maybe that ferocious storm of a few days ago replenished this tiny stream," suggested Saul.

"Whatever it is, it is a good omen," said Clara. "I am absolutely convinced."

"Perhaps we should continue," suggested Peter.

"My legs hurt. Can we rest a little longer?" begged Ljerka.

"Mine too," whimpered Rajko.

"Yes, let's sit a little longer," agreed Saul.

"Papi, when I grow up, will you send me also to Vienna to study medicine, like you promised Peter?" asked Ljerka. "I'd like that."

"When I grow up, I'd rather build buildings like that green marble one in Milan," piped up Rajko.

"That's called architecture," Peter instructed his brother.

"You know, children," Saul spoke with some hesitation, "I realized something recently, and your mother and I need to talk about this. The whole time that we have been away from Grad, we have talked about going back home the moment the war is over. It occurred to me a few days ago how different Grad will be when the war finally ends, and how many people we knew there who will not be there any more. With so many of our friends gone, Grad will be a different place, and I don't know if we will still fit in."

"Your father is right. We always thought about going back and picking up the threads exactly where we left them," Clara said, "but maybe this won't be possible."

"We are leaving behind us the immediate danger of war and ghastly persecution, but we are facing a very different world, and an uncertain future."

Peter spoke up, shrugging his shoulders. "I don't know why I couldn't bring myself to tell you this before, but I was in love with Silvia, and I think she loved me too. I need to find her and find out whether we still love each other when we are face to face."

"Son, you really have grown up," said Clara, and she gave Peter a hug and a kiss.

"I'm hungry," complained Rajko.

"Me, too," echoed Ljerka.

"Let us go now, and let us face the future with courage," said Saul, and Clara thought that she saw a faint twinkle in his left eye.

Peter helped Rajko, whose feet still seemed as if weighted down with lead. The Kestners continued on their path. They slowly descended, and from a distance they were like five insignificant little pebbles rolling down the slope towards Monte Fusco, one raising slightly more dust than the others as he dragged his feet. When they made it to the village Saul flagged down a jeep with a five-cornered white star, driven by two helmeted young men in moss-green uniforms. Saul was finally face-to-face with the Allies, his dream for years, but remembering the episode with the British prisoners of war, he restrained himself from embracing and kissing his liberators. Communication was difficult across the language barrier, and the sergeant waved the Kestners on with little interest. A moment later the two Americans exchanged some words unintelligible to Saul, changed their mind, perhaps realizing that this dusty bedraggled family had come down the side of the mountain and might have some information on German positions. They decided to take this "Italian" couple in threadbare clothes and their scrawny malnourished children to the headquarters and let the intelligence officer decide who they were, and what their disposition would be. The Kestners climbed into the jeep. The driver swerved the car abruptly, so that Ljerka nearly fell out, and then drove on into a cloud of dust. Saul breathed deeply. His family was finally safe, and for now that was all that mattered.

Breinigsville, PA USA
03 September 2009

223473BV00001B/12/P